David Lampe

Toronto
May '88

The Fisher King

Books by Anthony Powell

Novels
Afternoon Men
Venusberg
From a View to a Death
Agents and Patients
What's Become of Waring
O, How the Wheel Becomes It!
The Fisher King

A Dance to the Music of Time
A Question of Upbringing
A Buyer's Market
The Acceptance World
At Lady Molly's
Casanova's Chinese Restaurant
The Kindly Ones
The Valley of Bones
The Soldier's Art
The Military Philosophers
Books Do Furnish a Room
Temporary Kings
Hearing Secret Harmonies

Biography
John Aubrey and his Friends

Plays
The Garden God *and* The Rest I'll Whistle

Memoirs:
To Keep the Ball Rolling
Vol. I: Infants of the Spring
Vol. II: Messengers of Day
Vol. III: Faces in my Time
Vol. IV: The Strangers All Are Gone

The Fisher King

A Novel by

ANTHONY POWELL

Heinemann : London

William Heinemann Ltd
10 Upper Grosvenor Street, London W1X 9PA
LONDON MELBOURNE TORONTO
JOHANNESBURG AUCKLAND

First published in Great Britain 1986
© Anthony Powell 1986
SBN 434 59926 3

Printed in Great Britain by
Mackays of Chatham Ltd,
Chatham, Kent

For
Anthony and Tanya

I

Exile is the wound of kingship. When someone, recently returned from a transatlantic business trip, spoke of seeing a man on crutches taking photographs in the back streets of Oregon City, the rumour at once spread that Saul Henchman had settled in America. There could be a *prima facie* case. Nothing positive had been heard of Henchman's movements since withdrawal from London two or three years before. He liked extracting pungent overplus from superficially unpromising essences. Incertitude, seclusion, concealment, were at once suggested by mere association of his name with so obscure a myth as that of the Fisher King. As against those things, Henchman was not the only lame man to own a camera. No assistant of either sex was mentioned as the adjunct in the circumstances to be expected. Nothing was said of the crippled photographer's unusual cast of countenance. In short, this might or might not have been Henchman. At best it was an even chance. Were the rumour correct, he was now a king over the water.

The Fisher King label seems to date from the second

night at sea of one of the *Alecto*'s summer cruises round the British Isles; the evening the Captain was accustomed to invite a selection of passengers to dine at his table. On that particular cruise the Captain's guests, about eighteen or twenty in number, built upon a hard core of fairly non-descript veterans from previous *Alecto* cruises, had included Henchman himself (accompanied as ever at that period by Barberina Rookwood), Valentine Beals and his wife Louise, Sir Dixon and Lady Tiptoft with their daughter Dr Lorna Tiptoft, Professor Willard S. Kopf and Mrs Elaine Kopf.

No one else in the cast of Valentine Beals's later narration was present, though Gary Lamont, had he arrived on board earlier, would, as a Fleet Street notability, undoubtedly have taken up a place at the Captain's table that evening. The last two named guests were representative of several similarly academic American couples among the *Alecto*'s passengers. Later events indicate that it must have been Professor Kopf, who, halfway through dinner, spoke learnedly about a prehistoric Stone Circle of great antiquity in Orkney, one of the sites to be visited on the cruise.

By that time, wind blowing hard over the North Sea, resonant chatter pervading the dining-saloon, audibility was poor. All the same, Beals felt pretty sure that the responding voice – deep, ironic, sententious, preserving a purposeful touch of West Country speech – must belong to Henchman. The speaker, whether Henchman or not (he was sitting on the same side as Beals, therefore out of sight), commented that a no less congenial feature of this ancient Ring of Standing Stones lay in the fact that lusty trout (slightly mannered phrase) could be caught in the two great lochs nearby, adding that more than once in the past he had himself planned to fish up there, an intention never yet fulfilled.

That statement, together with other known information about Henchman, was instantly registered by Beals – who possessed an innate taste for pin-pointing archetypes – as confirming the Fisher King hypothesis. The neatness of the analogue was overpowering. Beals was later given opportunity amply to embroider this random fantasy of his, indeed to become one of the few comparatively authoritative sources for hitherto unventilated aspects of Henchman's life.

Beals's belief that he was a man of action was demonstrated plainly enough by the heroes (every one of them Beals), who fought their way through his, by then, twenty or thirty historical thrillers. He fended off a certain amount of not always particularly goodnatured banter as to this propagation of himself as hero, by answering that few people contrived to live in a dreamworld that was also highly profitable financially speaking. Whether a man of action or not, Beals always managed to create the impression of a person of consequence. His heavy aquiline features, dark complexion, fleshy neck, opulent shirts and ties, went some way towards suggesting a *Quattrocento* magnate.

In the context of Henchman, Beals might be envisaged standing or kneeling in the corner of an Old Master in the role of donor (not, as occasionally depicted, on a reduced physical scale, Beals being by far the bulkier of the two), where, making a reverential gesture, possibly holding an inscribed scroll, he points to Henchman as the paramount figure: mysterious, dominating, tormented, displaying a wounded body, holding in one hand a camera proclaiming his profession, in the other the fishing tackle emblematic of his regal counterpart.

Beals would afterwards recall – even to the extent of tedium for listeners not over-curious as to the workings of human nature and the emotion of love – the drama of the *Alecto*'s cruise. He might not have demurred at such pictorial treatment of its subject-matter. He always saw to it that his own book-jackets were vigorously illustrative of whatever was inside. Possibly he would have insisted that Barberina Rookwood also took a prominent place.

Alternatively, Beals might have judged Barberina Rookwood to deserve a canvas to herself, a picture belonging to an entirely different school from that celebrating Henchman. Barberina Rookwood's Old Master would have been one of those allegorical works that cause argument among art-historians and iconographists, in which such abstractions as Love, Fame, Chastity, Sacrifice, Dissimulation, Betrayal, Jealousy – of course Death – are corporeally symbolized. Which Immances were most appropriately attached to the figures portrayed might very reasonably become a matter for pedantic controversy.

2

The overture, as it might be termed, struck up when Beals was leaning over the side the afternoon the *Alecto* sailed, watching fellow passengers come aboard. Trains convenient for joining the cruise arrived at different times (if a car was not brought to be garaged at the dock, collected on the way home), so that individual parties turned up early or late according to taste.

Beals, contemplating the figures approaching the gangway, sometimes in groups, sometimes singly, had

Henchman and Barberina Rookwood in mind, together with a general curiosity about some of the other names on the passenger-list; a competition with himself to guess them correctly. He was in any case keeping out of the cabin as a matter of prudence, while his wife unpacked. He had never seen Henchman, nor his secretary assistant, though familiar with photographs of both.

Identity was at once established when this couple made their way across the quay. Henchman, a camera swinging right and left from the neck like a pendulum, moved with almost startling velocity on aluminium shoulder-crutches. Barberina Rookwood, keeping up effortlessly, seemed to glide over the ground. Beals, who held strong opinions about clothes, decided the tweeds in which Henchman's small shrunken body was enclosed were well cut, but of an insistently bold design. They over-emphasized a taste for catching the eye, and were in any case too smart for a holiday cruise of this kind. Their pattern alone disposed of any doubt, had that arisen, as to whether or not Henchman liked to draw attention to himself. Beals considered something quieter would have been preferable as an ensemble for a photographer recognized as so distinguished in that field.

Apart from suit or crutches, Henchman's face alone guaranteed that wherever he went his presence would be remarked. The deep lines and scars which pitted its surface recorded uncompromisingly a chronicle of reiterated carvings-up at one time or another undertaken by army surgeons, no doubt civilian medical men too. Even so, allowing for the appalling mess shell splinters had made of his features, Henchman would have passed for less than a few years off sixty, not much older than Beals himself.

The girl, Barberina Rookwood, in her early twenties, had a small head, slanting eyes, long legs. At first sight Beals thought her beauty greatly surpassed photographs of her. Her face, in such violent contrast with Henchman's, was of almost absurdly delicate cast. It stopped just short of absurdity (could such a term qualify beauty) for several reasons. One of these was the formality exacted by training on a dancer's physiognomy, a discipline by which grace, elegance, tradition, can be imposed upon even irregular or harsh features. She moved as if in time with Henchman's crutch-impelled acceleration.

All this, if he turned out lucky enough to catch their arrival, was more or less what Beals had expected to see. He was glad to have brought that off in so well coordinated a manner, rather than later to have come on them aboard. While he watched, he saw something quite unexpected take place, even at the time regarded by him as a scoop.

Just before Henchman and Barberina Rookwood reached the gangway, a man appeared from out of the cluster of Customs sheds and offices beyond the quay. Evidently recognizing the backs of the couple ahead, this person, smallish, with a keen leathery look, began to run. He caught them up, and gave an exuberant greeting. Beals recognized this new arrival at once from caricatures at the top of articles and 'profiles', the weasel-like outline of nose and chin, look of perpetual awareness, restless enquiry. It was undoubtedly Gary Lamont.

Beals and his wife were travelling with old friends, the Middlecotes, both of whom would be greatly interested in Lamont putting in an appearance in this manner. Middlecote, who approached all matters in terms of publicity, liked to gauge with exactitude the value of any individual in that field. In Middlecote's eyes, Henchman and Barberina Rookwood, unless otherwise defined, would belong to a run-of-the-mill gossip-column region, where they rated fairly high; Lamont, liable to be mentioned in such latitudes too, was a person of far greater note, as a rising newspaper tycoon. Beals remembered Middlecote, who had done business with Lamont, speaking admiringly of him. 'When the Lebyatkin Vodka ads were appearing in Gary's paper he uttered sage words about them. Gary is a man who understands advertizing perspectives. Really knows something about the theory of the thing.'

Beals was surprised to have missed Lamont's name in the passenger-list. He was surprised, too, to find him on a cruise of this sort at all. Flying visits to New York were more in Lamont's line, between life-and-death struggles going on round about him, take-overs, sackings, NATSOPA, possibly even divorcing wives, changing mistresses, though latterly Beals had the impression that Lamont had been solidly married for some little time.

So much did Beals feel convinced that Lamont would not stoop to a holiday cruise round the British Isles that this appearance on the quay seemed accountable only as seeing friends off on the *Alecto*. That seemed almost equally unlikely, though for a second or two the surprise also shown by Henchman and Barberina Rookwood at finding Lamont beside them to some extent helped to bear out the seeing-off possibility. So, too, did Lamont's shabby lounge suit. He looked as if he had come straight from the office.

Now in his early forties, Lamont retained in middle life a boyish facial expression, which caused an habitual look of cunning to seem amusing, larky, open natured, rather than menacing, as some of his business opponents had found it to be. Beals later put the paradox of Lamont's appearance succinctly. 'It's the air of an enormously sharp Victorian office-boy about to ask for a rise. He knows his increase in salary is assured, because he has found out something unusually gruesome about the private life of the boss, and the boss suspects that. I can't explain why Lamont should look Victorian. No one is more up to date. Perhaps a rags-to-riches approach to life makes him appear comfortably oldfashioned.'

Beals, plausibly enough, went on to suggest that Lamont regarded himself as a kind of latterday Gatsby, a Gatsby retired from a life of open illegality, while retaining the

13

Midas touch in commercial dealings; buccaneering ventures tempered in his own eyes with a few high ideals, one of them probably the image of the Perfect Woman. Lamont was known to read novels, even liked meeting novelists – rather another matter – though never allowing such literary contacts to inhibit instincts that were intrinsically tough and practical.

Watching the group on the quay, Beals tried to recall more clearly the episode connecting Lamont with Henchman and Barberina Rookwood. He knew this had importance, while failing to bring the precise details into focus. That a comparatively close connection existed was suggested by her putting an arm round Lamont's neck, and kissing him quite effusively, though some women did that to almost all men. While the embrace was taking place Henchman's face had displayed no visible displeasure at the fervour of the act. He simply watched sardonically, continuing to do so after the greeting was over. Lamont appeared now to be explaining why he was coming on the cruise.

At that moment three further arrivals emerged from the background of sheds, and walked briskly across the asphalt towards the gangway. Having noted the names on the passenger-list, Beals at once put them down as Sir Dixon and Lady Tiptoft, with their daughter, Dr Lorna Tiptoft. Sir Dixon Tiptoft was a retired civil servant of whom Middlecote had been known to speak. The Tiptofts were plainly occupied on a family row. Henchman, noticing their approach, took the opportunity of disengaging Barberina Rookwood from Lamont, with a view to reaching the gangway ahead of this trio.

Sir Dixon, stockily built, had an expression of immutable bad temper on his face. Like Lamont, he was wearing what might well have been an office suit, though one less deliberately baggy at the knees, and designed to express Lamont's open contempt for sartorial dandyism. Sir Dixon probably shared the attitude of mind. He carried a camera tripod. The complaints he was uttering in a rasping voice were in connection with some ineptitude committed in regard to the luggage.

Lady Tiptoft, the taller of the two, of skeletal thinness, was returning her husband's attack with vehement counter-allegations, evidently directed towards undermining the whole premise of his charges. She spoke with fanatical conviction of the justice of her case.

Their daughter, Dr Lorna Tiptoft, also some inches taller than her father, his same swarthy complexion, must have decided to put a stop to this controversy out of hand. Her manner was by no means placatory. Its sharpness at least as aggressive as her parents'. 'For goodness sake stop grousing. You're both in the wrong. In any case we don't want to begin a holiday with a silly to-do about luggage. That doesn't matter to anyone now. We can sort out all that when we've seen our cabins.'

These words did little or nothing to quell her mother's indignation. Her father, having established his point, remained silent, without abandoning a look of rage. Beals formed an unfavourable impression of the three of them. At the same time the firmness of the daughter's personality impressed him, her utter disregard for compromise. She might even turn out to be one of those potential models for an historical character in a future book: the She-Wolf of France or Sarah Duchess of Marlborough, though no doubt Lorna Tiptoft lacked their looks. Such reflections were dispelled by a sudden action on the part of Henchman.

Resting the weight of his body on the crutches, he must have grasped all at once the intensity of Tiptoft family disharmony. Raising the camera almost imperceptibly, he took a photograph of their fierce quarrelling. The movement was so rapid as to be scarcely observable even at close quarters, certainly not from several yards away.

Immediately after doing this Henchman began to move towards the gangway. Its ascent required a degree of attention in placing the crutches on the slope. Barberina Rookwood leant a hand. Lamont did not follow at once. He allowed the still unreconciled Tiptofts to precede him up the gangway. Then he boarded the ship at his own pace.

Myth presented

3

On the day following the Captain's dinner, Beals was sitting with his wife and the Middlecotes, having drinks before luncheon in the *Alecto*'s main saloon. The wind of the previous night had dropped to a mild breeze. There was a slight swell, little sun, the air fresh. At an appropriate moment Beals released what had been so transcendentally disclosed to him. He asserted that Henchman's peremptory demeanour, bodily disablement, spectral aspect, had already combined to hint strongly at the plausibility of identification as the Fisher King. Now, all such elementary qualifications were clinched by the *sine qua non* of fisherman.

Louise Beals, dwelling by nature in an unmapped interior

world of her own, where the Fisher King played little part – although one could never speak with absolute assurance as to the secret recesses of Louise Beals's reflections – remained content to leave Henchman's greater or lesser resemblance to so misty a personage unexplored. Dreamy, puzzled in manner, a shade *triste*, her quiet goodlooks had faded no more than consonant with the age she had reached, eyes light blue, hair within a shade to be called amber. She had been in love with a homosexual doctor, treating her for some female ailment, when she met Beals. They had settled down happily enough. Louise Beals was not in the least polemical like Fay Middlecote. Persons to whom she had taken a dislike rarely noticed they were being teased unless possessing susceptive antennae.

The Middlecotes at once questioned the credibility of Henchman's fishing, thus conveniently abstracted from the Beals cultural ragbag to add a literally crowning touch to one of his only too familiarly far-fetched disquisitions. This might well be a try-out for a new book. Piers Middlecote, as an adman professionally disputatious, enquired whether the Fisher King legend had comprehended a cycle of pristine photographic lore. His wife abetted him in not accepting Beals's proposition out of hand.

During the war Beals and Middlecote had been in the RNVR together, commissioned from the Lower Deck almost simultaneously. Then Middlecote found himself attending to the account of the firm for which Beals sold Scotch. Personal friendship developed from the circumstance of their wives getting on well together in spite of very different temperaments. Louise Beals had been chiefly responsible for Fay Middlecote inducing her husband (who usually preferred more energetic forms of holiday) to come on the *Alecto* cruise.

Beals regarded his naval service as consituting his strongest claim to be a man of action, a vigorous interlude extenuating the too personal drift of some of his romantic fiction. Friends were apt to put down the mere writing of historical thrillers to an undiagnosed psychological hang-up. Rather good at languages, Beals had served at sea in Naval Intelligence, intercepting and decoding on VHF enemy spoken R/T signals. Apart from its claims as action Beals was in other respects less nostalgic about his naval incarnation than Middlecote.

Middlecote had been in a destroyer escorting material of war for Russia on the Murmansk run. Notwithstanding rather too curly hair (only just beginning to go grey), he retained some of the bearing of a naval officer. Middlecote held himself very straight. An open clear-eyed smile went down well with clients. In spite of a lacerating quotidian regime of business luncheons, occupational hazard of his calling, he looked in better condition that Beals, who fitfully attended a gym to reduce weight. After a few drinks Middlecote would refer to the Royal Navy as The Andrew, speak of his 'naval occasions' or 'days when I was wont to go down to the sea in ships and occupy my business in great waters'.

Fay Middlecote, nowadays settled to a reasonable degree of plumpness, had lost none of her attack, nor taste for being at the centre of whatever was going on. Her black hair, retrousse nose, demurely assertive air, had captured Middlecote's fancy when both had been working as copywriters in the firm of which he was now on the board. This foundation in advertising imposed on Fay Middlecote's clothes a taste for clear bright colours, in contrast with Louise Beal's filmy floating dresses.

Beals at once cut short Middlecote criticism by remorselessly launching into whatever he could remember of the Fisher King myth. 'Let me recall the story. Perceval – Peredur – Parzival, if you're feeling Wagnerian – had been turned down as below the standard of the Knights of the Round Table. He was too young, too uncouth, too lacking in the sort of chic required of an Arthurian knight. So, saying farewell to his widowed mother, Perceval went out into the world, seeking adventure, sophistication, a lady for whom to fight. In a word, acquire attainments making him eligible for a seat.'

'If he became too sophisticated he might have refused a knighthood when offered,' said Middlecote. 'Are any potential Arthurian knights on record as doing that? Besides, would a really sophisticated man become involved in a fight about a woman?'

'You've often told me you did once during the war,' said Fay Middlecote. 'It was before you got your commission, and you were mixed up in some squalid scuffle about a Wren petty-officer in a pub. But then sophistication was hardly your thing, darling, before we married.'

Middlecote ignored a matter that had clearly been much worked over in the past. He returned to the subject of knighthood.

'That verray gentil parfait knight Sir Dixon Tiptoft used to cause me a lot of trouble when we were handling an account for one of the Ministries. I never met him, but can now see why he was such a plague in the background.'

'Dr Lorna's a formidable young lady, too,' said Fay Middlecote. 'An old girl called Mrs Jilson, who's sharing a cabin with her, told me she's got quite a reputation for her age in her own branch of medicine. I couldn't shake Mrs Jilson off. She then began on her son, who is travelling with her. She said he was a typical Virgo. I got away after that.'

Beals refused to be diverted by Middlecote red herrings. He continued with his own discourse.

'One day, during Perceval's wanderings in search of adventure, he came on two men fishing. One of them was crippled. The lame fisherman – the Fisher King, as it turned out – invited Perceval to his castle, which was in the midst of barren fields. The Fisher King had been wounded in the thighs. He was never out of pain. Fishing was the only pastime open to him.'

'Valentine, you must admit this story of yours is becoming rather a rigmarole.'

Beals made a gesture to indicate that, so far as consonant with the art of narrative which he practised, he would soon end. Middlecote, unconvinced, flagged a steward.

'While Perceval was banqueting with the Fisher King at his castle, a Spear and a Cup were brought into the hall by a page and a maiden. If Perceval had enquired the meaning of these objects the Fisher King would have been cured of his wound, the barren lands made fertile again. But Perceval was too diffident, too naive.'

'Perceval obviously wasn't going to get very far,' said Fay Middlecote. 'He was probably pondering his own future career when he became a knight, how to acquire a suit of good cheap armour, where to find the sort of lady whose looks he really fancied – not too PreRaphaelite – whether a knighthood would prove extortionately expensive to keep up. After all, he was a poor young man.'

'Whatever he pondered, he remained silent. In the Middle Ages, these objects were identified with the Spear of the Crucifixion and the Cup of the Holy Grail – the latter a vessel never precisely defined, in any case frowned on by the Church. In true fact –'

'The Tiptofts have just come in,' said Louise Beals. 'I do agree that Dr Tiptoft looks pretty bossy.'

The steward had at last noticed Middlecote's signalling.

'The same again. I can't produce a spear, Valentine, but a cup – a full one – will be in your hands in a matter of minutes. Meanwhile,

> If you be mad, be gone:
> If you have reason, be brief.

I've often found that quotation effective in business dealings. I recommend it to you.'

Middlecote, who always quoted Shakespeare as if the only person who had ever read him, made Beals even more obdurate.

'In true fact the myth goes back far beyond the Christian era. The Spear and the Cup are symbols of male and female sexuality. The Fisher King's wound had deprived him of his virility. As King he was emblem of Fertility to his people. The realm would remain barren as long as the King was sexually mutilated.'

'But poor Perceval,' said Fay Middlecote. 'How could he possibly have known all that? What happened to him? Did he ever make the Round Table?'

'Yes, after many adventures he did. But when he was feasting there, a maiden called The Loathly Damsel, a hideous young woman riding on a mule, upbraided him for letting down the Fisher King.'

'Do you think she looked like Dr Tiptoft?' said Louise Beals.

'But, Valentine,' said Fay Middlecote. 'Haven't we heard a lot of this before from T. S. Eliot, and all sorts of other people. Besides, we *are* supposed to be on a holiday. And where does Henchman come in? I can't see any resemblance, except that he uses crutches. And on the slenderest evidence you say he likes fishing. Oh, I suppose you mean . . .'

'Surely the accumulated facts make my point? I will now argue against myself, and agree that Henchman's kingdom, if by that you mean his photographic business, doesn't at present seem in the least barren. On the contrary, it couldn't be more flourishing. There may, even so, be facts of which we are ignorant.'

Fay Middlecote changed her ground.

'Then what about Barberina Rookwood? Is she a sort of female Perceval, who came to be photographed, and didn't ask the right questions, so was forced to stay as prisoner in the castle? Or was she the girl who brought in the Cup? That must be roughly speaking what she has to do as Henchman's assistant, except it's carting round heavy photographic equipment all day long, not to mention acting as secretary and nurse.'

'I've thought about Barberina Rookwood a lot,' said Beals. 'And not come to any definite conclusions yet. Dancing plays an important part in some fertility rites. Certain peoples kept a man dancing all the time the harvest was being reaped to make sure the crop was plentiful.'

'First of all Barberina Rookwood is not a man, but a girl. Secondly, dancing is just what Henchman has prevented her from continuing to do.'

'All will no doubt be revealed in the course of the cruise,' said Beals. 'By the way, have you noticed Henchman's eyes? They are reported to be one of the chief elements he brings into play to unnerve sitters, and produce those very remarkable photographs of his.'

'Do speak more quietly, Valentine,' said Louise Beals. 'People at tables round can hear all you say. Lady Tiptoft is beginning to look particularly alert.'

Beals slightly lowered his voice.

'If you find yourself near Henchman, observe his eyes, Fay. Like Banquo's eyes, there is no speculation in them.'

The simile had just occurred to him as a suitable one for rubbing in that Middlecote had no monopoly of Shakespearian quotation.

4

Even if archetypal figures were a hobby of his, Beals allowed himself only in private conversation flights of fancy like comparing Henchman with the Fisher King. Such fantasies (as Conrad might have expressed the mood) were Beals *en pantoufles*. In the more majestic role of international bestseller he geared any imaginative flashes that might come his way to purely commercial requirements; in practice limiting them severely to the capabilities of his regular readership, which he did not overestimate.

Beals used his wife as a reliable judge, almost rough-and-ready computer, of what would go down with his public. Notwithstanding a pensive bewildered air, Louise Beals was rarely unsound in her arbitration, especially in relation to the area, where Beals had been something of a pioneer, of embedding explicit sex into the historical novel. Louise Beals would adjudicate just how far to go. She did that well. In the development of otherwise pretty earthy passages Beals might once in a way indulge in an exotic metaphor. More often he rigorously controlled, as bad for business, eroticism of too intellectual a tone.

That he was a shrewd man Beals would have been the first to agree. He had been doing quite nicely in a wellknown firm of whisky-distillers before taking up writing as a fulltime profession. He did not make the change until he felt solid ground beneath him. Beals himself used to define his aims as to provide entertainment, while at the same time earning a pittance. He would willingly concede that he had achieved the last with a little over.

Unloved by reviewers – indeed rarely if ever mentioned on the literary pages save in some charitable Yuletide round-up of the not-forgotten in a comprehensive survey of books published during the previous year – Beals could set such supercilious neglect against increasingly heartening royalty statements. There seemed no reason to suppose these did not bring their recompense. At least Beals, unlike some less stoical writers treated with far more humanity by the newspaper critics, had never been heard to complain that he was victim of prejudice.

All the same, whatever the chosen range of a writer, whatever method brought to the business of writing (especially fiction), the mere routine is apt to play odd tricks with the mind of its exponents, not least in breeding there allusive or collatable images. As a novelist committed by genre to a fair amount of historical research – if only through involuntary reflection on such matters as the similar or disparate nature of one historical epoch or individual figure with another – he found himself peculiarly vulnerable to the pull of motiveless comparison.

After the prosperous years had come (he did not have to wait very long), when much of the donkey-work was done by deputy, Beals himself drudged away at making sure his narratives were easily grasped by readers 'under the dryer', or clutching tattered paperbacks at the launderette. Unwieldy contextures of history, inconvenient complexities of human behaviour, had to be adapted for the tired and harassed. In effecting these laborious simplifications Beals

24

found he could not prevent himself from begetting *aperçus* of no commercial value whatever (even potential stumbling blocks), like the fanciful vision of Henchman as the Fisher King, which, should it come to Henchman's ears, might well offend a man not lightly to be transformed into an enemy.

The best to be said for such strained analogies, however aimless, was that they impressed acquaintances with the possibility that Beals himself was something more than an untiring purveyor of packaged fiction, an imputation that had never in the least abashed him, except perhaps in resenting the accordant conclusion that he knew nothing about writing. Having learnt at a lowish literary level to get a lot of information down in a readable form, Beals may have wished his own utterances on books to be taken more seriously than they usually were. He could, in fact, sometimes surprise those regarding themselves as his intellectual superiors by passing unexpectedly acute judgments on contemporary writers made much of by the pundits; once in a way dispatching into the quivering ever sensitive flesh of an established reputation a poisoned barb that was positively lethal.

Beals and Middlecote had been by no means certain that, as old friends, they could tolerate each other's company, in the close juxtaposition of a cruise, during so comparatively extended a period. Beals was not always prepared to go the whole way in accepting Middlecote's conviction of his own omniscience, while neither Middlecote nor his wife was likely to allow any suggestion of the profession of writer taking precedence of that of adman. Beals's apostasy from whisky had been something of a blow to Middlecote, depriving him, so to speak, of representing art and letters, even if in commercial form.

Refusal of Louise Beals to engage herself at junctures when Fay Middlecote's contentious moods threatened discord always kept the peace. Most of the time the two wives discussed the problems set by children who were growing up, while the husbands, conversing in an idiom of their own, were generally equally amicable. Beals was anxious to show that he knew more than most writers about the ways of business; Middlecote, while feeling no proof necessary that his own cultivation outran that of the average adman, did not at all mind occasional opportunities to confirm the truth of that conviction.

5

Apart from material mustered on the cruise, earlier information about Henchman's life had been until then very limited. Little or no biographical matter had ever been released, what existed being both scrappy and sporadic. One or two interviews, appearing at long intervals from each other, had for the most part concentrated upon crustily phrased statements on the subject of photographic technique.

A few rather more intimate autobiographical details had been added to these by a radio programme, in which Henchman, rather resentfully, had agreed to take part. This *divertissement* adumbrated banishment to a desert island, where the musical tastes of the exile were revealed by choice of records taken there, additional indications of character given by a favourite book and special luxury, to alleviate solitude. The interview was also calculated to enquire, though not too closely, into personal origins. From this slender foundation no doubt most of Beals's knowledge of Henchman's beginnings was gleaned in the first instance, flavoured later by Henchman himself.

An obviously vulnerable physical condition had exempted Henchman from questioning as to whether he felt competent to look after himself, build a shelter, or raft for attempt to escape. Henchman had not been asked, for example, if he had ever done any fishing. In fact, during the programme, Henchman showed not the smallest wish to minimize his disablement, rather the contrary. He did that without the least implication of self-pity. Henchman's lack of self-pity was often a positive embarrassment to people who made something of an industry of that response.

After stating a single musical prejudice (detestation of The Beatles and all their works), Henchman chose Marie Lloyd's once popular music-hall number *I'm one of the ruins that Cromwell knocked about a bit*, followed by various selections of music for ballet. He terminated with Handel's *Dead March* in *Saul*, which he stated also as his preference, could he take only one disc with him. He enlarged on that opus.

'When my nonconformist parents christened me Saul, they no doubt had in mind that biblical busybody subsequently recycled as Paul. By temperament, however, I have always found more in common with the ruler of that name, who was given to throwing javelins at his best friends, when in the mood, hewing his enemies to pieces, finally ringing down the curtain by falling on his own sword. In this last connection, I have often contemplated suffocating myself under a camera-cloth, while photographing someone who particularly outraged me.'

For luxury on the desert island Henchman requested a camera, one equipped with an interval shutter, an infinite number of films, and means to develop them. There was some demur at allowing quite so much photographic equipment. In the end all was granted, the interviewer by then perhaps a little disconcerted by Henchman's manner and choices, both more than a little combative. For example, the book he demanded was Stendhal's *Armance*.

'His first and unfinished novel, as you probably remember. Not one of his best, but as it deals with the problems of an impotent man . . .'

'Ah, yes,' said the interviewer. 'And thank you, Saul Henchman . . .'

That closed a performance felt to have rested without complete equilibrium on the knife-edge that can divide good from bad taste. Some of the more factual stuff that emerged was that Henchman came from the less prosperous end of a widely spread clan of farmers, builders, local government officials, living in and about a small West Country town. As Henchman had observed, he owed the professional eligibility of his first name to the dissenting tradition of his family.

'My father sometimes preached in the chapel we attended. I managed to slough off most of my relations early in life. They were equally glad to see the back of me.'

He was revealed, not surprisingly, as a problem child from the start, awkward combination of inconvenient intelligence, unwillingness to do any of the things expected of him. Henchman emphasized, too, that from birth his physical appearance was regarded as against him. Beals was only partially in agreement about that.

'Even before he got shot up, Henchman's looks may well have upset people, though there must always have been something compelling about him. That face, I mean. Full of interest in all sorts of ways, especially if you know his history. I agree it would be a shock to come on him

28

round a corner suddenly, if you were in the jumpy state one so often is. Then, on top of that, comes Henchman's spiky personality. His own comparison of himself with King Saul is important, not only as showing self-knowledge but in conscious acceptance of the royal dignity.'

The truly extraordinary thing was the juvenile age at which Henchman had recognized in himself a vocation for photography. This childhood dedication appears to have made itself known several years before possession of means to satisfy the urge. Patient saving took place – early example of Henchman's self-control, if determined to practise that quality – resulting at last in acquisition of a battered old box of a Kodak that had passed through many hands, and was long out of date even at the period of purchase. In days of photographic eminence (usually with the object of disconcerting sitters judged self-satisfied) Henchman would once in a way return to this relic of professional immaturity.

'He described himself rather acidulously as, to coin a phrase, the sort of child whose nose was always buried in a book,' said Beals. 'Spoke of the moment when he could read to himself as one of the turning points of his life. A pity none of my novels were on the market in those days to start him off on easy history. He might have learnt a lot about the Lollards from *The Wizard on the Heath*.'

'A lot about other things too, darling,' said Louise Beals. 'You don't want a little boy to get bad habits.'

In spite of being tricky, indeed impossible to handle, as a child, Henchman's progress was steady enough. He won a grant from elementary school to local grammar-school, would certainly have had the chance of going to the university, if war had not come along at about the time when that would have been in question.

'All the same,' said Beals, 'Henchman's real education – like that of so many people who have been laid up in bed for long stretches, when still relatively young – came from wolfing down everything on earth in the way of reading matter, when lying in hospital. Talking to him, one is astonished at the ground he's covered.'

At some stage, probably before advancement from elementary to grammar-school (that seems uncertain, possibly during holidays), Henchman worked as errand-boy for a local firm selling agricultural accessories: gardening tools, fertilizers, wire-mesh, suchlike goods. Stock was stored in a warren of rambling buildings on the outskirts of the town. Henchman, from earliest age capable of getting what he wanted, persuaded the boss to allow him to use a shack or cubby-hole among the tumbledown warehouses at the back of the premises for a dark-room and depository for photographic paraphernalia. Henchman being Henchman, he probably also induced his employer to have a lock fixed, and may well have retained rights over this hide-out after leaving the job.

The same ability to obtain what he had set his eye on was additionally illustrated by the manner in which he used to corral children into acting for him as photographic models. When reminiscing on the subject to Beals, Henchman would complain of the obstinacy, thick headedness, of the childish mind, at the same time rejoicing that he would never be saddled with offspring of his own.

He would photograph picked children in loosely connected groups, rigging them out in odds and ends of fancy-dress, an old top hat, scraps of ceremonial army uniform (anticipating the hippies), a Fifth of November mask, trappings of that sort. These child studies were eventually published in an album (now hard to obtain), with an introduction by a wellknown poet, then a friend, later falling out with Henchman on the subject of the merits of some building or landscape.

'If you haven't seen those pictures of children they might sound quaint,' said Beals. 'Let me assure you that, whatever else they were, quaint they were not. Nothing could be less. The word sinister might come to mind. As with truly original productions, it is impossible to describe them. Something of the stylized convention of figures in a stained-glass window – mediaeval rather than nineteenth-century – young comedians by Watteau, except that everything by Henchman was peculiarly English. He never at any stage showed signs of that international gloss certain excellent photographs acquire, probably in spite of themselves.'

Beals said that Henchman warmed up, when speaking about these early photographs of his, in a manner that nothing else – certainly not skirting round the subject of love – ever quite quickened.

'One of the photographs in the album, taken when he couldn't have been at the most more than fourteen or fifteen, was of a village tart. That was looking ahead in a way to the post-war years, what might be called Henchman's Blue Period. I don't know what his relationship with this girl was. Anyway matey enough for her to act as model for him. She must have been older than Henchman, though age doesn't seem to have meant much to him when sexual development was taking place. He started early. All the sadder that what happened did happen, though you might look at it the other way, and say how lucky he was not to have wasted time, leaving so comparatively much experience behind him.'

Beals tended to ruminate a moment on that question.

'To return to the point, he took a series of photographs of this girl lying naked on her back in a shallow pool among some beech woods. Absolutely everything on display, not a hair missing. That was rarer in photographs of those days than now. Round the naked lady were floating bits of garbage, empty beer bottles, a tin or two prised open, an old boot, possibly a dead dog. I don't remember all the items. There was rather a row about this early experiment in Henchman realism. People were extraordinarily fussy in those days. Of course Henchman totally surmounted all that. Even then he had complete self-confidence.'

Probably in consequence of these embryonic photographic ventures, Henchman, after the errand-boy stint, seems to have obtained some sort of employment with a photographer in the town. Again, that could possibly have been during school holidays. There he no doubt picked up a certain amount of technical information about lenses, camera speeds, trick effects, all that. Otherwise, the job was likely to have offered no more scope at the time than by lending a hand posing wedding couples who wanted the occasion to go on record, or dealing with minor administrative details connected with causing the flash to go off at the right moment in the Market Hall at the Annual Dinner of the Ancient Order of Buffaloes.

What would have happened had opportunity arisen, owing to age, of proceeding on to the university a year or two earlier, is hard to say. As things were, war broke out. Henchman – doing a certain amount of his own photographic work on the side all the time, as well as whatever else involved him – seems positively to have welcomed changing his mode of life for that of the army. Beals looked on that as destiny.

'Henchman knew that he must be made a sacrifice, become the Fisher King, a foreordained figure down the ages.'

6

The afternoon he came on board the *Alecto*, Gary Lamont was already aware of suffering one of those intestinal attacks to which he was subject. Without much hope of success, he decided to attempt warding off the disorder with a drink or two, probably no more than prelude to retirement to his cabin for the rest of the evening, cutting out dinner. In some respects this course of action did not too much frustrate him. In any case he felt he needed a rest, and, like many devotees of power, was not much concerned about what and when he ate. Now that he was physically removed from the normal tumult of daily life he wanted to think out several matters directly concerning himself.

First, there was the diagnosis a specialist had given about the condition of his heart. Lamont did not propose to make a drastic alteration of habit on account of that formal statement. At the same time certain suggested minor adjustments were for consideration. Unexpectedly enough, this warning, however ominous, might be used with advantage in connection with another matter occupying Lamont's reflections. By coming aboard *Alecto* he had now entered the tactical area in which a plan of campaign would be required over and above the general strategic principles he had decided upon regarding this last objective. He would have to make what the army called an appreciation of the situation.

The military approach was not, as such, particularly sympathetic to Lamont. He was too young to have been conscripted into the war, though belonging to a generation still liable for national service. Lamont, his ambition – unlike Henchman's – taking other than military forms, had little to chronicle in his brief career as a soldier, which carried him no further than being promoted corporal in the Army Education Corps. The limitations imposed by rank alone must have made him disfavour the army.

Both Lamont's parents had been commercial artists. They were Londoners with roots in the North, probably ultimately in Scotland, as Lamont was said to have relations in Glasgow, where he had met his first wife. His own journalism had begun on a North Country paper, from which, through column-writing and minor editorships, he had quickly leapfrogged into a distinctly promising position in Fleet Street. Among other useful attributes, Lamont could write capably on financial matters. By now he had a finger in various pies replenished with appetizing ingredients.

Possessing exceptional abilities for getting on in the world, Lamont had also experienced more than usual good luck. An easy social manner helped. Lamont's air always suggested that he would be a good man from whom to seek advice on almost any practical matter. If consulted, he never made any difficulties about offering specific recommendations, whether familiar with the matter in hand or not. That always created a pleasing impression. Enquirers in this field reported counsel given as on the whole sound.

As usual in such cases a minority grumbled. That was much the same in the office. Most of his subordinates spoke well of Lamont, some with near adoration, while a small but articulate caucus hated him unreservedly. It was easy to hate Lamont. He was open to being hated for himself, or simply on account of the success he was up to now making of life. Lamont himself was well aware of possessing an eminently hateable side. That did not at all worry him. His own capacity for hatred, equipping him to reciprocate in kind, was not at all to be despised. The further he ascended the ladder, the more blood feuds simmered within Lamont's professional environment.

So far as current jobs were concerned, what could not be judged other than a plum of the juiciest ripeness, hung at that moment swaying on the branch, waiting to be picked. Opinions differed as to whether or not this would fall into Lamont's hands. In the eyes of those well instructed as to where such fruits were likely to come to rest, he was one of two or three favourites. The same master-minds also agreed that there was always the chance of an outsider bearing off the prize.

'These things are dicey,' Middlecote said. 'Only a man with steady nerve would risk being out of London, when a matter of such moment to himself hung in the scales.'

If Middlecote had known about the heart condition, he would not have judged Lamont's strength of nerve less firm. Lamont's own view may well have been, if time were likely to be short (though such was no more than a possibility), that additional impetus was given to having some fun with the job, while the going remained good. As long as he stayed alive, there was also an emotional goal which he hoped to attain.

7

The *Alecto*'s small bar, at the far end of which was an exit
to the deck, stood in the corner of a large saloon extending
across most of the ship's breadth. In the other corner, at
this end of the main saloon, a door gave on to a lesser
saloon used for continental breakfasts and buffet meals.
Between this last door and the recess which enclosed the
bar, a platform had been raised for the five-piece band,
which played in the evenings. A dance-floor of no great
size was set in the centre of the room, where a few persons
would dance after dinner, as a rule not occupying the floor
for long.

Lamont took a high stool at the short end of one of the
bar's two right-angles, and ordered a drink. Several stools
away, on the long side of the bar, another drinker had
already established himself in good time, the evening being
still not far advanced. This personage, not at all young, in
fact probably well into his seventies, shared with Lamont
an oddly boyish look, without any of Lamont's cheeky
office-boy air. So far as this elderly man resembled a boy
at all, that was an overgrown schoolboy, an unsatisfactory

boy, full of excuses for lessons unlearnt, slovenly turnout, lack of cleanliness, undesirable habits.

He wore a linen coat and darkish trousers, a tie of variegated stripes, which seemed likely to simulate rather than actually represent, collective association with club or regiment to which the wearer belonged. Any implied boyishness was at once flatly denied by the puffy blotched complexion which recalled the foxed parchment of an ancient document. Hair, fairly abundant, hanging round the bald summit of the skull, texture like damp thread, was not so much white or grey as the same tone as the face.

In spite of this relentlessly seedy exterior, a seediness bordering on rank squalor, in another direction – unexpected as the boyishness, perhaps slightly associated with it – a kind of half-remembered panache was detectable. A plea seemed somehow being put forward without any very strong conviction even by the defendant himself. There could be no doubt about being battered by Time, nor for that matter by excess in one form or another, probably most known forms. All the same some sort of shy pretext, however feeble, as to regretted better days, rescued the ensemble from sheer repulsion, even if the apprehension stopped only just short of that. This appeal, not to be judged too harshly, was also made with a touch of humour, admittedly humour of a rather machine-made sort.

'Bit more ice, Tino.'

'Yes, Mr Jack.'

It was not clear whether this early drinker's surname was Jack – possibly known to the barman from previous cruises – or, in the assurance that he would spend a good deal of time in the bar, he had imparted the name as a matter of convenience. On this or another trip he might even have requested the barman to dispense with a distancing formality, and call him by a christian name. Possibly the barman, unable to stomach an absolute familiarity of that kind with a customer, had himself added 'Mr', preferring a

mode of address not wholly lacking in respect, even having
something of the old retainer speaking to a son of the house,
indulged since childhood.

So far as bars were concerned, Mr Jack certainly showed
every sign of being a son of the house. A first-name seemed
more than possible, nor did that necessarily rule out this
customer's possible affinity with the *Alecto*'s staff. After the
call for ice Mr Jack appeared to become lost in melancholy
reflection.

Lamont did not take in all this at once. He was not given to
analysing the character of strangers who came his way,
beyond keeping an eye out as to how their behaviour might
affect himself. If for no other reason, he had too much to do as
a rule on his own account. He was almost startled to hear his
name suddenly spoken by so apparently inanimate an adjacent
body. The tone, hoarse, slurred, deferential, yet at the same
time slightly matey, indicated a person whose profession
required getting quickly on to terms with a diversity of
people; a door-to-door salesman, popular broadcaster, political public speaker, someone inured to ingratiating himself
with a potentially unfriendly audience.

'It is Mr Lamont, isn't it?'

'That's my name.'

Where a man was put at risk by bores − using that
terminology in its widest connotation to embrace not only
individuals of tedious personality, also those probably
harmless in themselves, who through no fault of their own
happened to obstruct his intended course of action −
Lamont felt in general well able to grapple. In this area
bars, for which Lamont had an ingrained taste, always held
endemic hazards. Lamont faced that. He was a steady, not
excessive, drinker, who, as an unaccompanied traveller, also
judged himself safer in the bar, rather than at a table in the
saloon, where a single man could easily be enveloped by a
large unprofitable group of fellow-passengers without
means of quick escape.

'Thought I knew your face, Mr Lamont.'

'Have we met somewhere?'

'No, never actually met.'

The words died away, their dwindling leaving no sense of embarrassment, only deep sadness. Notwithstanding the comparatively early hour, Mr Jack had evidently buoyed himself up already with a few drinks. Now he made an effort to explain why Lamont's face was familiar to him.

'Seen you in the chair sometimes at meetings – then of course your picture in the paper, when something's been on.'

Lamont diagnosed a journalist of fairly lowly order, possibly an employee on the business side of a newspaper, now retired, become more than ever alcoholic with loss of occupation. He was accustomed to strangers knowing something of his own activities, while at the same time possessing no very clear idea as to what those activities amounted to. Lamont had no objection to being regarded as a public figure. He rather liked that. Even so, it seemed best to find out a little more before committing himself to too much cordiality.

'How do you come to attend the sort of meetings where I've been in the chair?'

Lamont asked the question as if such occasions had not been brought to a close by retirement, which outward appearances of the dilapidated figure seemed to make fairly certain.

'I was standing in on some PR job when I saw you once – twice, I think. Done a certain amount of free-lancing in Public Relations. Been in the travel business too, off and on, courier and the like. That was in my younger days. Always managed to be fairly free from the office-bound state.'

Mr Jack mentioned several wellknown travel agents, who had employed him at one time or another, tailing off into names unknown to Lamont, who uttered some

39

commonplace about the advantages that freedom and travel had to offer. He was preparing to freeze off too much chat. Mr Jack, on the other hand, having momentarily overcome depression of spirit, wanted to talk.

'My relations sent me on this trip. Couldn't have afforded it myself, living as I do on a small annuity I arranged. Always kept my head on that, if not much else. When I made a tidy sum I'd put a bit away. Then, having been in the racket myself, I get a cut rate. My brother told me he'd stump up the money, just to get rid of me for a week or two. My brother was in chemicals. Did pretty well. I'm not the sort of relative any family wants hanging about in the neighbourhood. I can see that myself. My brother always though I was after his wife. Even these days, if you'll believe me. Wish I was. That's what comes of having a bad reputation with the opposite sex. How about another one, Mr Lamont?'

'No, thanks. I'm a bit off colour, as a matter of fact. Going to turn in early and have a good rest.'

The drink, at least temporarily, had caused Lamont to feel better. He made preparations for closing down on all further contact, if necessary without undue politeness. Should matters become no worse than at present he was prepared to sit it out until he felt ready for bed.

'I think I will,' said Mr Jack. 'Tino, same again. What I mean is those free as air jobs have their own dangers. When you're on your own, earning a living by moving from place to place, very pleasant in a way, easy to get into trouble too.'

Lamont idly concurred, without giving the least thought to what Mr Jack might be rambling on about.

'Women, I mean. I expect you're a married man, Mr Lamont?'

'My wife died last year.'

'Oh dear, I am sorry to have asked that.'

Mr Jack was overcome with remorse at having put so

unhappy a question. He really looked dreadfully upset. Tears even appeared in his eyes. He had to wipe them away with his knuckles. Lamont, annoyed at having been forced involuntarily into this reference to the loss of Doll (which he still hated to think about, however much he planned to replace her), spoke some banal sentences to ward off too pressing a display of sympathy. The last thing he wanted was a flood of sentimentality from someone like this bar loafer on a subject that could still disturb him. Mr Jack, on the other hand, in the manner of persons instantaneously stirred in such a manner, showed equal ease in recovering from his gaffe.

'Really am sorry to have asked that. Very sorry. Shouldn't have done it. Can't apologize enough. Sure you won't have another one?'

Lamont shook his head again. Mr Jack, having established an opening, now warmed to a subject that turned out to be chronically on his mind.

'Now married is something I've not been. Never really seriously asked a woman to marry me. Don't know why. Always seemed to get on all right with them without doing that. Well, come to think of it, I may have sometimes spoken in a manner that made one or two of them think that marriage was on the *tapis*. Even then the thing didn't amount to much. I mean I could never quite see the advantage. Might easily spoil everything. Often does.'

Lamont laughed. At least this was better than having to talk about Doll. Mr Jack was not a man with whom to be serious. Mr Jack seemed to feel that himself. At the same time he was anxious to define his own position.

'Not that I don't like women. Not at all. Like them all too well, I'm afraid. But you need to know them.'

'Aren't you talking of women in a very oldfashioned way for these days? Very macho, as they say,'

'I'm an oldfashioned man,' said Mr Jack. 'Wouldn't wish it otherwise. I fall in love very easily. Do to this day. If I

41

haven't married, that certainly isn't because I don't fall in love. You wouldn't believe the girls I've fallen in love with, if that's what you call it, and I don't quite see how you could give it any other name. You'd laugh at the messes I get into even at an age when I ought to know better. Of course age does limit you. No doubt about that. Most disastrous effect. And this too.'

He tapped his glass.

'So people say.'

Mr Jack thought for a moment. He screwed his face into an angle that implied doubt as to the propriety of the question he was about to pose, fearing perhaps another blunder like asking Lamont about his deceased wife. Finally he decided the enquiry was permissible.

'Ever fallen in love with a tart?'

Lamont took the question lightly. He could not quell all curiosity as to what might be coming next, though doubtful of the wisdom of allowing a toper of this kind to maunder on. For the moment no decision had to be taken. Having levelled the question, Mr Jack sank back into meditation. Lamont took the opportunity of nodding to the barman to provide himself with another drink unhampered by anyone else's hospitality. He made up his mind not to pause long over it, just allow himself to hear whatever might be said about falling in love with a tart, then retire to bed. Mr Jack came to with a jerk. Now he spoke gravely.

'I don't mean a girl who just sleeps round a bit, doesn't even mind a little monetary sweetener once in a while. I mean a real whore. A prostitute. A girl who walks the streets.'

Lamont shook his head.

'Happened to me a year or two after the war. I'd been in the army. You know, I didn't particularly mind the army. I was always moving about in the mob I patronized. Having some experience of shunting bodies by rail and other means, I did a lot of jobs in Army Transport and the like. Embarkation Officer, and so on. And the girls – my goodness.'

Mr Jack became lost in thought again, then remembered he was giving an account of a specific experience.

'Where was I? Girls. I was saying I hadn't been long out of the army – stayed on a bit, having nothing better to do – and, become a civilian again, rather at a loose end, picked up a tart one afternoon when I was wending my way through Soho. It was in Dean Street, I remember, the Oxford Street end. Wasn't particularly enjoyable, but for some reason I took her telephone number, and went again. Happened several times. Never liked it all that. She was as cold as a slice of fish on a block of ice, and very keen on the cash side of the romp. All the same, to cut a long story short, I fell in love with the girl. She wasn't even a girl, to tell the truth. Forty, if a day, yet I couldn't get her out of my hair. Would you believe it?'

Lamont hardly could believe it. He was distinctly shocked. A strong undercurrent of respectability had run through his upbringing. If he had himself ever picked up a tart that would have been an episode he preferred to dismiss entirely from his mind. The idea of falling in love with a prostitute was not only repellent to him, but in his own case unthinkable. He was appalled at the notion. Mr Jack's flow of revelation was not, however, to be stemmed.

'As I was saying, she was a real whore. Looked every inch of it. Worked that end of Dean Street in the afternoons. Her name was Theda, and about the same age as myself. Rather broad in the beam. What I'd call a good armful. That's my taste. To tell you the truth Theda wasn't all that unlike a lady in front of me in the queue at the Purser's Office, the afternoon we came on board. She gave her name as Dr Tiptoft, and was having a rare row about what she called the insanitary odour in the ladies' toilet. I was interested, because many a time I've had to deal with complaints like that, when I've been taking a party of tourists abroad. She was younger than Theda, no beauty either by any manner of means, but not so bad. Not one of those little flibbertigibets. Quite a lot of them have come my way too in the line of duty. Now that's a very goodlooking girl attending the lame photographer. Not my type, but a real beauty. He's a famous man now, I believe.'

'You could call him that, I suppose.'

Lamont was not too keen on hearing Henchman's celebrity rubbed in.

'Remarkable, too, the way he gets about. I expect you know him, Mr Lamont? In your position you've probably been photographed by him yourself?'

'I have as a matter of fact.'

'You have?'

'Some years ago.'

Mr Jack sighed.

'You won't believe it,' he said, 'Henchman once photographed me.'

'Why shouldn't he?'

'Well, I'm not the sort of person he usually photographs now. I suppose I might appear in one of those low life pictures Henchman does sometimes. I saw a series of them in a Colour Supplement. Must have been the best part of thirty years ago he took me. Wouldn't remember it himself. I might even remind him, when I've had just the right amount to drink. It would have to be just the right amount. Not too much, not too little. Very hard to hit always.'

Mr Jack had failed to do so at the moment of speaking. Drink was beginning to tell on narrative powers, which, suddenly come into being, were now steadily diminishing in lucidity. Further conversation in the same vein, projected across the bar from some little distance off, was in any case cut short by entry of two more passengers, who appropriated the stools across which Mr Jack had been transmitting fragments of his life. Waves of intoxication,

44

lapping against the Plimsoll Line of articulation, now rose in a powerful swell. Even if continuation in anything like a similar strain had been possible the narrative would certainly have been less than welcome to the new arrivals. The two middle-aged American male friends, who were travelling together, formed an effective *cordon sanitaire* in sheltering Lamont from further confidences had these been proffered. He saw that he would not be able to finish his second drink in peace.

Grey-moustached, sprucely dressed in dark blue blazers with brass buttons, impeccably barbered, an aura of almost self-conscious conventionality was only a little gainsaid by the shared whim of one wearing under his blazer a red T-shirt inscribed in blue lettering with the slogan BASICALLY BACH; the other, seeming to respond, possibly challenge, with an analogous garment, colours reversed, which proclaimed MARGINALLY MAHLER. After ordering drinks they immediately embarked on musical discussion. More than once Lamont caught the name of Boulez.

Beals reported this musical controversy to be maintained throughout the whole of the cruise.

'One supposed them to have booked on the *Alecto* to find a venue where their self-sufficiency would remain safely undisturbed. They never spoke to anyone else, so far as I know, until the dramatic moment that changed everything. I suppose, for one thing, they had so much musical ground to cover with each other, there was no time for that. It might be that only at sea they felt they could settle once and for all whatever musical difference it was that divided them. My own opinion is that violent musical debate was their immutable condition, without which neither could have survived. A kind of life-machine. That state of existence would not have been affected by taking a holiday, or any other change of regime.'

Lamont, whose interest in ballet made some of these

scraps of musical talk comparatively intelligible, listened for a time. Then, aware of an augmenting interior uneasiness, he went off to his cabin. He intended to remain there for at least twenty-four hours.

8

Beals, continuing to hold forth to his wife and the Middlecotes on the subject of Henchman, transmitted a creditable amount of information, considering how recently the subject had come to engage his thoughts.

'When people tried to make trouble about the alleged obscenity of Henchman's photographs when he was young, or indeed grumble about the sort of thing he says now — which I imagine must always have been much the same — he found no difficulty in seeing them off. Henchman has an extraordinary instinct for putting himself in the right. I only wish I had the same capacity.'

'Oh, you have, Valentine,' said his wife. 'You have that gift to perfection.'

'Yes, you don't do yourself justice,' said Middlecote. 'But how was Henchman employed in the war, when he got messed up like that? He was a pongo, I presume.'

'How extraordinary,' said Louise Beals. 'I always thought Henchman was English.

She said that just to tease Middlecote, having often heard him use the expression.

'Pongo is a naval nickname for a soldier,' began Middlecote. 'When Valentine and I –'

'Louise is only pulling your leg,' said Fay Middlecote. 'We don't want a lot of wartime reminiscence, except what happened to Henchman.'

Beals continued the Henchman saga on his own terms, though later able to add a good deal to what he had then known.

'I suspect Henchman volunteered before the statutory eighteen-and-a-half, possibly before his eighteenth birthday. The requisite amount of time must have been passed in the ranks to get recommended for a commission, then to go through all the process of becoming an officer. What is more obscure is how Henchman arrived on the Staff. In the light of his photographic interests, job in civilian life, already formed determination to make photography his career, he might easily have been absorbed into some technical branch dealing with interpretation of air photographs. Even gone into camouflage. He would certainly have been good at both of those. Possibly he did get sent on the Air Photography Course at the Intelligence Training Centre. Then, seeing other students in the same building doing the War Intelligence Course made an ambitious fellow like Henchman dream of higher things. He may have deliberately intrigued to get his name on the WIC list, so as to be equipped for duties on the General Staff. Henchman would have been well up to that. On the other hand, it could have been sheer chance. In the Services you never can tell. My own guess is that Henchman engineered himself into what he regarded as a form of military activity superior to interpreting photographs taken by the RAF, though no doubt he would have done that very well.'

Whether or not Beals was right, Henchman, still in his

early twenties with one pip, was appointed Intelligence Officer at a Divisional Headquarters. The rapidity of the whole performance, especially in the light of Henchman's early circumstances and specialized qualifications, underlines his own enterprise, ambition, tenacity, not least powers of making his abilities known in a world that could easily have proved mutually antipathetic. Beals emphasised all that.

'These things stick out even more when you think of Henchman's personal appearance. I know some women find him attractive, but quite a lot don't. Still, you could argue that no one would overlook a face like that. To be noticeable in the Services is by no means always an advantage in a subordinate. Gets all the bullshitting duties for catching a superior's eye. I served under an admiral, for instance, who only liked tall good-looking blonds, officers or ratings, didn't matter. He was a man of perfectly normal sexual tastes. Known in his younger days in Portsmouth as rather a *coureur* I believe. Just preferred that physical type, when there was a job to be done. Accordingly, tall goodlooking blonds were often called upon for tasks not always the most agreeable ones.'

'But, Valentine, don't you think your admiral must –'

Beals cut his wife short.

'Henchman would be selected for quite opposite reasons obviously. As I've said, Henchman's face could – undoubtedly at time does – physically repel people. That doesn't mean he wouldn't have been picked on. Quite the contrary. A pongo – as Piers would call him – who'd been on the WIC at Matlock with Henchman told me he was called The Monkey there. Up to a point that nickname may have been a tribute. Meant that Henchman had made his mark, even was liked. Not that his features are really what you'd describe as simian. He hasn't any of the monkey's innate pathos. In spite of everything, Henchman is entirely without pathos. Almost embarrassingly so. It's one of his outstanding characteristics. But I've always been interested in his fellow students calling him The Monkey. Like so many nicknames, it expresses only very indistinctly what is felt by the bestowers. It just shows they felt something quite strongly. When they pinned it on him, it was simply the nearest thing they could get to the impression made by Henchman's face on the community – in this case it just happened to be a military community – in which he found himself.'

'I think he does look rather like a monkey,' said Middlecote. 'Some rare species. Make a good brand mark.'

'I ran across this fellow who talked about Henchman in Sicily some years ago, when there was a certain amount of gossip about Barberina Rookwood going to live with Henchman. He was a journalist. He said that another reason that might have caused Henchman to be called The Monkey on the Course was that he was going through some dietary fad at the time. He used to go into meals a quarter of an hour early, and eat all the salad provided for about fifty officers. Anyway most of it, which was no doubt little enough. Two points about that. First, it shows Henchman's determination to get what he wanted, but there's also an interesting second possibility. It may have been ritual. As a King he had to abstain from flesh at certain seasons. Partake only of the fruits of the earth. That is for consideration.'

'Valentine, you must try and keep sane on the question of Henchman being the Fisher King.'

'My own description of his face would be that of a Shakespearian clown, who has been treated to a quarter turn of the rack, before having time to explain that he is perfectly willing to confess anything required of him.'

'He's like Tiny Tim in *A Christmas Carol*,' said Louise. 'A diabolical version of Tiny Tim.'

9

Sir Dixon and Lady Tiptoft, sitting a few tables away, were reading. Sir Dixon had *My White House Years*, by Henry Kissinger; Lady Tiptoft, Marshall McLuhan's *Understanding Media*. They were now joined by their daughter, who brought a notebook with her. She took no notice of her parents, nor they of her. She began to look through the notebook. Fay Middlecote, tired of the subject of Henchman for the moment, began to assess Lorna Tiptoft's clothes.

'Don't miss Dr Lorna's white cassock trimmed with gold, Louise. It would pass for a hospital overall. What was the trouble you had with her father, Piers? You were saying he was such a nuisance.'

'It was when we were handling that governmental account' – Middlecote mentioned the name of one of the Ministries – 'I didn't deal with Tiptoft personally. He had to approve what my opposite number arranged. My contact was OK. It was Tiptoft. My opposite number hated him. Said he had been in the Treasury originally, then downgraded to some lesser Ministry, a demotion Tiptoft attributed to stuffy colleagues being disturbed by his dangerous brilliance, the contempt in which he held formal politeness.'

'He doesn't look polite,' said Louise Beals. 'I wouldn't like to be married to him. Lady Tiptoft's so thin he must starve her.'

'She was his secretary in one of the Ministries to which he was banished. Throughout his career Tiptoft has always made a virtue of being disobliging, awkward to negotiate with, forthright about other people's shortcomings, furious if his own are pointed out. Likes to refer to himself as a man who has never truckled to another man alive. This bureaucrat I did my stuff with told me Tiptoft would kiss an arse with the best when that was needed.'

'Well, you're always telling me circumstances arise when we've all got to do that,' said Fay Middlecote. 'I've seen you go through the motions once or twice.'

'I don't deny it for a moment. I'll compete with anyone. But I don't set up as Sturdy Piers Middlecote, the only executive in all advertising who doesn't know the taste of bootpolish and much else besides. My bureaucratic friend assured me that if any really knotty points came up, Tiptoft always took the line of least resistance, ostensibly with a bad grace, but choosing the soft option nevertheless. As bad manners became increasingly accepted as a sign of keeping up with the times, Tiptoft's methods paid off quite well from his own point of view. All his judgments were safely pedestrian, except for keeping a weather eye on promotion, also popular prejudice of the moment. I heard him explaining to someone on board that he was no élitist, nothing smooth about him, a man who'd come up the hard way. In point of fact few people can have had an easier run.'

Middlecote's breakdown of Sir Dixon Tiptoft's characteristics was halted by the sight of two more persons arriving at the Tiptoft table, a rather dishevelled middle-aged woman, with a young man, evidently her son. It appeared the mother wanted to introduce him to Lorna Tiptoft, with whom she was sharing a cabin.

'This is Robin. I've told you so much about him that you must feel you almost know him already. He always says I talk about him too much to people I meet.'

The young man, tall, pale, a little drooping in appearance, was subsequently subject of much argument as to his looks. Even those like Fay Middlecote, prepared merely in the interests of contradictiousness, to give support to his claims, agreed that such looks as he had were of a notably ordinary kind. In fact his ordinariness was never challenged by anyone. Aspects of him that were not ordinary emerged plainly enough from what happened, but Beals was always at pains to insist that this preview was interesting only because it gave not the smallest hint of what was to follow. Beals, whatever he might think, was not necessarily right. Neither his wife nor Fay Middlecote would subscribe to quite the low voltage he indexed as Jilson's. Beals's sense of drama exaggerated Jilson's dimness to make a better story. For once Middlecote supported the Beals view. Lorna Tiptoft introduced her parents.

'This is Mrs Jilson, who's with me in my cabin – and Robin Jilson, her son.'

Mrs Jilson exchanged a few words with Lady Tiptoft. The young man attempted to engage Sir Dixon in some sort of small talk without receiving much encouragement. He was taken on with much more enthusiasm by Lorna Tiptoft. They seemed to have found some taste in common almost immediately. Then the Jilsons passed on, Mrs Jilson giving her son instructions to meet her on deck later. She disappeared through the door at the end of the saloon, leaving him in a chair reading *The Focal Encyclopaedia of Photography*.

'Dr Tiptoft took rather a fancy to the young man, didn't she?' said Louise Beals. 'I thought she was going to eat him.'

'He wouldn't make a very substantial meal,' said Fay Middlecote. 'The poor boy doesn't look at all well.'

Beals, forced to endure this interlude of discussing Tiptofts and Jilsons, was by no means finished with Henchman's early life.

'The Division – I rather think an armoured one – to which Henchman was eventually posted as Intelligence Officer was one of those engaged in the Italian campaign. I'm not sure whether or not that was his first staff job. It was the moment when our forces were about to cross the Po, or had just negotiated the river. Henchman had only been with them for a matter of weeks. He was cruising along in a scout-car when a shell knocked the vehicle out, totally smashed it up. Henchman himself was very severely wounded. When they picked him up no one thought he would survive. He was in a terrible condition.'

In due course Henchman was moved to England, where a long series of surgical traffickings followed. Those were by no means at an end when discharged from hospital on the crutches to which he was now committed for life. For some reason of his own, possibly because more convenient for the stationary position Henchman often adopted, he always retained shoulder (rather than elbow) crutches. This may have been a characteristic eccentricity, combined with refusal to take on additional medical gadgets to make photography easier. He did, however, according to Beals, also wear some sort of surgical applicances on his legs.

How much of life remained to Henchman when he came out of hospital was another matter. Continued existence was certainly in question. The period in bed was no doubt rightly emphasized by Beals as that when so much reading had been achieved. Henchman told Beals that he used to read everything, good, bad, indifferent, whatever he could lay hands on. All this reading supplied one of the most formidable weapons in the Henchman armoury. His knowledge of books probably helped to give him more in common with Beals than might have been expected, when they talked together later.

The havoc brought about on Henchman's body naturally put him in a most adverse condition for earning a living, especially a living as a photographer, a profession he was still determined to follow. He totally ignored his own parlous state. That was Henchman's style, Beals said, ramming home the point that it was a regal style. Apart from other difficulties was that of accommodation. So many West End buildings had been bombed that studios were hard to find during the immediately post-war years. Henchmen's relative lack of mobility made a fashionable quarter essential on account of the clientèle he envisaged. He must have a studio people were prepared to visit. When he became known Henchman was sometimes prepared to go 'on location', if that suited him, which it did only rarely. He preferred everything to be on his own terms. The problem of his trade address was settled in an unexpected way.

How Henchman kept afloat during those early years is not at all distinct. He would have been paid off by the Army with some sort of gratuity, also disability pension, the combination of both not adding up to much. At the beginning there were undoubtedly dubious activities, not necessarily always photographic ones, of the kind Henchman liked to laugh about. These ways of earning a living seem to have been various, especially when not very estimable. He spoke of some of them to Beals.

'Henchman told me that he was fortunate enough to possess as few moral prejudices as a man could easily discard by the age of twenty-two or twenty-three. Connection with the Black Market seems to have been among the more humdrum of his enterprises during those years. One should add that he undoubtedly liked to exaggerate relatively sinister aspects of those undercover days. More picturesque than small commercial advertising jobs of a commonplace order that wellwishers would put in his way.'

Henchman, if close friends would have been hard to name, always possessed a wide acquaintance. He never wasted a contact. While struggling along in this way he was also, when opportunity arose, taking such photographs as offered of his own sort. During these days of scraping a living as best he could he willingly pleaded guilty to the charge of sacrificing aesthetic ideals to financial considerations, occupying himself with a little commercial photography like wheelbarrows and mowing-machines, objects he had handled in his errand-boy days.

The sordid nature of his lodgements was to some extent a positive advantage. One of Henchman's early studios, if it could be dignified by that name, was in a badly blitzed house in Soho. His two or three rooms were rented on easy terms, as being too uncomfortable for the whores who occupied the rest of the building. The whores – as may be seen from one of Henchman's later albums – turned out comparatively rewarding neighbours. There was also a little pornography on the side.

Speaking of the last, Henchman always insisted that his own pain and humiliation, although moral rather than physical, were far greater than any inflicted on predominantly sadomasochist customers. Reminiscences of that interlude in his photographic novitiate always dwelt on the tedium, once habituated, of going through the drill (sometimes more or less literally the drill) of such specialized commissions.

'I much preferred photographing gas-cookers or fridges to such sitters, though one could hardly call them sitters, as, understandably enough, the last thing they wanted to do was sit, either before or after their photographic session. In the end I had to summon up all my interest in the frailties of mankind, in his or her photogenic aspects, to go through with even the more exotic deviations – and believe me some of them were quite exotic. I don't think the sort of assistant I could afford in those days minded the routines at all. They kept changing to get better jobs, or else cease earning a comparatively honest living in favour of becoming wholetime tarts or criminals. If a client was prepared to ante-up enough, over and above the rake-off they got in any case, one girl especially, rather a creepy young woman, was far from averse to participating in the proceedings.'

A lot of this about what Beals called Henchman's Blue Period belonged, of course, to later Henchman narrations. Not surprisingly, these equivocal activities on the part of a young photographer, not only on crutches but of startling appearance, began to get round; over and above the fact that Henchman's serious work was becoming known among people interested in photography. Beals thought the Henchman pornographic industry was also quite popular.

'There were probably members of his less reputable clientèle who found the very fact of a crippled photographer of gruesome mien added to the fun of being photographed playing perverse games. Much the same principle as blind and naked musicians providing an orchestra for orgies organised by *faisandé* party-givers in days gone by.'

10

Dissension was at work again among the Tiptofts. Lady Tiptoft had enquired from her daughter what sharing a cabin with Mrs Jilson was like.

'She talks all the time.'

'About her son?'

'Mostly. Ate an orange yesterday she'd taken from the dining-saloon. I had to open the porthole, or rather get a steward to open it.'

Lorna Tiptoft returned to her notebook. Sir Dixon put down Kissinger, marking the place with an envelope.

'The son's a poor fish,' he said.

'Why should you think so?'

'Feeble type.'

'You know nothing about him.'

'I can use my eyes.'

'Your eyes don't tell you the young man's suffering from a rare muscular condition of the cranial motor nerves. If you're uninstructed in medical matters it's better not to pronounce on individual states.'

'I suppose his mother told you that?'

'She didn't have to.'

'I could see something was wrong with him.'

'You amaze me.'

Sir Dixon looked sullen. Lady Tiptoft joined in.

'Is his case of interest to you as a doctor?'

She spoke in a manner that left no doubt about Jilson's health being far from interesting to herself in that or any other sphere.

'As it happens, yes.'

Sir Dixon, returning the envelope to his pocket, went back to Kissinger. Then he got out a pencil and marked a paragraph. Lorna Tiptoft, conveying the impression that she hoped not to be interrupted again by inept comments, began to write rapidly in the notebook. Basically Bach and Marginally Mahler passed, gesticulating at each other. They were making for the bar. Mr Jack, who had just vacated his place there, no doubt to satisfy a brief natural need, passed them moving in the opposite direction. As he skirted the Tiptofts he threw a quick glance towards Lorna Tiptoft. He had perhaps not seen her since, making her complaint at the Purser's Office, she had reminded him a bit of Theda. For an infinitesimal second he seemed to pause, thought better of it, sighed, floundered on again to find whatever place of relief he had in mind. Sir Dixon put Kissinger face downwards open on his knees, and leant back.

'I was thinking of my own Memoirs.'

He spoke meditatively. No one made a comment.

'What I should call them.'

His daughter wrote more angrily than ever in her notebook.

'For instance,' said Sir Dixon. '*His Helmet Now Shall Make a Hive for Bees.*'

Lady Tiptoft demurred.

'I didn't know you ever wore a helmet. Was that when you were fire-watching?'

'I was speaking in poetic terms. It is a quotation.'

His daughter, without looking up, offering her own recommendation. 'Publishers prefer short titles. What about *Bees in My Helmet*?'

I I

'Has Henchman ever photographed you, Valentine?' asked Middlecote. 'I gather from colleagues who've had dealings with him that he's decidedly difficult to handle.'

'From a publicity angle I wouldn't at all mind a Henchman photograph, even if uncomplimentary. The réclame would make up for any psychological bruises suffered by the ego. He never suggested it. As interviewers usually employ the paper's own photographer the matter has never arisen. I should be interested to experience the running commentary on sexual subjects, which appears to upset some of his sitters. Not having heard it one can't judge the momentum. No doubt we'll all become experts during the weeks ahead.'

'It's probably only a form of self-consciousness on account of his state,' said Fay Middlecote. 'He's just terribly unhappy. Can't keep off the subject.'

'What sort of thing does he say?' asked Louise Beals.

'Henchman told a woman he was photographing that he thought it a great piece of impertinence on the part of clubs and suchlike associations to begin letters "Dear Member". It suggested an intimacy to which they had no claim.'

'That isn't very terrible.'

'Not everyone likes that kind of pleasantry. In Henchman's particular case it embarrasses them. People feel avoidance of such specific references to be preferable.'

'He probably had a lot of fun before he was wounded.'

'Henchman himself always implies that. What makes people uncomfortable is a tone that seems to indicate fun is not at an end – anyway up to a point. Some listeners feel that limit, whatever it may be, should be recognized, the subject left alone.'

'What was the next step after photographing the whores?' asked Middlecote. 'Did the smart world gradually seek him out?'

'It was going into business with Eugene,' said Beals. 'You must remember Eugene's photographs of debs being presented, celebrated hostesses, famous actresses, the last two categories not always in their first youth. Eugene rather specialized in ladies of mature age.'

Eugene's shock of white hair, neatly pointed beard, slightly exaggerated bow ties, made him look like a French senator in a *Belle Époque* comic-paper, Henchman told Beals, though in fact he came from Rhyl. Henchman said that, within what were already oldfashioned terms, Eugene possessed a mild strain of originality, had at least when he started. He also knew a great many useful people by the time he came across Henchman. Naturally these had become reduced by the end of the second war (in which Eugene had obtained some sort of official employment), but he returned to a blitzed studio, its reoccupation worth a little discomfort, as Eugene had made his name there, and settled down to work again.

Henchman's first contact with Eugene may have taken place, anyway indirectly, through the byways of the photographic art to which Henchman was committed during his Soho bivouac. It was scarcely more. Eugene, himself homosexual, was also extremely circumspect. He would never have become mixed up in anything about which the faintest whiff of impropriety was to be detected; not (in Henchman's picturesque image) with the extended leg of Sir Dixon Tiptoft's camera tripod. Eugene's photographic assistant, longtime boyfriend, seems to have held less stuffy views. He may not himself have patronized Henchman's pornographic lens, but must have heard about that from friends, who bought the photographs, or even participated in *poses plastiques*.

Whoever first mentioned Henchman to Eugene, whether or not the boyfriend, would certainly have enlarged on technical proficiencies displayed, exceptional personality of the photographer, in addition to Henchman simply as an erotic phenomenon. Even if the subject of Henchman first arose through curiosity that was less than professional, professional considerations must in the long run have gained ascendancy. Besides, Eugene was known to be a goodnatured man. His immediate impulse would have been, so far as he could, to help a deserving young photographer so handicapped physically. At the same time Eugene can scarcely have contemplated from the start taking on Henchman as assistant.

Then Eugene's boyfriend, not particularly young, suddenly died. By that time Eugene, the boyfriend, Henchman, must all have known something of each other, even if uncertainty exists as to just what terms they were on. Probably, in the first instance, the boyfriend was conversant with Henchman's more shady incarnation; latterly Eugene with the reputable – indeed enormously talented – photographs that Henchman was simultaneously taking. Everyone agreed that few photographers of

Eugene's age, experience, standing, would have gone out of their way to pick an assistant on crutches.

'Engagement of such a subordinate suggests that sentimental benevolence spilt over into something not much short of professional masochism,' said Beals. 'None the less that was what Eugene did. Within a week of the boyfriend's demise Henchman was installed as Eugene's assistant.'

'Eugene may have spared a thought for the publicity angle,' said Middlecote. 'Crutches. Facial disarray. An unimaginative man might have seen those only as a disadvantage. A man who'd digested what makes an impact on the public could have looked beyond that. Eugene was after all a competent showman in his own right. It may have been a touch of promotional genius.'

If Eugene, anyway in the past, had possessed good connections for his trade, Henchman, with less extended experience and of a different kind, had managed to get to know quite a lot of serviceable people too. Some of these were a welcome addition to Eugene's depleted list. Eugene was also reminded that his methods needed bringing up to date forthwith. He was probably aware of this already. If not, Henchman made that clear in the plainest terms.

'One talks as if Eugene was a free agent,' said Beals. 'That may well be to miss the point. He could simply have been unable to withstand Henchman's will. Compared with his will, Henchman's mastery of such technicalities as posing and lighting could even represent comparatively minor elements in the birth of the partnership – for partnership it almost immediately became. From the day he entered Eugene's studio, Henchman was launched. He was more than launched. To all intents and purposes he took over in a matter of months.'

12

Beals was forced by the others to break off again to watch the Kopfs pass through the main saloon. He was not entirely unwilling to do that. Both he and Middlecote agreed that Mrs Kopf was uncommonly pretty. Beals had noticed her at the Captain's dinner-party, when her husband, Professor Willard S. Kopf on the passenger-list, had spoken so enthusiastically of archaeological sites to be seen in the Orkneys.

Middlecote, as in most fields of human activity, claimed a smattering of lore on the subject of educational foundations in the United States. He said that Professor Kopf was head of the English Department of a Middle Western college to be categorized as of eminently respectable standing. To prove that, Middlecote mentioned the name of one of its alumni, not only distinguished in the world of international advertising, but known to himself as a colleague of congenial personality.

Professor Kopf looked distinguished too. He was tall, greyhaired, lanky, with the figure of a man much younger than he could have been. Mrs Kopf – greeted as Elaine by some American cruise acquaintances they paused to have a word with – was a good deal younger than her husband. Small, dark, somewhat Latin in appearance, she too was said to have academic affiliations, though there was nothing in the least school-marmish about her.

'Obviously not his first wife,' said Fay Middlecote. 'I should think they were married quite lately.'

'I wonder whether it was a prudent reselection,' said Middlecote. 'She looks a hot little number.'

'Only to libidinous middle-aged men,' said Fay Middlecote. 'She strikes me as a perfectly ordinary rather goodlooking brunette.'

'I like her shoes,' said Louise Beals.

The Kopfs moved on to a table by themselves. Professor Kopf, having ordered drinks, began to glance through what looked like a learned journal he had brought with him. Mrs Kopf seemed happy enough to gaze round the saloon, while she appraised her fellow-passengers.

13

'Once settled in Eugene's studio,' said Beals, 'Henchman immediately brought into play a system by which in effect he controlled all such matters as posing and lighting, while Eugene merely released the shutter. That had the advantage of not worrying sitters who came there for old times' sake on the strength of Eugene's pre-war reputation. After all, to speak literally, Eugene still photographed them. In fact Eugene's action was only a mechanical one. It was super-imposed on Henchman's art. That was no concern of the sitters. Photographic technique was none of their affair. What they wanted was the magic of Eugene pressing the button, and that was what they got.'

This meant that overnight Eugene became what amounted to Henchman's assistant, rather than the other way about. Eugene can hardly have remained unaware of this reversal of roles. Presumably, since he had brought about the transformation himself, he had no objection to the metamorphosis. Growing old, a little tired, he may even have welcomed the Henchman takeover.

In matters of technique that was absolute. The social side,

all the patter, remained in the hands – more precisely on the lips – of Eugene. Patter had always been rather a feature of the business. Eugene, no doubt with reason, regarded himself as adept where female sitters were concerned. Since his earliest days Eugene had specialized in 'great ladies', a favourite phrase, which he employed to cover all overwhelming forms of female presence, social, theatrical, political.

This retention of interlocutory control confirmed, anyway to Eugene's own satisfaction, that he had not surrendered all prestige once attached to his position. Even partially to silence Henchman was agreed to be an achievement in the circumstances. There can also be no doubt that Henchman himself learnt a lot from watching how Eugene dealt with sitters; how he spoke to them (possibly the origin of Henchman's stagey tones); what lines to follow; what lines to avoid; much else beside. This is allowing for the fact that Henchman would often choose to do the exact opposite.

The fact that Eugene had never experienced physical desire for a woman – lady great or ungreat – gave freedom from certain sorts of admiration that might have been photographically inconvenient. It may even have contributed to Eugene's photographs possessing exceptional merit in representing aspects of womanhood other than sexual. In that respect Henchman was in very different case. He let his own tastes be known immediately after Eugene was in his coffin, doing that unambiguously. While Eugene remained alive Eugene ruled the roost when it came to talking; talking, in Eugene's view, playing a not inconsiderable part in creating the 'portraits' for which he was chiefly admired. Henchman never attempted to dilute that element in the partnership, which (in spite of rumours, probably true, of savage mutual recrimination) held together and did good business. Then, after a year or two, suddenly as the former boyfriend, Eugene himself was gathered in.

After (as Henchman put it) Eugene had faded from life's negative, many things were changed. Henchman moved from the neighbourhood of Bond Street to north of the Park, where, paying incomparably lower rent, he rightly judged he could do just as well. The new studio was the one from which Henchman's fame dated. How far that fame was at first to some extent vested in personal peculiarities is hard to estimate. No one – not even rival photographers who disliked Henchman personally, of whom there were several – denied that he was an accomplished performer. At the same time the characteristics, physical and moral, that made up the Henchman *persona* would always have brought notoriety of a sort, in some eyes not particularly desirable notoriety.

'There is nothing at all unique about a man sexually *hors de concours* adopting a flirtatious manner towards women,' said Beals. 'Plenty of irretrievable homosexuals behave like that, not to mention exuberant heterosexuals, who for one reason or another may happen not to be physically available for action that goes beyond the flirtatious. I can supply names if parallels are required, though I would admit both categories usually fall short of Henchman's demeanour.'

Henchman played this line to a point where it seemed to some people to become not much short of sexual bullying, inoperative sexual bullying at that. He always sounded as if possession was what he wanted, and he couldn't wait. This social gambit, implication that he was going to make a pass at any moment, might be just detectably satirical when the woman in question was patently lacking in attraction. Even then the onslaught was not so much relaxed as varied. If it came to that, there was always a touch of satire in Henchman's manner of handling anyone, male or female. Even those who made allowances for his circumstances had been heard to reprehend some of the things he said.

None the less for many women, arguably for most, Henchman's behaviour, perhaps even his condition, seemed to produce a taste for his company. The affection of being a Don Juan – a figure like Mr Jack at a higher level, for ever on the warpath – in no way lessened what some regarded as a faintly perverse partiality for Henchman on the part of the ladies who made up his court.

'Whether they think it a situation like Wycherley's *The Country Wife*, I don't know,' said Beals. 'As against that, a few of Henchman's sitters – though surprisingly few – just frankly dislike him. Their alarm and despondency is recorded in the photographs Henchman takes of people who feel that way.'

For those accustomed to the gentle coaxing small talk of Eugene this was a big change to swallow. In the natural course of things some sitters were dissatisfied for reasons of vanity. Others simply desired a more humdrum approach to their outward appearance, less visual comment on inner peculiarities, perhaps secret habits.

Henchman had two methods of dealing with discontent. He might apologize abjectly for having put such captious persons to the trouble of sitting for him at all, assuring them that he would never dream of charging for photographs, the proofs of which a customer had taken against. By the time he had finished with dissidents of that stamp they had usually not only withdrawn reservations expressed, but ordered more copies than originally intended. Alternatively, Henchman would persuade waverers that he had brought out points of character missed not only by other photographers, but by the sitters' own friends, possibly even the sitters themselves. No doubt that was often true. Even those still uneasy as to whether Henchman's summing up of them was what they inwardly coveted, departed thinking better of themselves, full of praise for Henchman's art.

14

'But what an extraordinary life for Barberina Rookwood,' said Fay Middlecote. 'It must have been going on now for at least six or seven years. She was only seventeen, if that, when she went to be photographed by Henchman, with a dazzling career as a dancer ahead of her. She'd been marked down when quite a child. Then, most definitely, in the *corps de ballet*. She had such a huge success as one of the Fairy Godmothers in *The Sleeping Princess* that they were going to give her the lead in a new ballet that was being planned. It was in connection with that she went to be photographed by Henchman. Fate struck. Everything was all over. I believe she's very talented in other ways too, but mad to dance from infancy.'

'All little girls are horse-mad or ballet-mad,' said Louise Beals. 'Ours are horses.'

'How did she get into ballet?' asked Middlecote. 'Parents in showbiz?'

'Showbiz doesn't often produce dancers now for some reason. I can't think why not. They're teachers' children, doctors' children, that sort of thing. I believe Barberina

Rookwood's father was a teacher. Anyway her parents are dead. She was brought up by a grandmother.'

'The grandmother must have had her wits about her.'

'She did. Arranged for ballet training from the start. She also changed her grand-daughter's name from God knows what to Barberina.'

'I see you, too, made an early investigation into the passenger-list, Fay,' said Beals. 'I can supply more. Barberina Rookwood was an only child, the grandmother an absolute dragon, determined that her grand-daughter should get to the top. What's more, also be the height of respectability. No man was allowed near her. At least not without a very sharp eye being kept on him all the time.'

'Glad I wasn't asked to the house,' said Middlecote.

'So you have Barberina Rookwood, mad about ballet, immense talent, five-star beauty, grandmother to promote her, also keep the wolves from the bedroom door. She goes to be photographed by Henchman. There is a *coup de foudre*. The present situation is the result.'

'That's what comes of wrapping a girl up in cotton wool,' said Middlecote. 'How much better to have introduced her to a capable fellow like myself, who would have set about her publicity in a proper manner. What did the grandmother think about Henchman?'

'The grandmother died a week or two after it all happened. Whether as a result, I can't say.'

'How soon did Barberina Rookwood go to live with Henchman after having her photograph taken?' asked Louise Beals. 'Was it at once?'

Her worried drawl made an answer urgent.

'She's supposed to have sent for a toothbrush and a nightie, and stayed on at the studio from that moment. Henchman's flat is above. She immediately gave up further thought of being a dancer, though I've been told she keeps up a dancer's exercises every day. That's why she moves so marvellously.'

'And now she's just Henchman's assistant,' said Louise Beals. 'But I understand her going on with her exercises.'

'For that matter, Henchman's nurse. He's always having crises from which he isn't expected to recover.'

'My own opinion is that Henchman's as tough as hell,' said Middlecote. 'He'd have packed it in long since were he not. When I was first in the firm one of the older copywriters used to sing a song called *Put It There*. It was about a man who got married, and the first night his bride took out her teeth, and her glass eye, and unstrapped a wooden leg, etc:

And so I simply said
As I pointed to the bed,
"If there's anything left over, put it there".

That's what living with Henchman must be like.'

'You're horrible,' said his wife.

'But think of it,' said Louise Beals. 'A real *Prima Ballerina Assoluta*.'

'One story runs that Henchman, developing negatives of the photographs he'd taken, decided on inspection that he couldn't live without her. He's got such a strong will she had to agree.'

'Still, she must have had a bit of a fancy for him too,' said Louise Beals. 'But, just like Little Red Shoes, he cut off her feet.'

'I bet she's got a strong will too,' said Fay Middlecote. 'You've only got to look at her to see that. Think of the will needed, after you'd tasted a little success already, to give up a career like hers. I believe there were one or two promising young men in the offing too, apart from anything else.'

'She looks wonderful, doesn't she?' said Louise Beals. 'I quite understand anyone being bowled over.'

'When Henchman's just about to croak – of course Piers doesn't believe that – she always brings him back to life. Tends him night and day, answers the telephone, types his letters, does all the photographic stuff. In fact it's Barberina Rookwood who actually takes the photograph.'

'The last is true in the the sense that she releases the shutter,' said Beals. 'Henchman himself does all the essential. That merely carries on what used to happen with Eugene. The method is not at all unknown among successful photographers. Naturally enough it's always been Henchman's way, owing to his restriction of movement. In another sense, as one can see on this boat, he can move quicker if he wants then most undamaged people.'

'You must remember that there are those nowadays who wouldn't think it in anyway a come-down to be assistant to a photographer like Henchman,' said Middlecote. 'Dancer or anything else. Photography has become a very smart profession. You pretty well have to be an earl to be allowed to practise it at all.'

'Balls,' said Fay Middlecote. 'You can't compare the two.'

'You're out of touch. Jealous that none of them have photographed you. They're just as highly thought of as dancers.'

'How many photographers have the whole of Covent Garden standing up in the stalls and shouting for them to come back after the twentieth encore of a photograph they've taken? It's a bastard art anyway.'

'Tell that to Henchman.'

'I shall if he tries any funny business. I believe he's absolutely bloody to her, too, a lot of the time. Really bloody. Not to mention minor affectations like calling her Miss Rookwood in the studio – at least he used to do that, I don't know whether he still does – and tease her sadistically, if she makes the least slip.'

'I expect he suffers a lot himself,' said Beals. '*Tout comprendre c'est tout pardonner*. All that –'

'Oh, do you think so, darling?' said Louise Beals. 'Personally I always find the more you know about people, the less you feel able to pardon the way they behave.'

'That might be true of Henchman,' said Fay Middlecote. 'I'm sure the more I knew of Barberina Rookwood, the more I'd like her.'

'Henchman may treat her badly in public,' said Beals. 'Things could be a bit different in private. An actor I know, who'd just been photographed by Henchman, was leaving the house, when he remembered he'd forgotten a book or something he had with him. Turning back towards the door of the studio, he heard Henchman's voice, speaking quite differently from the highflown manner he adopts as a rule, say "Sweetest, come here, I can't live a second longer unless I kiss you". The man who told me that story is not the most reliable raconteur in the world. He may have invented it as the sort of story that ought to be in circulation about Henchman and Barberina Rookwood. People often do that. Present anecdotes that are totally untrue, but fit in with what the teller would like to think was true. I just repeat it for what it's worth.'

'So far as the kiss went,' said Middlecote, 'matters must have stopped there.'

'Apparently Henchman could never keep an assistant, male or female, until Barberina Rookwood took the job on,' said Beals. 'That was in spite of the prestige Piers alleges to be attached to learning from a photographer of Henchman's standing. They all found working for him too hard to bear. As you might expect, it's reported he didn't act too well to the one functioning when Miss Rookwood took the job over in this unheralded manner. Whoever they were found themselves thrown out on their ear at the shortest possible notice.'

'Were all the girl assistants treated as semi-mistresses?' said Middlecote. 'I mean so far as being even a semi-mistress was feasible in the circumstances.'

'I believe not. On the contrary just made to work bloody hard at their photographic duties. Kept in their place. I daresay Henchman's conversation remained as gamey as ever. They had the benefit of that.'

'Barberina Rookwood has to work incredibly hard too. Especially if she also does all those gruelling ballet exercises.'

'Keep her fit for the office work,' said Middlecote.

'But think of it. A girl of her looks. Not only giving up a career, but still a virgin. Hasn't that something magical about it? A matchless beauty. Never had a lover. And of course Henchman . . .'

'Oh dear,' said Louise Beals. 'I don't think that magical at all. I think it's perfectly awful. Is it really true, Fay?'

The concept threw her into profound dejection. Beals saw another aspect in virginity.

'The fact that she remains a virgin is magical, not in the sense Fay uses the word, but in supporting the point about the Fisher King. Virgins play a great part in the Arthurian Legend, which is based on Courtly Love.'

Middlecote had been irritated by his wife's downright affirmation of virginity.

'How on earth can you pontificate as to whether Barberina Rookwood has ever had a lover? Apart from anything else, you don't know what she and Henchman may do together, even if that may not be quite the usual thing. She could be a lesbian. Or just not interested in that side of life. It's been known. Everybody nowadays behaves as if no one had anything else to do but screw.'

'If she's a lesbian she may have had women lovers,' said Louise Beals.

She spoke as one seeing a faint ray of light flickering in a hitherto ever darkening sky. Fay Middlecote began to get cross at having her assertion so much questioned.

'Well, she isn't a lesbian. Not in the least. I happen to know that for a fact. She's just very good, a sort of nun, if you like the comparison.'

'There are nuns and nuns,' said Middlecote. 'Think of some of the stories about nuns, not to mention limericks.'

'She loves Henchman in her own way. Adores looking

74

after him. That may not be everyone's cup of tea. It happens to be hers.'

'Her face has that rather too perfect harmony which Balzac thought signalled frigidity,' said Beals. 'And if she had been, so to speak, a nun of art, she would have remained with her dancing. You can't deny it's an interesting situation.'

Middlecote, also rather cross by now – shown by his allowing Balzac's name to pass without some capping comment – now brought up what had remained unfocused in Beal's mind until then about Lamont and Barberina Rookwood.

'Do you really believe she remained a virgin after all that thing with Gary Lamont?'

Fay Middlecote allowed this as at least worthy of consideration.

'I'll admit that was probably the only occasion when there seemed the least likelihood of her leaving Henchman. That's why it's fascinating Lamont being on board. Rather surprisingly for someone of his sort, Lamont happens to have a mad passion for ballet. He knew about Barberina Rookwood as a dancer quite early on. Before she went to Henchman. About the moment when she was lined up for the new ballet in which she was going to dance the lead.'

'Did he meet her backstage?'

'I'm not sure about that. May have done. The thing didn't flare up – so far as any flare up took place – until several years later. By that time Lamont too was beginning to make a name, and went to be photographed by Henchman. It started then.'

'But is all the thing about Lamont and Barberina Rookwood generally accepted?' said Beals. 'I agree with Piers in bringing it up in the virginity connection, and of course one's heard rumours. But Lamont is always in the public eye about something or other. Was it more than that? Gossip-columnists having to earn a living. I thought

Lamont was firmly married anyway. I agree that doesn't necessarily mean no one's gone to bed.'

'Lamont's wife died the other day.'

'It was because of Lamont's wife that nothing came of the Barberina Rookwood business,' said Fay Middlecote. 'Only marriage would have got her away from Henchman. Lamont didn't want to bust his own up. That is what people say. I don't believe she would ever have left Henchman myself.'

'Is Gary Lamont attractive?' asked Louise Beals. 'I haven't seen him yet.'

'Nor me. He seems to have disappeared since Piers saw him coming aboard. He's attractive enough for Henchman to have been disturbed about him at the time. She might have married Lamont, and gone back to dancing. Retired ballerinas quite often do that.'

'I'm not sure I believe all Fay's stuff about nothing happening,' said Middlecote. 'What form did Henchman's resentment take?'

'He behaved with the greatest calm. Showed no jealousy. Always welcomed Lamont to the studio. That method worked.'

'I've heard that one before.'

Louise Beals was doubtful too.

'But if Henchman's . . . as you think he is . . . I mean . . . Is there any reason why someone else . . .'

'You suggest that if Henchman can't do it himself, why shouldn't some other man do it for him?' said Middlecote. 'I'm afraid that doesn't show a great grasp of human nature, Louise dear, just indicates what a nice character you've got yourself.'

'Perhaps Fay is right,' said Beals. 'It is merely how the lady feels. All the same, I don't see a man like Henchman not objecting to someone else cutting in.'

'There's always such a hell of a lot going on round Lamont that I'm surprised that even in those days he had time to sit for his photograph,' said Middlecote. 'Much less try and get Henchman's girl off him. I imagine loss of La Rookwood would absolutely bugger up Henchman's life by now.'

'He didn't lose her,' said Fay Middlecote. 'She stayed with him – and remained a virgin.'

The point, reiterated to exacerbate her husband, effectively did that.

'You know there aren't a great many virgins about these days.'

'None the less, she's one of them. I just know she is. I can tell. It's the sort of thing you don't understand, so cease worrying your poor old head about it.'

Middlecote was beginning to be bored by the conversation.

'The sea's getting quite choppy. We'll soon be shipping green water. Are we off oil-rig coasts yet? I'd like to sight one.'

'Here are the people we've been talking about,' said Louise Beals. 'Isn't she wonderful?'

15

Henchman and Barberina Rookwood had entered the saloon from the far doors. Owing to their combined appearance, it was not possible for this to be without dramatic effect. When they reached the dance-floor Henchman crossed without the least concern for the impact of crutches on a slippery surface. On the way to the bar the two of them passed quite close to the Beals/Middlecote table. As he did so Henchman cast an all embracing glance at those sitting there, which, if not positively unfriendly, made clear that he did not regard being on the same cruise as allowing any claim to mutual acquaintance.

Henchman was plainly used to being stared at, even conducting himself in a manner to extort that reaction. At the same time his personality, public in one way, was equally designed to be unapproachable. The implication seemed to be that admiration of his photography would not be accepted as an excuse for an informal introduction. That understanding was, so to speak, pre-empted.

'I see what you mean about Henchman's eyes,' said Fay Middlecote. 'Rather compelling, I must admit.'

Henchman, although he had already been seen about the ship, always came as a surprise. His aspect in no way refuted a name for being formidable. Barberina Rookwood's beauty offered so drastic an antithesis to this near monstrosity that their dual entrance had the impact of a piece of contrived 'theatre' sprung on an unprepared audience, an act designed to startle. Fay Middlecote gave expression to this visual effect.

'When they were crossing the dance-floor I felt Henchman would suddenly cast aside his crutches, and execute that Russian dance where you fold your arms and kick your legs out, while she would snatch the scarf from her neck, and pirouette round him like the ballerina in *Petrouchka*.'

'For my regular readers,' said Beals, 'Dresden porcelain is the phrase I should not hesitate to use. The comparison is hard to resist even among friends, with whom, so far as humanly possible, one hopes to avoid the more tarnished clichés.'

'It's her inner repose that fascinates me,' said Fay Middlecote. 'Even apart from the situation she's landed herself with. That alone could upset most people after a year or two at most. I've never seen waters so still.'

Barberina Rookwood's carriage, however much consequence of training, seemed also to come naturally to her. Her movements in no way demanded the forced attention of an actor's, still less were they the exhibitionist stride of the model draped in garments for display. On the contrary, far from concentrating on herself, she seemed wholly absorbed in the man beside her, her eyes resting on him from time to time, as if to make sure that all was well.

'She's really more extraordinary than he is,' said Louise Beals. 'I love her.'

That opinion was a very tenable one. Superficial impressions might be caught by Barberina Rookwood's looks. In the last resort these were less arresting than the sense of intense individual isolation to which Fay Middlecote had referred. Whether such emphatic detachment from the world round about captivated the observer, or the reverse, might be open to question. Certainly there would be differences of judgment. Indisputably this innate setting of herself at a distance removed from her beauty the faintest indictment of sugary prettiness, Beals's Dresden china princess. An intelligence, even a rather intimidating intelligence, might also be inferred from that enormous inner reserve, which seemed to veil her being. Once these things were accepted, Barberina Rookwood could be supposed no less formidable than Henchman, in some ways even more disturbing.

On reaching the bar, Henchman paused a second to gather impetus for launching himself upward on to a stool. The ship was rolling sufficiently to impede the convulsive jump required for swinging his body from the crutches to a seat. Barberina Rookwood, who had held out a hand as they crossed the dance-floor, did so again. She was evidently prepared for all Henchman's actions to be transacted with a violence sufficiently reckless inveterately to risk damage. When he had achieved the high stool he ordered drinks for them both. Then he gazed thoughtfully towards the other end of the bar, afterwards making a comment. This probably referred either to Mr Jack, sunk in one of his somnolent states, or the musical clinch in which Basically Bach and Marginally Mahler wrestled.

'Of course the moment I set eyes on them I realized they were Beauty and the Beast,' said Fay Middlecote. 'I mean before Beauty had finally agreed to take the Beast on.'

'Perhaps she took him on, and the magic didn't work,' said Middlecote.

'I always wonder whether Beauty went on fancying the Beast after he became a handsome Prince,' said Louise Beals. 'It was an awful risk for him to change like that so suddenly. After all, she may have secretly rather liked him as he was.'

'When we were first married I remember someone calling Piers and me Beauty and the Beast,' said Fay Middlecote.

'The compliment was by then undeserved,' said Middlecote. 'The bloom of my youth had already faded by our wedding. And even I failed to grasp your fractious possibilities while we were engaged, darling. So how could others have guessed at such an early stage. Besides, to describe you as a beast was going too far. Gross bad manners. I'd have called him out, if I'd known, no matter how much he admired my looks.'

Before his wife could adequately respond, conversation was brought to a stop by a sudden commotion at the bar. What exactly had taken place there was not clear from where the Beals/Middlecote party was sitting, except that Henchman's crutches had clattered to the ground. He himself was no longer upright on the stool, but leaning precariously between it and the counter, supported by Barberina Rookwood.

Although Henchman was exceptionally small and lightly built, she was only just strong enough to hold him more or less firmly in the awkward position in which he had fallen. Even the extent to which she prevented him from sinking to the floor probably owed something to a dancer's training in supporting the weight of other bodies in relation to her own.

The two stewards were both occupied in taking orders at the far end of the saloon. The barman, in any case engaged in an attempt to solve some perplexing alcoholic problem set by a comparatively renascent Mr Jack, was cut off by the bar. Basically Bach and Marginally Mahler, discarding temporarily musical animosities, had risen at once in a great state of agitation, but at the crucial moment had not been close enough to help.

The situation was saved from what might have been comparative disaster by the young man, Robin Jilson, introduced by his mother not long before to the Tiptofts. Having closed *The Focal Encyclopaedia*, and put the book under his arm, he was making his way past the bar to reach the door at that end of the saloon, which opened on to the deck. He arrived at the most critical stage of Henchman's slow steady descent to the ground, when Barberina Rookwood's strength seemed to be failing. Grasping at once what was needed, he caught Henchman's shoulder on the other side.

Robin's aid

Middlecote, always anxious to concern himself with any unusual event taking place within range, also perhaps foreseeing means of making himself known to Henchman, jumped up from where he was sitting, and walked quickly towards the bar. The rest of the table settled for acceptance of whatever was going on as a spectacle to be watched, rather than a happening in which to participate. Mr Jack, still holding the barman in earnest conversation, seemed taken aback when that was broken short by the barman leaving him in the middle of a sentence, and moving towards the mode of egress from behind the counter.

Henchman's fall appeared to have been brought about by increased roughness of the sea, in combination with a characteristically vehement gesture in reaching out for the potato chips or salted almonds. These unsteadying factors caused loss of balance. Barberina Rookwood, habituated to such crises, had effectively broken his fall without being quick enough to keep him in position, nor strong enough to shift him back to stability. Even the auxiliary efforts of the young man failed to do better than maintain Henchman more or less upright between the stool and the bar. The pitching of the ship, a contributory cause of the accident in the first instance, threatened the permanence of even this rescue operation.

Basically Bach and Marginally Mahler, by now at hand and anxious to help, were, as in their musical relationship, unable to agree as to the best form of concerted effort. The barman, together with the two stewards joined the mêlée, which now came to the notice of Mr Jack too, who watched with keen attention for a minute or two, before sinking back into one of his cataleptic trances.

Middlecote, whose intervention increased the number of persons involved within a restricted area in front of the bar, at first substantially added to the confusion rather than affording aid. As was his way, he began to issue orders to all those round about him. Possibly at the suggestion of Henchman himself − who had remained undisturbed by suspension between seat and deck, not speaking, only smiling. Middlecote and Jilson, pushing aside the rest of the persons contemplating the problem, picked up Henchman bodily, removing him to one of the large sofas, outside the bar itself, set along the sides of the saloon. Henchman began to laugh heartily, at least as heartily as his own sort of laughter permitted.

Middlecote − subsequently described by Beals as behaving as if he had been recommended for a VC after evacuating a wounded comrade under fire − reported Henchman to be as light as a child. Fay Middlecote asserted that Jilson had done most of the work in carrying out this operation.

16   Henchman's "Fall"

Not only had Henchman shown no discomposure throughout the ordeal, he made no real objection to resettlement
on the sofa. This suggested that he had not at all minded
being the centre of attention in this manner. When addressing Barberina Rookwood his tone only affected to complain.

'Why have I been taken in this remorseless way from
my drink, may I ask, and dumped in this place?'

'I'll get your drink for you at once. And my own too.
We can continue with them here. It's more sensible now
the sea's got up. But are you feeling all right? You came
down with quite a thump.'

She turned to thank Middlecote and Jilson for their help.
Middlecote said afterwards that only then did he notice the
small scar on her cheek, incurred in a motor accident
driving Henchman to some photographic appointment.
The mark was only visible when close to her. Middlecote
added that the blemish saved her looks from too great an
unimpeachability. It was almost an adornment, a deliberate
beauty spot to make her more than ever enchanting. That

was Middlecote's often expressed view. Henchman was reported to have remarked that the scar linked them together as a disfigured couple. Now he seemed in the best of form.

'I want for nothing except the restoration of my drink. Perhaps I finished or upset it. If so, please bring another with the least possible delay.'

'I thought you might have had one of your black-outs.'

'Merely an uncontrollable desire to possess myself of an olive. Greed as usual brought its own reward. One should be more careful. That Nineties poet, Lionel Johnson, met an early death falling off a bar stool, and cracking his skull. They are dangerous perches. Those who sit on them take their life in their hands.'

The young man laughed. Barberina Rookwood smiled at him before going off to collect the drinks. Middlecote (as Beals always said) not the most sensitive man in the world, for some reason noted that smile. Something about it struck him. Jilson seemed ready to offer to help with the drinks, but Henchman made a gesture to detain both him and Middlecote. Middlecote was, in fact, delighted with the manner in which he would now be able to meet Henchman in circumstances that had created him Henchman's benefactor. This was much better than accosting him on deck, or getting an introduction from some acquaintance in common.

Now the crisis was over, Jilson, on the other hand, was evidently at a loss to know just how to behave. He had perhaps been dazzled by Barberina Rookwood's smile, and was not yet quite recovered. He was also rather breathless in consequence of his exertions, indeed quite shaken, certainly more unstrung than Henchman after his fall. He seemed unable to make up his mind whether to go away, or offer further help, something that did not at all trouble Middlecote. Henchman fixed the two of them with his disconcerting stare.

'Most kind of you two gentlemen to act the part of All the King's Horses and All the King's Men. I am duly grateful. Your brisk efforts were in contrast with the failure of the Household Brigade to reconstitute Humpty-Dumpty, a personage I resemble both in obstinacy of opinion and uncertainty of balance. These twin failings on my own part lead to frequent tumbles, both physical and moral. You two, between you, unlike the royal troops, have put me together again with singular success, so far as that is possible, my structure being, as it happens, organically defective.'

'Only too glad to have been of help –'

Henchman interrupted Middlecote.

'Apart from my drink, I lack one other standby – my crutches. Will one of you oblige me even further by getting them from the bar, where they fell to the ground? I have developed quite an affection for my crutches over the years. We all have our crutches in one form or another, although not everyone needs the kind I use. That sounds rather like the beginning of one of those long sermons I found so wearisome as a boy. Much as I disliked them, I have always recognized the effect they had on my style, an over ornateness, too noticeable a tendency towards biblical language. Let me hasten to add – again rather in the manner of a sermon – that in my own case crutches are by far the least of the disadvantages under which I labour. On the contrary, they are not only admirable vehicles for speedy movement, but can if necessary be employed as weapons of defence or offence. You laugh? I can assure you I have used them more than once in the latter capacity, may well do so again. One of you get my crutches, then come back here and have a drink with me, as a small recognition of your kindness.'

Jilson, still panting a little, forestalled what was probably not a very sincere movement on Middlecote's part, suggesting acceptance of the errand. Middlecote's face betrayed that someone other than he would fetch the crutches, especially as Jilson's temporary removal would give providential opportunity to clear up with Henchman a small matter connected with busineess.

'My name is Piers Middlecote –'

'Yes, yes . . .'

Henchman mentioned Middlecote's advertising agency. Middlecote did not conceal the satisfaction he felt at the firm being thus fluently quoted. Henchman then got in first with the subject Middlecote himself had been about to embark on.

'I had dealings with your people a year or two ago. They may know all the facets of advertising, if so they failed to display them. In fact they got very much the wrong side of me. Incivilities were uttered. I expect you heard. Or rather incivilities were proffered on my part. Your firm turned the other cheek – if admen can be said to possess more than one sort of cheek.'

Middlecote laughed rather unnecessarily loud at that. He was in his element. Henchman was talking just as he had hoped.

'I heard something of the kind. No hard feelings so far as we are concerned. Not in the least. I hope we'll persuade you to do more photographic work for us one day, and relations will be happier, less frustrating, good news. All the same I must refuse your offer of a drink just now. I have one already over there, where I'm sitting with my wife and some friends. If you're really all right, I'll return to them. We'll meet again in the course of the cruise.'

While this exchange was taking place, Barberina Rookwood returned with the drinks. Jilson accompanied her, carrying the crutches. Middlecote took the crutches from Jilson, handing them to Henchman, who placed them side by side on the table in front of him.

From his comparatively distant vantage point Beals described this procedure as manifesting a ceremony at the court of the Fisher King; a lesser courtier, in the shape of

Jilson, not directly approaching the sovereign with the royal crutches, but presenting them through an intermediary of more august rank. Middlecote, in order to contradict, compared the ritual rather with a naval court-martial.

'The sword lying on the table still points towards the prisoner, if guilty, when marched in to hear the verdict. If acquitted, the hilt of the sword. The business-end of the crutches pointed at Jilson, so he was being tried, rather than being one of the accessories of the court.'

Whichever it was, Middlecote departed after presenting the crutches, Henchman having spoken no assurance on his side that he hoped further meetings would take place. On his way, so to speak, off stage, Middlecote smiled admiringly at Barberina Rookwood to ratify the fact of their acquaintance. She acknowledged that, then addressed Henchman.

'The drinks had been upset or finished. Possibly drunk by the old boy who's such a fixture at the bar. I had to get fresh ones.'

She put them down. Jilson now attempted to make his farewell. Henchman, preventing that, asked his name.

'Jilson.'

'Christian name?'

'Robin.'

A slight twitch passed over his face after giving this last piece of information. Nervousness was understandable in the light of Henchman's manner.

'It was most obliging of you to fetch my crutches, Mr Jilson, not to speak of earlier kind offices. As I was emphasizing to that very forthcoming adman, even the apparently hale and hearty resent being separated from their crutches, whatever form these take as their strength and stay, moral or immoral. What will you drink?'

Jilson, whose paleness had turned almost to a blush, began to refuse. He did not look at all well, though his eyes were bright. He gave the impression of possessing a kind of fitful energy that had shown itself in stepping in so opportunely to prevent Henchman's fall. Clothes and general demeanour revealed nothing about him.

'It's very kind of you. I don't think I will. I'm just on my way to find my mother.'

'A drink will give you strength to search for her. It can be a difficult business finding one's mother. Not everyone is satisfied with the mother they begin with. Some people spend a lifetime looking for a mother, and fail wretchedly at the end of it. Come on. What is it to be?'

Barberina Rookwood laughed.

'Yes,' she said. 'Stay on a moment.'

She seemed to have taken a fancy to Jilson. Henchman glanced at her. He was amused.

'This is my assistant, Miss Rookwood. She is named Barberina. Being nearer to her age than I am, I expect you will call her Barberina, and she address you as Robin. Just as crystallization of surnames was one of the steps in human civilization, their relinquishment gradually increases as we revert to savagery.'

Jilson, seeing a combined insistence would be too powerful for denial, agreed to tomato-juice. Henchman, about equally bearing out Middlecote's comparison of the scene to a court-martial, or Beals's to exercise of Royal Prerogative, now began to satisfy his own curiosity as to all aspects of Jilson, and why he was on the cruise.

'I've been ill, as a matter of fact.'

'So your mother booked on the *Alecto* for the sake of your health?'

Barberina Rookwood glanced at Jilson to see how he would answer that question. He must have decided that to tell the whole story from the beginning would be best; in the long run simplest, less of an expense of spirit than continuing to spar against Henchman's mandate. To express to an inquisitor like Henchman the precise position in which he found himself may even have been something of a relief, providing in his own eyes a degree of clarification, self-definition, that he was inwardly seeking. That was especially in the light of the disclosure he was to make a minute or two later, which must have strongly affected his attitude towards Henchman from the start.

'My father died not long ago. He'd just retired. He and my mother were going to celebrate retirement by taking a cruise. My father always had archaeological interests of an amateur kind, but was never able to do much about them. Then I got ill, and had to leave the job I was in. My mother decided she and I should use the money they'd set aside for the cruise, and we'd go together.'

'So this trip is with a view to convalescence?'

'In a way. Not exactly.'

Jilson looked almost as if he might collapse entirely, perhaps even die, in consequence of being forced to divulge these intimate details about his life. Henchman, with complete disregard for any such possibilities arising from the strain he was imposing, went on relentlessly.

'As a fellow-crock, may I ask what you are suffering from?'

'I've got a sort of muscular complaint. One of those things that work slowly, you can only hope not too surely. My mother thought I needed a holiday before trying to find another job.'

'What are your symptoms?'

'I get tired very easily. Can't always keep my eyes open for long periods of time. Also have difficulty at moments in holding my head upright. But I'm not too bad if I have plenty of rest.'

Jilson spoke apologetically. He undoubtedly wanted to avoid giving an impression that he was feeling sorry for himself. That wish would certainly have appealed to Henchman, though he showed no particular sympathy now that specific medical information had been released. On the contrary, he looked even more severe than when he had begun the cross-examination. None the less, Jilson's attitude towards his troubles may have made its mark. Barberina Rookwood's face had changed from friendly amusement to something more serious. She was probably familiar with such procedures in Henchman's life.

'What was the work you had to give up?'

'I was in a bank.'

'And that from which your father retired?'

'He was in a bank too.'

'High up in it?'

'He got along all right, but was never really happy there. He was the organizer of the Local History Society where we lived in North London. That was what he really liked.'

'You don't share these archaeological pursuits?'

'Not much, though my father used to make them sound quite interesting.'

'I fear you will have a good deal of history and archaeology on this cruise.'

Jilson managed to laugh.

'I've nothing against history and archaeology. They just don't happen to be my hobby.'

'Are you going back to the bank?'

'They won't have me. I'm not physically fit enough for them. I don't blame the bank. I'll just have to find another job.'

Jilson had begun to look more than ever as if Henchman's grilling might bring on one or other of the vitiated bodily conditions to which he was subject. Henchman pressed on nevertheless.

'If not history and archaeology like your father, what is your hobby?'

Jilson paused for a moment before answering. He seemed to be having an inner struggle to make up his mind about something. Then he spoke in quite a low voice.

'Mr Henchman, I hardly like to tell you. I want to be a photographer.'

Henchman's laughter, never very reassuring to the hearer, must in the circumstances have chilled Jilson's photographic aspirations to their depths.

'With you photography takes the place of your father's archaeology?'

'Yes, but I want to be a professional photographer. It isn't only a hobby. That's what I want to do now.'

'I see.'

Henchman's manner had changed a little.

'It showed a certain delicacy on your part to give photography the designation of a hobby,' he said. 'One far below the place it really held in your heart. Not pouring out a lot of stuff to me about yourself, and how you dreamed about being a photographer. Believe me, not everyone behaves like that. Let me congratulate you on good manners at least.'

'I didn't like to speak of taking photographs to someone who can take the photographs you do.'

'Thank you. Some people think that a good reason for badgering me.'

Jilson's photographic ambitions had for some reason caught Henchman's attention, perhaps something about the young man himself, though afterwards everyone agreed about his intense ordinariness. He had a kind of firmness too. Probably the flattery did no harm, more acceptable from having been extracted from a façade of diffidence. At the same time flattery alone would not have captured Henchman's aimiability. People had tried that, and failed. He turned towards Barberina Rookwood. She smiled gently back at him, then at Jilson.

'What steps are you taking to initiate yourself into this gruelling trade?'

Jilson, not very coherently, spoke of training, governmental grants, photographic courses at universities, colleges, acquiring technical knowledge, outlining generally the direction in which he was heading. Henchman listened impatiently, making no attempt to conceal his own contempt for such things, nor what he plainly considered Jilson's lack of true enterprise. Jilson himself had the good sense to grasp that the sooner he cut short this account of his plans, the less alienated from him would Henchman become. He stopped almost in the middle of a sentence, and prepared to leave. Henchman prevented that once more.

'Wait a moment. I don't expect you've got any photographs you've taken you could show me?'

'I have, as a matter of fact, I –'

'Bring them along then. Let me speak a word to you about my own reasons for coming on this cruise. First and foremost, I wanted a holiday, which I haven't had for some time. Secondly, something of which you may not be aware, as it is a tribulation not generally apprehended, I am suffering from a sense of my own photographic powers running dry.'

'Oh, I'm sure –'

'Photographers have been known to find that they can take no more photographs. The art has left them. They have exhausted their powers. Like writers who have written themselves out, painters whose touch has gone. Of composers I know nothing, but the same law must apply. In the physiological sphere, I might add womanizers who have lost desire, or are unable to possess. I suspect from what I hear that we have at least one of the last on board.'

'You might add dancers who can no longer dance,' said Barberina Rookwood. 'Dancing, too, can go – not necessarily from growing old.'

Jilson gazed at her as if he could believe in her existence as little as in that of Henchman. He seemed like a man struck by lightning at the sudden onset of her looks. This slow but violent receptivity could have been connected with his ailment, a temperament formed by thinking chiefly of himself, sudden rays put out by Barberina

93

Rookwood, possibly elements of all three. Henchman concurred.

'Dancers, but of course. For that matter, <u>actors</u>. On the other hand, some actors continue to practise their art until the last breath leaves their body, in a manner that other artists can only envy. I have naturally a fellow feeling for Sarah Bernhardt, who lost a leg, yet continued to play her later roles with a wooden one. If you have ever been to a French theatre, you will know the three knocks that announce the rise of the curtain. After the Divine Sarah had her artificial limb inaugurated, when the three knocks sounded at a play in which she was performing, a wit in the audience remarked, "Here she comes". A dancer could hardly carry on in the same manner.'

Jilson was getting restive.

'My mother —'

'Has a wooden leg?'

Jilson laughed.

'No, but I mustn't keep her waiting any longer. She will be wondering what has happened to me.'

'That will worry her?'

'It might.'

Jilson was torn between wanting to stay where he was, yet fearing to distress his mother. The strength of the last sentiment was not lost on Henchman. He shook his head, gave one of his uncomfortable smiles.

'Only a minute longer, just to round off what I was saying about the <u>declension of my own photographic driving force</u>. Several things promised on this trip attracted me as possibilities to photograph. Unlike some professionals, I do not limit myself to professional occasions. When I am in the mood I am prepared to compete in abundance of shots and triviality of subject with any Japanese tourist you can produce. That is by the way.'

'You really oughtn't to keep him,' said Barberina Rookwood.

She had certainly taken a liking to Jilson.

'No, that's all right. My mother can wait a moment longer. I'm thrilled to hear about all this, that you will be taking photographs on the cruise.'

'There is Hadrian's Wall. In Orkney, a Stone Circle. More than one, in fact, but one I specially have my eye on. Some of its stones have been defaced during the last hundred years by modern graffiti. Destruction wrought by vandals on monuments of the past is sometimes worth photographing. It has characteristics of its own. In any case I have long had in mind exploration of the Northern Isles, Ultima Thule, the limits of the known world, beyond which it was unwise, indeed madness, to penetrate. We might even leave the ship, and I would fish. I have made arrangements for that, should the mood take me. That is by the way. If your photographs strike me as of sufficient merit, it might be of interest to you to talk about subject and method, while I myself tackle whatever the cruise may put in our way. Would that appeal?'

Jilson, astonished at such an offer, muttered unintelligible phrases of thanks. He was overwhelmed. Henchman swept aside all acknowledgment of gratitude.

'You have to develop a more inspired approach. I mean how you're going to set about things. You show no inspiration whatever at the moment. Not a sign. You must, if you're going to do any good. I don't pretend to have by any means all the answers myself, but I have accumulated a few useful experiences, some of them relatively rare. While we are on board together I might be able to pass on a little of that.'

'Thank you again, Mr Henchman. I'm very fortunate indeed. It's more than kind of you to say what you have. There's nothing in the world I'd like more than to watch you at work. It never crossed my mind when I saw you were going to be on the cruise that we'd even meet, much less get such a break.'

'No, you're very lucky indeed. At least you may be. You don't know what I'm going to do or say. Neither do I. We'll have a further talk about your prospects when I've seen what sort of thing you are doing now. And, on my side, thank you again for lending a hand in at least delaying my physical downfall. Now run off and find your mother, and don't keep her waiting like this again.'

17

Henchman rearranged the crutches in front of him. He raised his eyebrows in the grimace of the monster in a horror film.

'Unlike you to commit yourself in that sort of way,' said Barberina Rookwood. 'At least you seem to have committed yourself. Perhaps you haven't.'

'It's always hard to tell how I shall behave.'

'I agree.'

'What did you think of him?'

'Rather sweet.'

'So I imagined.'

'He doesn't look at all well.'

'A condition always attractive to you.'

'He's rather like a fern that has been pressed for decades within the pages of an old book. Looking up something for you in one of the early volumes of *The Photographic Journal* that you bought the other day I found a flower that must have been preserved there since Victorian times.'

'Young Jilson certainly has that faded air. I mean morally speaking. His mother seems much on his mind.'

'Have you a hunch that he might make a good photographer?'

'Degas is on record as expressing astonishment at the manner in which dangerous implements like a paint-box and paint-brushes are allowed in the hands of even small children, much less irresponsible people. I feel the same about a camera and films.'

'So you're really going to undertake his instruction?'

'A few elementary hints perhaps, while we are on the cruise. Just an attempt to prevent in future some of the worst excesses. If he shapes well I can probably place him in goodish hands.'

'I shall watch with interest.'

'I felt sure you would.'

She ignored a tone, which might have been some sort of challenge, perhaps merely statement of what he knew by instinct.

'Besides, I could so easily recognize his predicament. A passionate desire to take photographs, enclosed within a body delighting to thwart its owner by incapacitating him at critical moments.'

'Poor boy.'

'He can get along all right at the moment in what he wants to do. That is all anyone can expect from life.'

'You mean it will close in on him?'

'I presume it may.'

'But at least a few years of doing what he wants, if he gets fixed up as a photographer.'

'Provided he's aware that even in Arcady – so far as any

life can be called Arcadian, especially that of a professional photographer – Death holds sway there too.'

'You mean the Poussin picture? The shepherds finding the tomb?'

'*Les Bergers d'Arcadie.*'

'It's a menace he can hardly forget.'

'When he was outlining his diseases and domestic circumstances it struck me that the inscription on the sarcophagus ET IN ARCADIA EGO might be varied to ET IN SUBURBIA EGO – Death rules even in Suburbia.'

'No one doubts that surely?'

'Still it makes another link between Jilson and myself. Well, I suppose in my case it wasn't actually Suburbia, but not so very different, and just as stifling, possibly more so, if you wanted to be the sort of photographer I had in mind to be.'

'The shepherds finding the tomb would have been a good subject for one of your photographs.'

'Perhaps photography is what the group is actually engaged upon. They are not shepherds at all, but a camera crew from Arcadia Television. All those beards, and their clothes, suggest some form of movie people. Talking of the media makes me think of Lamont. Where is he? The great man is not suffering from sea-sickness, I trust, and confined to his cabin.'

Henchman asked the question in the same light tone he used to speculate upon the figures in the pictures. Barberina Rookwood replied in an equally indifferent manner.

'Not sea-sickness, common or garden tummy upset. This morning I looked in on the ship's doctor to get a supply of sea-sick pills after last night's gale. I haven't felt at all queasy, but thought I'd be on the safe side. Gary was in the queue outside the surgery. He said he was not quite recovered from the gastric thing he had when he came on board, so retired to bed. He seems all right now, anyway so far as his stomach's concerned, so we'll probably be seeing him.'

'The digestive organs of these high-powered operators are so often more sensitive than their owners.'

'It's the price they pay.'

'When you say that, Lamont is all right so far as the stomach thing is concerned, do you imply something else is wrong with him?'

'As a matter of fact he said a specialist had told him to take care about a fairly ominous heart condition.'

'In fact you had quite a serious talk in the surgery queue?'

'Serious to the extent that he told me that.'

'You mean death from heart condition could hardly be considered serious by anyone except doctors?'

'I should have thought doctors, by definition, took it on the whole more as a matter of course than patients.'

'Serious or not, why is Lamont on the boat anyway? His own explanation, given on the quay, was quite un-acceptable, certainly did not explain the omission of his name from the passenger-list. I should have thought a cruise round the British Isles something quite outside holidays to be considered by him. If I were in the travel business, I should have sent him to the Costa Brava before he rose to eminence, to Bermuda now.'

'Even Gary has a right to choose his own holidays.'

'But not to share them with me. Why isn't Doll with him?'

'Doll died about a year ago.'

'Doll dead? Well, well. Why didn't I hear about it?'

'I did.'

'Then why didn't you tell me?'

'I thought you would probably have seen or heard about it, anyway her death would not particularly interest you. You never knew her.'

'On the contrary, I am greatly interested. I nearly asked about Doll on the quay, then forbore on the principle of never showing inquisitiveness about absent spouses.'

'Doll died suddenly in New York. She'd gone with Gary on some business trip. It may have been when we were away photographing somewhere, and I heard about it later.'

'Did he murder her?'

'He loved her very much.'

'But each man kills the thing he loves.'

'Doll got ill, and died quite suddenly, whoever told me about her said.'

'They told you because they thought you would be interested?'

'I was interested.'

'Naturally.'

'Gary is very upset still.'

'I'm not surprised.'

'He came on this trip at the last moment to try and cheer himself up. He was very devoted to Doll. They were devoted to each other.'

'And he hasn't got a girl with him? That certainly shows devotion. At least it might.'

'I don't know of one. If there is, she hasn't appeared yet.'

'She could have been tending his enteritis or heart condition.'

'Now I come to think of it he mentioned he was alone when we were all on the quay.'

'So I thought. It's odd.'

'Perhaps it is odd.'

'Very odd. He may hope to pick up a girl on the boat.'

'Possibly. I haven't noticed any likely ones yet, have you?'

'Yes, I have.'

Henchman made a face at her. She laughed. Nevertheless the atmosphere was not a happy one.

'I'm not sure you're right,' she said.

'Aren't you? I am. Very sure.'

'He didn't exactly say so.'

'I don't expect the queue outside the surgery offered the best of backgrounds for a declaration, even if he were prepared to ventilate the matter of his heart condition there, or in the passage outside after your consultations. I think he will soon make his reason for taking the cruise clear.'

She laughed again.

'We shall see,' she said.

'It would have been a friendly act to have let us know he was going to be with us on the *Alecto*.'

'He probably didn't have time. He said he had decided to come at short notice. Felt he must get away from everything for a week or two. He's got some important business move waiting for a decision, so that's understandable. He may not have known anything about our being on the cruise until he saw us on the quay. That was how he behaved.'

'I agree that was how he behaved.'

'Well?'

'I think that he heard by chance you were going to be here, confirmed that, then booked a cabin. What conceivable attraction could a cruise like this have for a man like Lamont?'

'You never know with journalists.'

'Lamont moved with all possible speed. I underline this obvious fact merely in order that everyone should know where he or she stands. Lamont got himself on this boat to ask you to go off with him now Doll is dead.'

'You may be right.'

'In fact I should be surprised if he has not asked you already in the surgery queue or afterwards. Am I not right?'

'More or less.'

'You retract what you said just now?'

'He didn't put it in so many words.'

'Are you going to go with him?'

'I don't know.'

'I suppose he suggested a return to dancing?'

'One of the things.'

'Naturally a temptation. Besides, I've not been at my best, such as my best is, for some little time. Neither personally nor photographically. As I said to that young man, I may be losing my grip. In that case I shall merely become a malevolent cripple without visible means of support. Talking of ill health, I am most interested in Lamont's heart condition. He has always been a man of many sides in putting himself in an attractive light.'

'Does a heart condition make a man attractive?'

'It might to some women. Just as men in women seem to go for bad lungs. On the other hand, I agree, some people actually dislike me for being disabled. They feel it gives a kind of power that they lack. They are in a sense envious.'

'You mean Gary's heart condition draws me towards him?'

'Of course.'

'But I don't like Death.'

'No, but you like saying there's no one at home, when Death puts his foot in the door. To have stayed so long with me shows you may have to receive him one afternoon.'

'Death or Gary?'

'Death. You haven't revealed enough about Lamont for me to say.'

'But Gary is by no means certain to die.'

'Is not all humanity under sentence of death?'

'Naturally I did not mean to imply that Gary is immortal.'

'The *Alecto* seems to have several entries at short odds for the mortality race. What you have said is at least a warning to myself that days with you are likely to be numbered. That is an admission for which I was sooner or later nerving myself. Even though I know how lucky I have been, how unbelievably fortunate, I am not sure yet how I shall be able to bear a reversal of that.'

'It has not yet been reversed.'

The conversation seems for the moment to have ended there by Henchman pointing with one of the crutches towards the window above the sofa upon which they were sitting. From time to time the sea was sending up sprays of whitish-yellowish spume, which spattered across the thick glass surface.

'Don't miss the <u>gothic effects in the sky</u>. Jagged mountain peaks, donjon keeps, knights in armour, ladies riding pal-freys, ogres, witches, warlocks, dwarfs. But what about lunch? Everyone seems to have disappeared. Let us make for the buffet.'

18

Beals only had Henchman's word for what had passed on this occasion, but felt pretty sure the phrase about being philosophical must have been authentic. He used to mull it over.

'Rather a cruel thing to say. What I mean is that one

sees Barberina Rookwood had various sides. All that sacrifice, then feeling rather different about things. When we had those talks, Henchman asked me if I knew the poems of an Elizabethan called George Gascoigne. I had to admit I did not.'

'Didn't you really, Valentine?' said Middlecote. 'You surprise me.'

'Henchman said one of them contained the best account he had ever read of having trouble with your girl. I looked it up, and agree. As you are so familiar with Gascoigne's works, perhaps you would like to quote it for us, Piers. You must know the one I mean.'

'It's slipped my memory at the moment. I just did not expect you to be ignorant of Gascoigne's name.'

'The first verse is sufficient,' said Beals. 'You will notice the specific connection to Henchman's case:

> And if I did, what then?
> Are you agreev'd therfore?
> The Sea hath fishe for every man,
> And what would you have more?

It's a familiar theme, but Gascoigne's girl seems to have put it rather unusually well.'

Beals often reiterated that he never seriously considered basing one of his thrillers on the *Alecto* experience, naturally with mutation of chronology, but he seems to have contemplated that at least to the extent of pondering whether Henchman should be the dominant figure as hero, or Barberina Rookwood as heroine. He once admitted as much. At first the answer had seemed obvious. Henchman must have that place, and in the end Beals was convinced he must have it. All the same the instincts of a romantic novelist seem to have momentarily gravitated in the direction of putting the accent on Barberina Rookwood as heroine. Beals always maintained that going to live with Henchman in the first instance remained both the most dramatic, least explicable, aspect of the whole affair. She was the pivot upon which all subsequent action turned.

Alternatively – again speaking, of course, as a thriller-writer, rather than man of the world – Beals sometimes saw that impulse to surrender herself, abandon a career, simply as another facet of Henchman's powerful personality, rather than her own. All this was no more than a writer's daydream. The story, for a thousand other reasons, would have been impossible to transform into Beals's terms of narrative. Beals himself saw that absolutely. Such a tale would have been disastrous for sales, even had he been competent to write it, which he doubted.

One of the points Beals was fond of making was that the paradox of writing romantic fiction consisted largely in transforming imaginary improbable events in a manner to make them appear realistic. That ruled out most of the far more improbable events of real life.

'Henchman's eidolon is in itself unbelievable,' said Beals.
Middlecote was not going to let that pass.
'Eidolon?'
'Spectre, phantom.'
'Why that word?'
'Is it unfamiliar to you? It seemed the best one.'
Beals merely followed that with a quotation.

> 'By a route obscure and lonely,
> Haunted by ill angels only,
> Where an Eidolon, named Night,
> On a black throne reigns upright,
> I have reached these lands but newly
> From an ultimate dim Thule –
> From a wild weird clime that lieth, sublime
> Out of Space – out of Time.'

'Poe is not greatly regarded as a poet these days.'
'Maybe rightly. None the less, he has his moments. I don't put these lines forward as one of them. Only to show the use of eidolon for those ignorant of the word.'
'You don't think it an insufferable affectation?'
'If you require additional authority, Meredith used it in

The Egoist. He says "his naked eidolon, the tender infant Self".'

'I stuck in *The Egoist* many years ago.'

'Then you will also have missed a passage equally applicable to Henchman, which says something to the effect that people feel a compassion akin to scorn for those who have an opportunity to excite pathos and decline it.'

'You seem well up in Meredith.'

'I tried him again recently, but without complete success.'

Middlecote was content to leave things there.

19

Women liked Lamont. In earlier days he had taken advantage of that to some considerable extent. Later he avoided involvements, finding them handicapping in undertakings which possessed him more profoundly. In that respect Barberina Rookwood was to be looked upon as an exception. There seemed reason to suppose that she must have dominated his thoughts for a long period by the time he shipped on the *Alecto*.

Lamont's first marriage (to a pretty rather silly girl by whom he had a daughter) lasted only four or five years, if that. His second wife, Doll (married previously to a Labour

MP, whom she left before meeting Lamont), had been not least in the elements of Lamont's luck. Doll had coped dextrously with his volatile temperament, highly pressurized social life, marked by a steady upward mobility in the professional scale. She kept him on a reasonably tight rein. In the light of being rather a temptation to women, that may have been regarded by Lamont himself as a useful restraint in remaining free from other distractions during the power struggle.

While Doll was alive Lamont's personal life had been too much merged with hers (though he had no children by her) for any serious risk to have arisen of the marriage coming apart. On Lamont's side, one or two probably baseless adventures had been rumoured, never proved. Doll, since leaving her first husband (by whom she had a son), appeared always to have been discreet. Certainly there were no stories about her.

The matter of Barberina Rookwood had been the sole occasion when Lamont was thought to have come near losing his head. People knew that only because Lamont himself used to talk with ostensible openness in those terms about the Barberina Rookwood interlude. It was Lamont's system to speak openly about most things. He was no doubt right in adding that was the surest method of mystifying the world. In the particular case, however far what he said was accepted at the time, precisely the opposite may well have been proved by his words.

Because Lamont and Barberina Rookwood were occasionally seen out together, certain persons insisted that they must sleep together. More determined inventors of scandal stated that unequivocally as a fact, adducing the corollary that Barberina Rookwood had been heard to express a growing dissatisfaction with Henchman, was indeed declaring her intention of leaving him.

The argument in support of this view was that Lamont was the sole man with whom Barberina Rookwood had ever been seen alone in public after going to live with Henchman. Many men, given the chance, would have been glad enough to take her out, and try their luck. That was during periods when Henchman was away working on photographic enterprises he preferred to tackle on his own, which sometimes he did, getting such help as he needed on the spot. In the nicest possible way she always refused such invitations.

Lamont, Beals used to say, represented a kind of un-resolved sequel to the original story of Henchman and Barberina Rookwood. In their respective spheres both could be called wellknown figures, as noted in Middlecote's reactions to them. Lamont, wellknown in quite a different way, by his behaviour had caused renewal of talk about them. That too had in due course died down. Each aspect of the triangle attracted its own adherents when the supposed entanglement was being discussed. In the course of such debates the magnitude of Barberina Rookwood's abnegation of her career tended on the whole to excite less interest than her acceptance of Henchman's nullity as a lover.

When it came to analysing Lamont's conduct, the general opinion was that a man of such essentially practical ap-proach would not waste time over a woman, unless con-vinced that he had a good chance of sleeping with her, if his cards were played adroitly. At least people regarding themselves as of equally practical approach put forward that apprehension. Others, possibly nearer the mark, were more subtle. They considered so easy an answer open to criticism. This latter school of thought held that Lamont wanted to marry Barberina Rookwood (which, in his case, would certainly have included sleeping with her), and (irrespective of whatever she herself might feel in the matter) was prevented simply by the more dominant in-clination of wishing to remain married to his wife Doll.

In these already convoluted relationships, Lamont's

passion for the Ballet created another imponderable factor. Although delight in watching her dance may have influenced a first attraction – hers, too, in at least partial response – since she no longer danced, Lamont's love of ballet became a link the force of which was hard to gauge between them. At the very least it must have created a topic for talk that was always absorbing. The inventors of rumour asserted that, when Lamont removed Barberina Rookwood from Henchman, he would reinstate her as ballerina.

Whether she had been to bed with Lamont was no doubt a matter of legitimate concern only to themselves, and to Henchman as an interested party. Some might even have demurred at the last, at least argued that Henchman's right of veto was limited. None the less, the question focused a good deal of curiosity for a time. If the dual relationship had been less unusual, Lamont would probably have excited no more comment than that aroused by the average third party intervening between two people previously united; which is not to deny that third parties, even if only briefly, are chronically calculated to excite comment.

Beals, whatever highflown or farfetched improbabilities he might play with in his novels, was a man difficult to tax in 'real life' with labouring under romantic or idealistic illusions about human behaviour. In some ways Middlecote, anyway when it came to the craft of advertising, possessed a more romantic strain. Accordingly, Beals's wholehearted agreement with Fay Middlecote (who, in the latter part of the cruise, heard a good deal of the story from Barberina Rookwood herself) in dismissing out of hand any suspicion of 'bed' in regard to Barberina Rookwood and Lamont, must be allowed weight.

Beals himself was far more engrossed in other aspects of a situation he was much concerned to unravel. For example, did Barberina Rookwood not feel drawn to going to bed with anyone, yet experienced in a high degree the emotions of love in quite another manner? Did she, indeed, experience that other kind of love with such acuteness that she was prepared to make so absolute a sacrifice because Henchman was the man she loved?

'After all,' said Beals. 'Plenty of ballerinas fall desperately in love. Desperation in love is almost their endemic condition. Some have many love affairs, others settle down and marry. Neither sort necessarily gives up dancing. Why did she feel she had to undergo that renunciation? On the face of it there was no absolute requirement. While devoting every moment of her spare time to Henchman she could have continued to dance.'

'Dancers don't have all that spare time,' said Fay Middlecote. 'Besides, Henchman needs a great deal of attention. If Henchman's love was to be gained, he would accept nothing less than complete surrender. Henchman's love was what she wanted, so that was what she gave.'

Beals then began again on <u>Courtly Love</u>.

'I once planned to write a novel about the Troubadours, the humble lover and the haughty lady. There was no bed. That is the sexual situation reversed, of course, to the couple we're talking about. Anyway, how many lovers of either sex achieve surrender in totality? There are always areas of doubt. Henchman must have wanted to prove that, in spite of his handicap, he could, so far as humanly possible, accomplish such an ascendancy. Henchman's colossal self-esteem may have required the suppression of a great artist – in this case a great dancer – as expression of a physical love of which he was incapable. Perhaps this, Henchman accepting nothing less than complete surrender, made him, in the particular circumstances, irresistible. In other words it was Henchman's inability to possess that caused him to triumph, where other men had failed.'

'How long are other men going to fail?'

'Ah, there's the rub, if one may use the metaphor.'

'I think she regards Henchman as her child,' said Fay

Middlecote. 'The relationship proves not so much his power over her, as her power over him.'

In the end Beals always returned to his original contention.

'Which ever way you examine it, the Fisher King image lurks in the background. All the additional aspects of the myth. Who was to be the Fisher King's heir? Who will make the barren lands fertile again? Who – to consider the meaning from another angle – cause Winter to give place to Spring?'

'I could do with Winter giving place to Summer on this trip,' said Middlecote. 'After all it's nearly August.'

20

Mr Jack's pervasive presence in the bar did not take long to become the subject of comment on board. Apart from multitudinous experiences with women, which did not seem at all limited to periods when employed as a courier, a profession notoriously exposed to sexual responses, his background remained shadowy. He evidently possessed exceptional abilities for looking after himself in that or other callings, always showing encyclopaedic knowledge of guide-books and time-tables, relating to every part of the world.

There were occasional interludes in the bar between melancholy reflection and manic garrulity, when he would express his mood by flicking at the barman the round pasteboard mats placed under glasses. That would be chiefly when alone, or all but alone, at times when the barman was making new dispositions with the bottles on the shelves at the back. Considering the amount he drank, Mr Jack was a surprisingly accurate shot when indulging in this pastime. He would flick the mat lightly, so that it caught the barman with quite a sharp percussion in the back of the neck. The barman took this horseplay in only moderately good part, no doubt curbing any temptation to exposulate more violently by reminding himself that Mr Jack, already established as by far his most steadfast customer, showed every likelihood of remaining so. The diversion was also, as a rule, quickly brought to an end by shortage of mats.

Beals, accustomed to have drinks in the saloon, did not often use the bar, but, the night following Lamont's encounter with Mr Jack, Louise Beals had wanted soda-water in the cabin. Beals went to the bar as the quickest means of getting a bottle. Mr Jack, who possessed the innate instinct of persons of his type for momentarily catching the attention of whomever he wanted to involve in conversation, asked Beals, who was signing a chit for the soda-water, some question about what a lecturer had said the previous day about late Roman tombs. Before Beals was fully aware of what was happening, he was listening to an anecdote about a baronet's widow, with whom Mr Jack found himself alone in Theodoric's Mausoleum at Ravenna, while conducting a tour.

Beals, who, as a professional teller of stories, was impressed by the mastery of compact narrative, then found himself entrapped by the common enough bore's decoy of apparently having something of further interest to say. When Mr Jack moved on to the statement that an aunt of his had been briefly mistress to Frank Harris, Beals nibbled the bait, the trap closed, and he had to listen to a series of verbal vignettes illustrating Mr Jack's picaresque life-style: the girl with a stutter picked up in Bruges, where the two of them lay in bed listening to the carillon; something about a married woman and a fire-escape in Buffalo, halfway through which Beals managed to extricate himself.

All this did, however, turn out to make a point of contact with Lamont, when Middlecote introduced them, conveying at the same time that Beals was lucky to have a friend conversant with a world in which such a galvanic figure operated in dramas of back-stabbings and take-overs. Beals was far from prepared to accept condescension of that kind, pointing out that there was nothing to prevent him from speaking to Lamont on deck, or during one of the tours. All the same it was true that he preferred a meeting to come about in an entirely unforced manner. Lamont's media connections were potentially useful. Having gone so far as to benefit Beals to that extent Middlecote plunged into his own preoccupations.

'What sort of a price-tag do you suppose they'll put on this new scheme for bus-shelter advertising, Gary?'

Lamont made some noncommittal answer. He did not propose to have his brain picked, nor was Beals prepared to be kept out of the conversation by adman talk.

'The company's reputed to be flush of cash,' said Middlecote. 'There's a yawning hiatus for someone who knows how to fill it.'

'I don't want posters in bus-shelters to take the bread out of my mouth,' said Beals. 'I've seen fans of mine devouring tattered and rain-soaked paperbacks in bus-shelters before now.'

Middlecote laughed.

'Physically, expectation of public transport,' he said.

'Mentally, sacrificing their last drop of blood as a dangerously handsome boy-page of Richard Coeur de Lion, or fighting unsuccessfully to keep their virginity from sex-mad pirates on the Spanish Main.'

'Exactly,' said Beals. 'I won't have my readers distracted by Piers's mundane recommendations as to what shampoo to use, confectionery to gorge, or financial institutions in which to stow away their money.'

'You seem to have a good grasp of poster ads yourself,' said Lamont.

He knew Beals was not the sort of writer whose acquaintance offered the smallest intellectual cachet, indeed rather the reverse, but Beals might possess other assets. In any case a capacity to make money on the scale Beals did simply by writing books was not to be looked upon as negligible. If Lamont might be useful to Beals, Beals could conceivably be useful to Lamont, who in any case made a point of being agreeable to persons encountered by chance in these sort of circumstances. *Compagnons de voyage* could turn out handy contacts during the next week or two.

'There's no clash between consumer ads and your fiction, Valentine,' said Middlecote. 'The condition of trance induced by reading it, which I've described, is just what's required for subliminal digestion. Has the pirate about to rape me noticed my shampoo? What brand of chocolate did Richard Coeur de Lion's page favour. We shan't do your novels any harm.'

'Talking of rape,' said Beals, 'have either of you come across an elderly figure who haunts the bar, and tells you about his former conquests? The Ancient Mariner was a terse reporter compared with him.'

Beals was prevented from saying more about becoming Mr Jack's victim by Lamont claiming priority in relating his own experience.

'He appears to be the ship's Don Juan,' said Lamont.

That was too much for Beals, embarking him at once on archetypes.

'But, of course, you are right. He is Don Juan. The name itself is of obvious significance. I should have seen that at once. Mr Jack is the Great Lover, condemned to travel from place to place – just what Jack's life seems to have been – eternally seducing women, eternally suffering sexual ennui. He is old, weary, probably impotent, sunk in a hell of memories and drink.'

That sort of talk was not to Lamont's taste, although he had brought it on himself. The arrival of Fay Middlecote gave an excuse for saying a word to her, rather than answering, then moving off. Beals was absorbed in this opportunity of transforming another *Alecto* passenger into a myth-figure. He was still explaining to Fay Middlecote that Mr Jack was Don Juan, when Louise Beals turned up.

'I always imagined Don Juan rather a handsome dashing fellow,' said Middlecote. 'You can't call old Jack that.'

'He may have been better when younger, and those qualities are far from prerequisites in the role. Think of some of the Don Juans one has known.'

Louise Beals was not going to accept that.

'Oh, Valentine, I've known some very pretty ones. Makes me swoon to think of some of them still.'

'So have I,' said Fay Middlecote. 'They may have been awful creeps, but some quite goodlooking. After all, the lead in *Don Giovanni* is always got up to look handsome, even if like most singers he's become a bit plump. I wouldn't mind hearing *Don Giovanni* once a week.'

Beals refused to be sidetracked into the musical area.

'When I was writing *Songs of Seville* I went into the evolution of Don Juan as a legend. He starts off in Spain as nothing much more than a player of unpleasant hoaxes. The sort of man who likes getting a girl into trouble just for the fun of the thing, and by any trick he can. No nonsense about love. Then Molière saw possibilities in Don Juan for a play. The first thing Molière did was to smarten the Don up a bit, present him as a wit.'

'Molière ought to get to work on old Jack,' said Middlecote. 'He needs both smartening up, also improving conversationally.'

'The Eighteenth Century viewed Don Juan with classical detachment. If you like seducing women, seducing women is what you like. Nothing to make a fuss about. It was the Nineteenth Century that brought romanticism in, actually managed to turn Don Juan into an idealist – the man who's always looking for the perfect mate. Of course that works well for a Don Juan Do-It-Yourself system, but doesn't hold much water as an explanation of Don Juanesque behaviour. I bet old Jack's often applied the looking-for-an-ideal-mate technique in his own particular way.'

'I've met a few of those,' said Fay Middlecote. 'Haven't you, Louise?'

'Then there was Byron's contribution. Even if no one ever enjoyed feeling romantic so much as Byron did, he also saw the richly comic side of Don Juans.'

'Can one get these lectures on literature on this wavelength every Tuesday at this time of day?' asked Middlecote. 'You shouldn't be doing this free, Valentine.'

Having begun his theme, Beals was as usual determined to go through to the end.

'Modern psychology has divested Don Juan of almost all his male characteristics. He is at best a complete narcissus. All he is thinking about is presenting himself in a flattering light. He is not even very interested in sex, except to possess every woman he meets. He is hopelessly neurotic, intensely feminine, with a strong streak of concealed homosexuality. Macho, perhaps, in outward bearing, really much more in need of psychiatric treatment than a woman to go to bed with.'

'Oh dear,' said Louise Beals. 'Are Don Juans really as bad as that? I've met some quite nice ones – anyway nice to sit next to at dinner.'

'You have to discount unsuccessful men's propaganda,'

said Fay Middlecote. 'Still I'd admit there are some awful heels in that line. I haven't seen much of poor old Jack being homosexual. It's just the booze.'

'Permanent intoxication is always an ominous sign, where concealed homosexuality is concerned. Then flicking those cardboard things at the barman shows a touch of homosexual sadism, aggressive desire to call attention to his own charms.'

'Rubbish,' said Fay Middlecote. 'It's to call attention to the fact that he's without a drink. What about Gary Lamont. Would you call him a Don Juan?'

'Good heavens, no,' said Beals. 'Lamont's an immensely domesticated animal, even if he did have a few affairs earlier on. At the same time I think he's got his eye on Barberina Rookwood pretty seriously.'

'I'm not sure he won't bring it off,' said Fay Middlecote. 'Gary's got a way of bringing off what he wants.'

21

Middlecote usually breakfasted earlier than his wife. In any case he liked eggs-and-bacon in the dining saloon, rather than her preference for coffee and rolls in the smaller breakfast place on the deck above. He sat down at an empty table near the doors on the opposite side to that from which he had come in. Only a few passengers were present. Middlecote had just given his order, when Henchman and Barberina Rookwood entered by one of the doors close to his table. Henchman, after looking round the room, took the chair beside him.

'Good-morning,' said Middlecote.

'I doubt it,' said Henchman. 'Simply because it will be so uncomfortable on The Wall if it is not a good morning. I feel the Fates are much more likely to decree bad weather.'

'You're bound for The Wall too?'

'We are. Have you introduced Hadrian's Wall into any of your ads? Thracian legionaries drinking Scythian vodka, Batavians consuming low calorie health-foods from Phrygia?'

'Not up to now. Since you mention it, we'll have to consider The Wall's possibilities for innovative images.'

Henchman seemed in a relatively good humour, though Middlecote thought the mood might easily change at any moment. He reported Barberina Rookwood as looking ravishing, particularly pleased about something. Middlecote had been not a little overwhelmed since first setting eyes on her, and admired her even more now the impression of melancholy had lifted. Since the to-do when Henchman had fallen from his stool she seemed more prepared to accept fellow passengers.

'Have you seen The Wall before'? she asked.

'Never.'

'I feel rather excited about it.'

Middlecote said afterwards that he had begun to prepare an answer that would at once do justice to the promise of the expedition, express homage to Barberina Rookwood, set himself in a brilliant light, when, before he could devise the exact turning of phrase, a steward, with the aim of filling vacant places at already occupied tables, steered Sir Dixon and Lady Tiptoft to seats opposite.

'Good-morning,' said Middlecote.

Sir Dixon looked preoccupied, as usual rather angry. He did not answer. Lady Tiptoft made some slight acknowledgment, adding that she thought it was going to be a nice day. Henchman and Barberina Rookwood began a conversation together about their cabins, which appeared to be opposite one another. They ignored the Tiptofts' arrival. The Tiptofts, for their part, seemed not to notice them.

'May I be allowed some toast, Sybil?' said Sir Dixon. 'You are sitting on the butter, too.'

'There are only rolls in this basket. I have taken the last piece of toast.'

'Can't we get some more?'

'You had better order it.'

Gaunt, withered, beaky, in a general way unnoticeable, Lady Tiptoft would spring to life, when at odds with her husband or daughter. On such occasions she could display a pugnacity unguessable from a normally impassive exterior.

'Try to get some honey, too, while you're about it. There is only marmalade on this table.'

Sir Dixon, having himself in some degree acquired what he wanted for breakfast, took no immediate notice of this request. He drank his coffee, continuing to ponder some weighty matter. Then he looked up, glanced across the table – perhaps with the idea in his mind of asking a steward for honey – and seemed to take in for the first time that Henchman was at the same table as himself. He now addressed himself to Henchman.

'I believe you are a photographer?'

Henchman looked up. He made no answer at once. He considered the question. His reply took so long to formulate that Middlecote wondered whether he was going to utter one at all. Then Henchman, too, drank another cup of coffee. By that time Sir Dixon, temporarily engaged in securing honey, began to show signs of expecting an answer. Henchman spoke.

'What makes you think so?'

'Are you not a photographer?'

'Yes – and no.'

Sir Dixon, probably inured to receiving a certain number of disobliging or teasing replies on account of the manner in which he approached people, must have grasped that Henchman was resistant material. He did not smile. At the same time he showed no resentment at Henchman's bantering tone, beyond the normal exasperation with which he confronted life.

'Am I wrong in supposing your name sometimes appears in the papers in connection with photography, even photographs taken by you?'

'Not wholly.'

'In fact we may assume you are a photographer?'

'Some people might call me that.'

'What do people call you, may I ask, when they do not call you a photographer?'

'Ah,' said Henchman. 'That is a big question. There are many and complex answers. Let me ask you a question in return. Are you a man of power?'

Sir Dixon appeared by no means displeased to be placed in that category. Middlecote reported that his face contracted, into a bureaucratic simper. He must have recognised that Henchman, even if only an amateur of power compared with himself, was not a wholly unqualified judge of the status.

'I'm retired now.'

'Once a man of power, always a man of power. Like being a Boy Scout.'

'I suppose I have wielded a certain amount of power in my day. I would not deny that. But what I wished to talk about was not power, but photography. I have taken up photography in my retirement. There are certain questions I should like to ask you.'

'Let us stick to power for the moment,' said Henchman. 'Has it never struck you that a photographer imposes his or her will in a manner unparalleled on the person photographed. The painter supplies his own version, essentially idiosyncratic. Everyone can see that a painted portrait is the painter's personal view of the subject. People are far less aware of that in the case of photography, yet the photographer forces the sitter to defer to his whim no less than the painter. The sitters themselves think that they submit only to a representational instrument. On the contrary, they hand themselves over bodily just as much as when painted or drawn.'

'I am not sure that I understand you.'

Sir Dixon's passing good humour at being recognized as

a man of power was diminishing. Henchman must have observed that with satisfaction. There could be no doubt that he intended to be as annoying as possible.

'Savage races are quite right in objecting to being photographed. The mysterious power of the photographer twists them to his own ends, so they believe, and they are perfectly correct. This is quite a different story from, say, drawing an offensive caricature of someone. That is merely the cartoonist's notion, from which the subject has every right to differ, saying that he has not got such a long nose, or her eyes are not so close together. It is useless for the photographic victim to apply that sort of objection. The camera is thought – quite erroneously – not to lie. What has been recorded has been recorded by what might be called scientific means.'

'I agree that some photographic portraits are not in the least like their subjects. Most of us have had such incompetent photographs taken of ourselves.'

'But you seem unaware that, if the photographer is an American, in nine cases out of ten you are made to look like an American. If by a Frenchman, like a Frenchman, and so on. I agree that it is sometimes an American or a Frenchman's idea of what an Englishman looks like.'

'I hardly see what relation such things have to power, even if what you say is correct. For my own part I have never noticed it.'

'Only because you are both unobservant, and take a narrow view of power. You should broaden your horizons.'

'Power over whom?'

'The Living and the Dead. Especially the Dead.'

'Please explain yourself.'

'Photography is one of the aspects of Death and Regeneration. Those who live more photographic lives than one, have more photographic resurrections than one, as well as more deaths. Nowadays a dead person depends

122

almost entirely on photographs for the manner in which he or she is physically remembered. In the past it was the painter. The painter, even if competent, may have been subservient or malicious. A painting or drawing can therefore be discounted as untrue to life. The photographer is far more difficult to disparage on that account, provided, where verisimilitude is in question, the print is reasonably clear. If that is not power, I don't know what is.'

'You are like the Victorians, and attribute importance to verisimilitude?'

Sir Dixon evidently felt he had scored a point.

'People mean different things by verisimilitude. It was something early Nineteenth Century photographers, admirable as they were in many ways, did not always understand.'

Sir Dixon seemed divided. He had assumed an expression that denied such arguments as specious. At the same time he must have hoped to extract what technical information he could from Henchman without being teased more than was absolutely necessary. Middlecote saw him as finding difficulty in steering a passage between these feelings.

'I would like to discuss with you methods of using light to measure optical density. What you regard as the best coating for paper or film. Such things as the way underexposure leads to a dense positive in the direct reversal process. Remedying that by chemical reduction. Densitometers, emulsions, and so on.'

Again Henchman did not answer immediately. He continued to gaze at Sir Dixon as if considering whether, as such an unusual specimen of his kind, he might himself be worth photographing, then and there once again, as he had been done on the quay. Henchman took a roll. He began to butter it. He spoke in a measured voice.

'To answer such questions to my own satisfaction I should require an X-ray photograph of the brain, to speak more technically, a pneumoencephalogram, preferably taken after replacing the cerebrospinal fluid with air or oxygen, so that the brain cavities show more clearly. Suitable equipment for such an experiment is unlikely to be available in this ship. The test, were you anxious to proceed with it, would have to be delayed until our return.'

Before Sir Dixon had made up his mind how best to deal with this piece of insolence (if he so regarded it, Middlecote was by no means certain), whether or not to show that he did not mind having his leg pulled, the subject was brought to a close by Lady Tiptoft.

'I think we have had enough photography at breakfast. I get sufficient while we are on expeditions.'

'I agree,' said Henchman. 'Me, too. Yet how encouraging to see a retired man so keen on a hobby. I often wonder what I shall do myself when I retire.'

'As I've finished, shall I go and look for Robin?' said Barberina Rookwood. 'If he is coming with us?'

'Do,' said Henchman.

He turned towards Middlecote, and smiled. For some reason the smile made Middlecote feel embarrassed, a process he himself admitted difficult to bring off. There were all sorts of matters connected with advertising he would have liked to raise with Henchman, since he seemed willing to speak of such things, but he felt that inopportune. The chance was removed a second or two later by Henchman abandoning his roll, and departing.

22

Beyond The Wall, rolling northward in bright sunlight until lost in the horizon, stretched a green campagna, rugged and empty, tenantless uplands, where the huge expanses of grass were diversified by a few clumps of dark trees and squat conical hillocks that marked pre-Roman Iron Age strongholds. The only hint of human infiltration of these pastures came from distant sheep or cattle, isolated specks grazing the meads far from one another, shadowy herds of nomadic tribes.

Only about half the *Alecto*'s passengers, in preference to another excursion, had opted for The Wall. They were now spread over the neighbouring country, some trailing a lecturer from archaeological point to archaeological point, others wandering off on their own to contemplate the remains of imperial military quarters, the occasional propitiatory shrine, or simply rambling about without specific aim.

Louise Beals, untroubled by Romans, archaeology, photography, subjects for future novels, TV advertising rates, newspaper takeovers, at the same time not indifferent to the behaviour of fellow passengers, had settled under a tree, one of the few thereabouts. She was reading a detective story. The place she had chosen was not far from where recent excavations were more or less fenced off. The dig seemed uncompleted, but a tablet or altar had been cleared in a manner that made it available to the public for examination.

Lamont was scrutinizing the inscription on this stone. He was not much interested in the past, as such, at the same time recognized that concerns to which he was committed might require a certain grasp of changing fashion in ideas, how those had come about. The ebb and flow of history could illustrate aspects of the power principle. Lessons were undeniably to be learnt, while history could also be used conversationally, if not too often. At the moment his mind was no doubt on things other than the Roman occupation of Britain. Although staring at the altar, he was more likely to be thinking of Barberina Rookwood. At least he had made a start. All looked hopeful again.

Having settled his wife under a tree with a book, Beals was for a moment uncertain what he wanted to do himself. He had visited The Wall before, some little time before, when he had travelled up here with the specific purpose of making notes for *Mistress to Maximus*, a novel about Magnus Maximus, the usurping Emperor of Britain. Beals conceded it owed something to *Puck of Pook's Hill*. He had liquidated the children, and added a generous flavouring of sexual adventure.

Mistress to Maximus (selling well enough, if not one of his most popular) had caused Beals to acquire a fair amount of miscellaneous information about Roman Britain. Seeing how Lamont was engaged, Beals thought he might renew their acquaintance by displaying some of his own grasp of the terrain. He strolled across. Lamont looked up. Beals opened with a mildly imaginative foray.

'What a solemn sense of untamed ancientness is to be

found up here. To all intents and purposes the Romans might never have left the place. Don't you expect a centurion to challenge your presence from behind one of those ruined embrasures, or a cohort of Dacian cavalry to canter towards the gate from the Caledonian side of The Wall, on their way back from a patrol in Pictish country – though strictly speaking the Picts were a good deal further north, beyond the abandoned Antonine Wall, not, as Kipling represents them, right up here, where there were just more Britannic tribes.'

Lamont nodded, but said nothing. If not entirely meaningless to him, such mental images, on account of their over imaginative nature, were suspect. He liked what was easily apprehensible. The partly effaced lettering, over which he had allowed his mind to wander, at least represented a practical problem of decipherment.

'Is this a gravestone? I was trying to make out the lettering.'

Beals gave the stone his attention.

'A sort of memorial shrine, I think.'

'Can you read any of it?'

Beals began to intone the opening line in an incantatory manner. Lamont, to be on the safe side in case Beals broke down, assumed a sceptical smile. This began to fade as Beals progressed.

'I O M ... Jupiter Optimus Maximus ... Jupiter, the Best, the Greatest ... No, let me see ...'

Beals was glad Middlecote, a scholarship boy of some classical attainment, was not present. Middlecote might have reeled the inscription off like a headline in the morning paper. Beals, whatever he had mugged up for *Mistress to Maximus*, had to rely on pretty average Latin.

'CETERIS QUE DIS IMMORT ... It's difficult to read the way they run all the words together ... And the Other Immortal Gods ... ET DEO BELATUCADRO ...'

Beals stuck there. Even so, Lamont was unable entirely

to exclude admission of respect. His own education would not have risen to this amount of metaphrase.

For the moment Beals was floored. He was anxious to put on a good show for Lamont, who, having ceased to smile, had nodded once or twice in a serious manner. Achievement of any kind tended to impress him. Beals saw what he produced could conceivably influence getting one of his novels on television, possibly even the comparatively unsuccessful *Mistress to Maximus*. That would be a pleasing late harvest. Then the next words brought inspiration.

'GENIO LOCI ... The spirit of the Place ... Belatucadrus is the name of a Celtic god. He was a horned god, equated with Mars, and called the Fair Shining One. I'm not sure whether he himself was Spirit of the Place, or that was another yet more minor deity, like a nymph.

Beals saw there was going to be trouble ahead. The face of the stone deteriorated soon into damaged surface and illegibility, when release would be brought about from showing off to Lamont. Before that came at least one other fairly legible series of letters remained.

'CUNITT ... I think I may be stumped ... another proper name perhaps ... Could it be another god? ... Cunittus? That sounds Celtic too ... I have it. He was probably the fellow who put the stone up, or to whom it was raised. A Brit in the Imperial Forces. There were quite a lot of them, some of whom Magnus Maximus took with him, when he had a crack at making himself Emperor. That was the real withdrawal of the Legions, such as it was. There wasn't a kind of D-Day. When Maximus was beheaded, they stayed on the Continent, and probably founded Brittany. That was nearly fifty years before the Rescript of Honorius, when all Barbarians were told to look after themselves.'

Lamont wilted a little at the volume of information Beals had launched at him. All the same, he was not incapable of praise, when he felt a job had been well done. Beals had surprised him.

'Very interesting. Remarkable the way you did that.'

Beals brushed aside, as if nothing, what he hoped had represented to Lamont a dazzling display of learning.

'I find something sustaining in the thought of a local deity,' he said. 'I should like to have one at home where we live.'

Lamont, perhaps contemplating a series of religious articles from Beals, looked at him narrowly.

'Do you go for religion?'

'To the point of not wanting to offend Belatucadrus. I should like to feel that Belatucadrus was keeping a friendly eye on us while we are up here by The Wall. I'm sure trouble would follow if he took against any of the *Alecto*'s ship's company.'

Lamont gave a short laugh. He did not react well to that sort of observation. Nevertheless, Beals's epigraphical performance had established good relations, in spite of Lamont being allergic to vignettes of imagined history. If Beals, as he was showing signs of doing, continued too long in that strain, he could easily lose what marks he had accumulated. Beals himself was perfectly accustomed to a reception of that kind. He could usually tell by instinct the exact amalgam of romanticism and popular history his public could take, without too great a strain, though he had not for a moment placed Lamont in the category of his public. He now changed the subject to one he judged more in Lamont's line.

'When you were editing . . .'

Beals mentioned the paper from which Lamont had resigned not long before, adding a question about the proprietors. He was surprised by the uninhibited manner in which Lamont began to expatiate on that matter to an acquaintance set eyes on for the first time so shortly before. Lamont's personal and business affairs were his own favourite subject. When speaking of either, he gave the impression, so often illusory, of complete openness. Beals, as diplomatically as possible, settled down to cross-questioning, something Lamont greatly preferred to speculations about Roman Britain. As a matter of common politeness (which Lamont did not wholly lack), also because such information could prove useful when filed away in the mind, Lamont threw in intermittent enquiries as to Beals's own manner of earning a living. Beals treated that airily.

'My sales? Well, it's not at all easy to assess them. Different titles sell very differently in different countries. I suppose, to strike a kind of Dow-Jones average . . .'

Beals hoped the last metaphor, with its throwaway suggestion of familiarity with international money-markets, would amuse or impress Lamont, who either failed to notice, or thought the image inept. Talk soon drifted back to Lamont's own concerns, which Beals hoped to beam, before too long, towards the subject of Henchman and Barberina Rookwood. Meanwhile, he was content enough to hear something of the devious business negotiations, which had occupied Lamont's last few months. Beals enquired about one of Lamont's more notorious adversaries.

'An unrivalled asset-stripper.'

'An asset-strip-tease artist?'

Beals thought he could again risk a pleasantry. Lamont accepted the parallel only in moderation. He may have disliked such a subject to be spoken of in jest.

'It's the concern he's abandoned that's left without a rag, not himself.'

Beals, for his part, was enjoying the conversation. He planned to repeat as much as he could remember to Middlecote, who would be envious of some of the information. Then the direction in which they had been moving offered opportunity to switch to what was for Beals a more interesting topic.

23

Some little way ahead, on the path in front, a group consisting of Henchman, Barberina Rookwood, and Jilson, had stopped. Henchman was making some announcement to the others. After concluding whatever he had to say, he turned towards The Wall, which at this point ran along a high natural parapet of crags and turf. Henchman, camera round his neck, began to lever himself up its steep rocky slope. This ascent was evidently directed towards finding an advantageous spot from which to take photographs.

The causeway along the top of The Wall, which led over this parapet, fell for thirty or more feet on the Caledonian face, the drop continuing for a longish stretch of the battlement. From ground level, even for a climber unhandicapped by Henchman's disabilities, crutches, dangling camera, the scramble would have been quite arduous. A foothold was nowhere easy to maintain. More than once, Henchman, who was dragging the crutches after him, nearly slipped. At last he reached the summit, moving across the causeway to the far edge of The Wall itself. He advanced onward to a crag jutting forward on the outer ridge above the descent. There, squatting down fairly hazardously, he began to experiment with camera sitings.

Barberina Rookwood and Jilson (who also carried a camera, although not yet allowed by Henchman to take any photographs), followed up the slope as quickly as they were able. Earlier that morning Jilson had been given instructions by Henchman to remain within range throughout the expedition, in case any useful photographic tips were let fall. After Henchman's inaugural display of benevolence, Jilson, in response to this command to make himself of the party, had more than once repeated that he did not want to become a bore. In answer to this expressed hope, Henchman always replied that Jilson would be immediately apprised, in the plainest terms, at the first sign of vexatiousness in him being detected. Pending notification of that, Jilson was to remain close at hand as already informed, being also encouraged to make any comments, or ask any questions, he might judge relevant. Jilson was perhaps more sure of himself than Henchman guessed.

Beals admitted later that he was uncertain, at this stage, of the extent to which Jilson was aware that Barberina Rookwood had taken so strong a fancy for him; indeed, as it turned out, fallen in love with him. No doubt Jilson still found difficulty in crediting his luck in obtaining Henchman's expert advice on photography. He may well have been dazed by finding himself a kind of additional assistant to so beautiful a girl. At the same time the icy inner loneliness in which she seemed to live, captivating to some men, could have blighted him. Her silence alone may have been daunting to someone daily habituated to the unceasing chatter of his mother.

By this time Mrs Jilson had made herself known not only to Henchman and Barberina Rookwood, but possibly even to the majority of her fellow passengers. She was an energetic effusive little woman, who started up a conversation with anyone who happened to be within her orbit. This often took place to her son's embarrassment. Mrs Jilson would pour out miscellaneous information about him, her late husband, herself. She was at once very proud of her son, and ever anxious about his health. Jilson, much dominated by her, was always attempting to escape.

On first hearing that Henchman had promised his good offices in connection with photography, Mrs Jilson had attempted to proffer astonished and grateful thanks. Her words had been cut short not only by Jilson himself (who grasped that fervent phrases would only exacerbate Henchman), but even more brutally by Henchman, who indicated the utmost discouragement to Mrs Jilson, either in persisting with expressing a sense of obligation, or proceeding into any other form of communication with him.

Such brusque treatment did not at all discourage Mrs Jilson, at best tolerated as something of a burden, even by friends and relations. Undisquieted by inurbanity in human transactions, she moved away from Henchman without taking the least offence, or attempting, as her son was doing, to tabulate Henchman's prejudices and preferences. That was her habit with everyone. She would chat strenuously to all who came her way, not minding at all if, like Henchman, some displayed reservations as to how long they could put up with her company.

Mrs Jilson, who was making the excursion to The Wall, now appeared in the neighbourhood of Beals and Lamont, enquiring from a group of middle-aged ladies, not too dissimilar from herself, whether any of them had seen Dr Lorna Tiptoft within the last half hour or so.

'We are sharing a cabin, and were going to do our sightseeing together. I must have got on the wrong bus. I don't think Lorna can have done that. It would have been very unlike her. She is the most efficient person you ever met. She was just saying she so much wanted to meet my son again, while I was sorting my dripdrys, and I suppose I didn't listen properly, and got the bus number wrong.'

Nobody seemed to have seen Dr Tiptoft. Mrs Jilson forgot about her friend for the moment in the excitement of suddenly noticing her son in the company of Henchman.

'Why, there's Robin with Mr Henchman. It's so good of Mr Henchman, he says he'll help Robin become a photographer, which Robin is mad to do, though I tell him he'll end up by being one of those men who take photographs in the street. And look where he and Mr Henchman have climbed. Fancy Mr Henchman getting right up there with his crutches. He really is a wonder, isn't he? I don't know whether he ever photographs animals. I'd have given the world for him to have taken a picture of our basset, Bertie, such a wonderful dog, but we had to put him down when he got too old to spend a penny properly. Very sad, it was.'

Mrs Jilson's *obiter dicta* – so Beals called them – had been expressed in a tone sufficiently loud to give Beals excuse for bringing up with Lamont the subject of Henchman, which he was hoping to do.

'Look, indeed. Henchman certainly is a phenomenon in the way he gets about. I expect you know him well. I remember a very striking photograph he took of you in your office, with an extraordinary arrangement of filing-cabinets behind you. An extremely ingenious design. I'd never come across him, not even set eyes on him, before our cruise.'

Lamont seemed positively relieved to be given this opportunity to talk about Henchman.

'Yes, of course I know old Saul. That photograph of me? The whole bloody paper was disrupted for a week after we were rash enough to allow him and his camera on the premises. I thought he would take me in his studio, but he was determined to come to my office.'

It occurred to Beals that going to Lamont's office might have reduced at least one meeting between Lamont and Barberina Rookwood. The same thought could have been in Lamont's mind too, because he began to speak of her.

'I know Barberina even better. Are you aware of their extraordinary story? You must be. How she gave up her dancing for him? Christ, if you'd seen her at the Covent Garden Matinée of *Giselle*, which they lay on for the Royal Ballet star pupils.'

'It must have been a terrific sacrifice,' said Beals.

'Sacrifice? It's like something you read about in one of those pi books Saul says he used to be given as a child. I mean the legend of some female saint or something. I don't know, Florence Nightingale, Grace Darling, all that sort of thing. Simply destroyed her career for that crippled remnant of a man, who's a pretty fair shit into the bargain.'

Beals would have liked to hear more about the last estimate.

'I suppose you could say he is a very celebrated photographer.'

'Of course we know all that. I don't say he isn't gifted in his own line. A very clever bugger indeed, in addition to his photography. But, God, would you be prepared to sacrifice what she did? Have you met her yet?'

'Just spoken a word to her when we were getting into the bus. She was charming. And what a beauty.'

'She's a wonderful person. I don't mean her looks. Everybody can see they're absolutely marvellous, spellbinding, breathtaking, knock you off your feet. I mean herself, her character.'

Lamont spoke all that with much fervour. He seemed, so it appeared to Beals, just in the mood for self-revelation. In supposing that, Beals may not have allowed enough for the Lamont method.

'You talk as if you felt pretty strongly about her.'

'Feel strongly about her? I came near wrecking my marriage about her. I don't know whether I'd have done that, had it come to the crunch. As it was, Barberina wouldn't consider leaving Henchman.'

Beals was becoming partly aware that Lamont, in disclosing what appeared to be such powerful sentiments, might be doing so not from an inherent forthrightness of nature, but as policy judged best for future plans. In any case Beals was given justification for urging further unveilings.

'But you were close friends with her?'

'Oh, yes. We were friends all right. Close friends, if you like. But just that. No more.'

'Did you know they would be on this trip?'

Lamont looked hard at Beals. He certainly saw that he was being deliberately interrogated. That did not at all disturb him. If anything, he seemed amused by Beals's curiosity. Accustomed to life within a far from sensitive society, where individual privacy was neither respected, nor even highly regarded, he could afford to tolerate an inquisitiveness that he found flattering, rather than impertinent.

'Yes, I did. Since you ask that. I found out quite by chance that they were going on this cruise. Managed to get a booking for myself at the last moment.'

'The ship was filling up even when we decided to come.'

'I must have got about the last berth. As luck would have it, I'm sharing a cabin with that rather sickly young man, who, for some inexplicable reason, Saul Henchman seems to have taken up. I don't know whether he thinks some use can be made of young Jilson. I should have thought it unlike Saul to do an act of spontaneous kindness. Still, you never know.'

'He seems a perfectly harmless young man. He saved the situation when Henchman fell off his stool in the bar. Perhaps Henchman's just grateful for that.'

136

'Jilson can't get over Henchman cottoning on to him. He keeps me hourly informed about the two of them. I think he's probably got a crush on Barberina too, although rather afraid of her, as well he might be.'

'She's so nice to everyone, but very silent. I'm not surprised if he's fallen for her.'

The inference deduced by Beals from this recital was that Lamont himself derived some sort of personal easement by making it. He positively wanted to unburden himself to someone to clear his own mind – much in the same way that Jilson had revealed his situation to Henchman – and Beals seemed a suitable recipient. Beals reckoned, too, that information put out by Lamont was, anyway for the time being, as ample as could be reasonably hoped. By that time they had arrived quite close under the place on The Wall up to which Henchman and his two attendants had climbed.

24

Henchman, kneeling at a perilous angle, contemplated the green perspectives. Their immensities appeared not to satisfy him. He changed position, groaning loudly as he did so, then, not without all danger of toppling over into the comparative abyss below, tried to straighten himself. Barberina Rookwood, who was watching, helped to put him on his feet.

'I can't find anything here. I like the country. It's me, not the place, that's at fault.'

She picked up the crutches, and handed them to him. Henchman took them from her, then, without hesitation, hurled them down the slope on the near side. They ricocheted over the rocks to the foot of the parapet quite a long way below. Henchman watched them with apparent pleasure.

'Easier to get down without those bloody things.'

He began his descent, aiming more or less for the spot where the crutches had settled not too far from each other. Barberina Rookwood quickly began to move in the same direction, if possible to arrive first, help Henchman's landing, at worst break a fall. Sliding headlong over the declivity, he made no attempt to wait for her. More than once a crash seemed imminent. By clutching handfuls of turf or projecting stones he always managed to steady himself, arriving in a cascade of rubble on the grass below. Beals and Lamont came up a moment later. By that time Henchman was upright on the retrieved crutches.

'Good-morning, Saul,' said Lamont. 'Been mountaineering?'

'Only as far as snow level,' said Henchman. 'I do it every morning for my health.'

'Found anything worth snapping?'

'Not yet, Gary. I'm in hopeless photographic form today. I feel as you must when your paper has failed three times running to get a scoop offered on a plate.'

Henchman, in his characteristic position of resting on the crutches, smiled rather malevolently at Lamont, who now changed conversational direction.

'Good-morning, Barberina.'

Beals considered the smile she gave was sufficient to irk Henchman.

'How are your guts today, Gary?' she asked.

'Quite in order now, thank you.'

'No longer having to run?'

'I shouldn't be here were that so.'

'But behind a wall is a traditional place for relief,' said Henchman. 'And even in these wide open spaces, no one would notice if you were seen digging a hole for your own purposes. They would think you were an archaeologist.'

'You're looking better than when we met at the surgery,' said Barberina Rookwood.

'You're looking pretty blooming yourself, Barberina.'

Lamont was about to add something to this compliment, when everyone's attention was all at once directed to another matter. Jilson, perhaps suffering one of his attacks of dizziness, had been following the other two down the side of the parapet at a slower rate. His care possibly made its insecure surface more risky to negotiate than Henchman's slapdash approach. For that reason or another Jilson was less lucky in reaching the ground. He seemed to have caught one foot in a crevice used as a step down, losing his balance, pitching forward, finally descending the rest of the way on his face. At the bottom of the slope he picked himself up in some disorder. His cheeks were scratched, one hand bleeding quite profusely from a scrape on a jagged boulder.

'Just the way to damage a camera,' said Henchman. 'Surely if I can get down there intact, he can,'

Barberina Rookwood ran to help, followed by Lamont at a slower rate. Jilson seemed rather shaken by the fall. Left alone with Henchman, Beals saw this as the strategic moment to make the contact he desired. After expressing fears for Jilson's camera, Henchman stood contemplating the scene with his enigmatic smile. By then Mrs Jilson had moved on in her search for Lorna Tiptoft, but several other *Alecto* passengers came up to offer varying degrees of assistance. Barberina Rookwood at once took charge.

'Give me your handkerchief.'

Jilson rummaged rather helplessly with his undamaged hand, managing at last to withdraw from his pocket a fairly grimy rag.

'That's no good. Wait a moment.'

She searched in the bag, quite a capacious one, which she always carried on expeditions. Jilson, still shaking a little, seemed more overawed than soothed by this care for his wellbeing. He was like a man made understandably nervous by the sudden vision of an angel come to minister to him. At the same time he plainly fell naturally enough into the role of patient, a person in a moral position to be looked after by other people. His pale face lighted up a little, and he began to apologize for his clumsiness, at the same time looking nervously in the direction of Henchman, as if he expected a rebuke for being so feeble as to fall down, when Henchman himself had mastered the descent. He was no doubt right to suppose that to be Henchman's attitude, but by then Henchman's attention had been distracted by Beals.

'This will be better.'

Barberina Rookwood produced from the bag a clean bandage, roll of sticking plaster, surgeon's scissors, evidently emergency equipment for Henchman's routine accidents.

'Has he . . . has he . . . fallen down?'

It was Mr Jack. He had quietly joined the group standing round Jilson. An ancient Panama hat, the straw gone in places, concealed his baldness. It gave him the look of an elderly uncle acting in a charade at Christmas, an uncle about whom there were some doubts as to the wisdom of inviting to a family gathering. He spoke with the overflowing feeling of compassion that belonged to a man familiar with the difficulty of remaining in an upright position. Then he began to fumble in a hip-pocket.

'Always keep a small flask of brandy . . . just for emergencies . . . never know . . .'

Jilson refused the offer with thanks. Mr Jack, as ever when an invitation to drink with him was turned down, looked sad. He thought things over for a moment.

'Perhaps I'll . . . At my age these all-day expeditions make you feel a bit cooked. Only sensible to recognize Anno Domini.'

Removing the flask from his lips, he wiped the mouthpiece carefully with the typewritten sheet of coloured paper outlining the day's programme which he had produced from a breast pocket. Then he moved over to where Beals and Henchman stood. He held out the flask towards Henchman.

'Try a sip, sir. You'll find it does you good. You must get a bit weary at times on those things.'

'You're absolutely right. I do – and will. Thank you.'

Henchman spoke with the charm he could show when he liked. He took a good gulp, wiped the nozzle with his elbow, and returned the flask. Mr Jack smiled approvingly. Then his face became grave.

'You know, sir, we met a long time ago.'

'Did we?'

Henchman spoke indifferently. Mr Jack offered the flask to Beals, who shook his head.

'Long time ago . . . You wouldn't remember . . . Forget a lot of things myself these days. Penalty of old age. Always remember how understanding you were.'

Henchman seemed hardly to have heard. He was keen to get rid of Mr Jack, rather than enthralled by Beals, who was now trying to recapture his attention.

'Yes, I can be very understanding. One of my best points.'

Mr Jack nodded heartily.

'We'll have a talk sometime. The old days . . . things different then . . . Often think about them.'

Waving a hesitant farewell to those standing round, Mr Jack moved off down the track. His gait was almost pedantically steady. He was soon out of sight. Barberina Rookwood completed the binding up with a safety-pin, and returned the rest of the surgical equipment to the bag. She smiled at Jilson.

'Otherwise the rest of the day you'll bleed over everything. Do you feel all right? Not going to faint, or anything like that?'

'Absolutely OK. Thank you very much for doing what you have. It's made all the difference.'

Nevertheless, Jilson did not appear wholly recovered. His face, marked with scratches, was very white. He was going to say more in appreciation, when someone pushed through the several people who had been watching the bandaging. It was Lorna Tiptoft. She did not at once grasp that some disturbance had taken place.

'Have you seen your mother, Robin? We are spending the day together. She must have come by a bus with a different number to the one I told her we were going in.'

'She passed by a few minutes ago. She's gone on. Can't be very far ahead.'

Lorna Tiptoft looked him over. Unlike the sobriety of her parents' garments, she had adopted a conspicuously holiday outfit, butcher-blue knickerbockers, a man's check cap with a peak. Entirely without superficial goodlooks, she could, as Middlecote had remarked, have been found engaging by some men; probably even more by some women. Her features had firmness, her expression suggested a sense of direction. She was evidently unhandicapped by humour.

'What has been happening to you?'

'I had a fall coming down the slope.'

Jilson pointed towards the parapet.

'Why did you climb up there?'

'We wanted to see what it would be like to take photographs from the top.'

'We?'

Jilson invoked his photographic tuition from Henchman.

'Never mind that. It was a foolish thing to do in your condition of health. Your mother has told me a lot about that. What is the injury?'

'I scraped my hand on a stone.'

'Who put this bandage on?'

'I did.'

Barberina Rookwood had been watching Lorna Tiptoft with a look of amused horror on her face. Lorna Tiptoft stared back at her severely.

'Has the wound been washed?'

'There was nowhere to wash it. I cleaned the grit out so far as I could. There was hardly any dirt as a matter of fact.'

'That is not always easy to see. You may have done more harm than good.'

'I thought it best to staunch the bleeding as a first step.'

Lorna Tiptoft did not answer. Taking Jilson's bound-up hand in her own, she regarded the bandage with dis-approval. Jilson, laughing in an embarrassed way, tried to alleviate some of the awkwardness of the distinctly absurd situation of which he had suddenly become focus. Lorna Tiptoft continued to hold his hand. He did not seem to mind that at all, making no attempt to remove his own hand. On a smaller scale he shared Henchman's taste for personal attention.

'It was only a scratch. I wasn't at all badly hurt. Just bleeding rather a lot. The scrape looked quite clean.'

'I've just told you it is not always possible to judge that with the naked eye.'

Lorna Tiptoft spoke in a milder tone to that she had used with Barberina Rookwood, but no less inexorable, only more sympathetic to a patient, rather than someone she evidently looked upon as a meddler in medical matters. Jilson seemed to like her. In fact he was much more at ease with her brusque manner than Barberina Rookwood's probably Henchman-influenced carelessness of demeanour. Fussing was no doubt what Jilson was used to from his mother. He was well disposed to anyone who showed signs of fussing over him.

'We had better take this bandage off, so that I can look at the injury.'

Then Barberina Rookwood, hitherto merely amused, began to show signs of pique.

'Oh, come, is that really necessary? You don't want it off, Robin, do you?'

Lorna Tiptoft was magisterial.

'As a member of the medical profession I am not accustomed to being contradicted in the directions I give.'

Jilson seemed uncertain which tutelary goddess to obey.

When Lorna Tiptoft began to unwind the bandage, he made no effort to prevent what allegiance to Barberina Rookwood might have been thought to demand. In fact he gave in completely to Lorna Tiptoft. She examined the wound in a menacing manner, then pronounced judgment.

'This arm should be put in a sling.'

Barberina Rookwood was prepared to challenge that announcement.

'But he won't be able to hold a camera. Can't he just stick his hand in his coat like Napoleon. Take it out when he wants to use it?'

Lorna Tiptoft ignored this frivolity.

'He can use this scarf of mine as a sling.'

She took a multicoloured square of stuff from her neck, and began to fold it diagonally. When straightened out the scarf, like the T-shirts of Basically Bach and Marginally Mahler, revealed a preference or motto, in this case the words KEEP THE EARTH GREEN set within a laurel wreath.

'Do you really want that, Robin? It will mess up the day's photography.'

Barberina Rookwood spoke calmly, but no one could have doubted that she was angry. Jilson put up no fight. He had already capitulated.

'I suppose I'd better use a sling, if Dr Tiptoft says so. I mean she knows about my tiresome state from my mother. I don't want to get ill, and not be able to benefit from what I've been promised.'

Lorna Tiptoft arranged the scarf so that most of its message was legible on the exterior.

She looked up from what she had been doing.

'Come and see me in your mother's and my cabin when the party arrives back on board this evening. I'd like to have a talk with you about several things.'

25

Beals and Henchman had been standing sufficiently far away to be excluded from personal involvement in this confrontation. Henchman had glanced once or twice to see what was going on, and Beals had taken in some of the points, in spite of concentrating chiefly on Henchman. As Henchman presented a very different case from Lamont's, where making contact was concerned, Beals saw no harm in repeating a slightly differently phrased version of an opening tried on Lamont unsuccessfully. In new conditions it might not necessarily prove inoperative.

'I was just remarking to one of our fellow passengers that it's possible to feel the Romans are still about in these parts. A sense of Roman imperial power pervades The Wall. Have you examined that most interesting shrine over there, tombstone or whatever it is, which appears to invoke a Celtic deity?'

Henchman looked Beals up and down. He did not give anything away. Beals prepared himself for a rebuff. The rebuff did not come. Henchman spoke quite amicably.

'I shall be quick to photograph any Romans I see. Speed

is everything where the supernatural is concerned, often a useful photographic reinforcement in dealing with the merely natural, animals, for example. I remain old world in thinking that. Young photographers today tend to clamp the sitter's head into a metal vice for several hours in the manner of the photographers of the eighteen-fifties. At least not much short of that.'

Beals was uncertain whether or not his own popular renown as an historical novelist was known to Henchman. Apprehension of that, as Beals was well aware, could not be relied upon. Even when known, it did not always make a favourable impression on professional intellectuals, who had sometimes shown themselves actively antagonistic. Those were the occasions when Beals would shoot off a few poisoned darts after discovering what writers his adversaries admired. With Henchman he thought it best to authenticate right away some sort of historical seriousness.

'If the Romano-Britons had employed the services of Hengist, and his Teutonic mercenaries, up here against the invading Picts, or on the Welsh coast against barbarian raiders from Ireland, instead of fighting their fellow Teutons harrying the Saxon Shore, the Borders, or West Wales, would have populations racially akin to East Anglia.'

Henchman raised his eyebrows in one of his dreadful grimaces. Nevertheless the notion Beals had put forward seemed to please him. He showed his hand to a small extent.

'Have you written one of your novels about that? It is an amusing idea.'

This at least revealed that Henchman was aware of Beals as a writer of historical novels; whether well disposed to those, or not, remained to be seen. Beals looked on this as preferable to complete ignorance of his trade. It was one of the occasions when a little learning was the lesser evil.

'I once thought of doing so, then decided my public was

not up to the comparative complication of the idea. But I went into a certain amount of Dark Age history, when contemplating a book about all that. I might even return to the subject after this trip.'

Henchman nodded, and laughed. That may have been the juncture at which he decided to give his countenance to Beals – a royal countenance as, Beals put it – ultimately proceeding comparatively far in the disclosures he allowed himself.

'I will admit that I know of your books only from hearsay. I have never read any of them, though many people regard that as no handicap in discussing a writer's work. I think, however, I can guess some of the tone, as I was a great reader of historical novels as a boy. Stanley Weyman, Jeffrey Farnol, Baroness Orczy, Raphael Sabatini. I understand you have given them all cause to look to their laurels – anyway, regret their inadequate treatment of life's sexual side. Now tell me, <u>how would one of your heroes behave when his lady was under attack from two assailants at once?</u>'

'You mean in love, or war?'

'Oh, <u>love</u> essentially.'

'With the greatest dash. Run one through the body, hurl the other into the sea, were the sea handy.'

'Even if he knew his own battle over the lady was already lost?'

'I feel sure that would make him even more ruthless.'

Henchman laughed again. To the annoyance of Beals this pregnant conversation was cut short by Lamont, who, probably thinking it wiser to withdraw from the duel over how best to treat Jilson, now renewed with Henchman the subject of photography. This can only have been because, feeling himself put in a vaguely disadvantageous position, Lamont could think of nothing else to say.

'So the landscape isn't photogenic enough for you, Saul?'

'In principle, I approve the country. The landscape is

what people call magnificent. I am myself uninspired today. In fact at the end of my tether. Even you may sometimes be conscious of that feeling, Gary, when for some reason you have failed to shake Fleet Street to its foundations. You must wake up some mornings, and wonder whether it is all worth while. I feel today that, walking below The Wall, if not with the lowest of the Dead, then I am certainly with some of the lowest of the Living. That is purely a nervous reaction. Naturally I make the routine exception in favour of present company.'

Lamont and Beals both laughed, Beals flattering himself that only he appreciated the quotation, Lamont accepting it merely as one of those enigmatic sayings of Henchman to which he was long accustomed. Barberina Rookwood came across. She was slightly pink after her passage with Lorna Tiptoft, which had no doubt ruffled her more than she was prepared to admit. So far as Jilson's damaged hand was concerned, Lorna Tiptoft, medically victorious, had remained in possession of the field, even to the extent of having booked another consultation with the patient. She was sufficiently self-confident about her ascendancy to leave Jilson in the hands of whomever else wished to take him on, while she herself continued the search for his mother. Jilson, more uneasy than ever about all that had been happening in this contest over his body, strolled across too. Henchman took him by the slingless arm.

'Gary, you should employ this young man as war correspondent for one of your papers. As you can see, Robin Jilson has been in the thick of the fighting up here, and had several cameras shot out of his hands, while recording battle scenes with the greatest gallantry. To be more banal, he is a photographer like myself. This is the famous Gary Lamont, of whose daring exploits in Fleet Street you will often have read, especially in the financial pages, if you ever study them. Personally, I find that bit of the paper usually the best reading.'

Jilson at once began to protest at being classed as a photographer in the same breath as Henchman. When he spoke of Henchman's art, it was as if deeply moved, his words having a confidence lacking in any other matters. Lamont was perfectly equal to dealing with Henchman's playful introduction.

'Robin and I are sharing a cabin. We already know each other in the intimate way of men who have come to an agreement as to who is to shave first, or have to apologize for using the wrong tube of toothpaste.'

Henchman was greatly amused by this piece of information, which must have been new to him. It seemed to increase the malice of his tone.

'One is always reading of the overcrowding in prisons, how young offenders are confined with old lags, who teach them all sorts of wicked ways they did not know before. You'll be able to compare notes about Barberina's skill in binding up wounds, which, so far as I could hear, was found wanting by that very formidable-looking lady-doctor.'

There could be no doubt, Beals thought, that Henchman's words were intended to jar. In the more obvious sense, they would be taken to refer to Jilson's fall, for that matter to Henchman's own collapse at the bar. They could be judged to apply also, anyway in the mind of Henchman, to former wounding of Lamont's heart. If that were so, Lamont displayed no sign of being at all provoked. On the contrary, he became more than ever genial.

'Naturally we talk of Barberina a lot. The subject of First Aid can now be added to the agenda for discussing her gifts. You must be very familiar with that side, Saul. Others are usually less lucky. But, Barberina, who was the high-powered lady who stepped in so fiercely to take your place as a ministering angel? I thought the two of you were going to come to blows.'

'She's called Lorna Tiptoft, interfering old bitch.'

Barberina Rookwood spoke warmly. Brooding over Lorna Tiptoft had caused her to ignore Henchman's spiteful remarks. Perhaps she had not noticed them. Her manner with Lamont was always easy, without suggesting any strong emotional link, only that she liked him. Lamont on his side made no secret of the pleasure he took in her company. He wanted everyone to know that. Jilson looked intensely uncomfortable at all this.

A certain amount of tension was alleviated by the arrival among them of Fay Middlecote. After her husband's talk with Henchman following the fall at the bar, she had assumed herself to be on equally familiar terms. Henchman interpreted this as being an overture to become enrolled among the bevy of ladies-in-waiting who made up his retinue at parties or similar occasions. The *Alecto* would provide a typical setting for the bringing into being of one of Henchman's itinerant courts. Fay Middlecote's on-coming manner perfectly qualified her. Always on the look out to improve her standing, she stopped to talk.

'Has he hurt himself?'

She pointed to Jilson's sling, voicing the enquiry in the tone of one addressing adults responsible for a child, who seem to have inadequately safeguarded its wellbeing. That was the sort of attitude Jilson appeared to arouse in women, although on the face of it Fay Middlecote's sentiments were quite well under control, more pity than love. Henchman took upon himself to answer.

'He had a fall. Neither of us seem able to stand up or sit down for any length of time without requiring help. All this falling about on the part of Robin Jilson and myself will have to be curtailed.'

'But your fall was just due to a rough sea. It might have happened to anyone. I'm always catching myself on bollards and bulkheads, and other bits of ship's furniture of the kind Piers talks about. Isn't there a wonderful feeling up here of being on a frontier? I find that very stimulating.'

'Frontiers don't particularly excite me,' said Henchman. 'I'm too familiar with them. I spend a lot of time on the frontiers of Sanity, brought there by the way people go on – from the way I go on myself, if it comes to that. Then there's the frontier of Death. I'm always wandering off there too, when I've nothing better to do. After a time one becomes satiated even with the attractive prospects those two frontiers offer.'

Fay Middlecote was not at all reduced by such apparent discouragement.

'Oh, I love frontiers always. The frontier of Love. The frontier of Financial Risk – and of course the frontier of Good Taste. You can't say you don't enjoy those? There are a lot of others, too, I like negotiating when in the mood.'

She smiled invitingly. Henchman refused to be fascinated.

'For me there are none of the frontiers you speak of. They do not exist. Unaware of them, I always cross over.'

There were signs that he was becoming bored with her. His good temper, always limited, was running out. Fay Middlecote, having entered that particular area, was not going to be made to retire so easily.

'What a pity we aren't having a picnic on a gorgeous day like this.'

'Thank God we are at least spared that. People speak of hardships endured as no picnic. I fail to understand. Picnics abound in torment, not least of those often being hunger and thirst.'

Barberina Rookwood closed this conversation.

'Shall we move on? The light is changing all the time.'

Henchman nodded, then set off with his accustomed speed, abandoning Fay Middlecote and her whimsicalities. Barberina Rookwood turned to Jilson, who remained a little disorientated by all that was taking place.

'Come on, Robin. You'll be all right to photograph, won't you? You can always slip your hand out of that hideous rag of a sling.'

They caught up Henchman. He had evidently been meditating on Mr Jack, rather than any of the other recent happenings.

'I wonder where that tipsy fellow met me. Probably in my unregenerate days. There must be quite a few like him I've forgotten about.'

'When did your days become regenerate?'

'When you walked into my studio that May morning. But regeneration takes a long time. And, like most ailments, it is subject to relapses. I'm not sure it's even an aim any longer.'

26

Fay Middlecote remained wholly undamped by Henchman foresaking her. She shifted her position to where Louise Beals lay on the grass. Louise Beals had put down her book, and was gazing at the knot of people that a moment or two before had included her husband. She was perhaps trying to make up her mind whether or not to rise and follow him, though her look may have indicated no more than a state of abstraction. Fay Middlecote settled herself on the grass alongside.

'You're having a very peaceful time, Louise.'

'I've been so much enjoying myself.'

Fay Middlecote picked up the paperback, and examined it.

'Any good?'

'I guessed who'd done the murder after a few pages, then looked at the end, and found I was quite right.'

'And now you're just having a rest?'

'I've been watching how everyone's love affairs have been going.'

'I haven't noticed any, except my own mad passion for Barberina Rookwood. I love her almost as much as I do Henchman. Do you think I shall ever dare call him Saul? Even Barberina never seems to use his first name. The only person who calls him Saul is Gary Lamont.'

'You might say: Saul, Saul, why persecutest thou me by being so attractive? Except a lot of people must have said that to him. You'll have to dream up something new.'

'Do you think anyone has said that? It could sound like teasing him in rather a horrid way. Couldn't it?'

'A passion for Barberina is far healthier than one for Henchman, Fay. I'm sure of that. I don't know where a passion for Henchman might not lead one. Nowhere nice, I'm sure.'

'Oh, I do agree. And she's been behaving like a perfect angel. That rather dismal young man, whom they've for some reason taken a shine to, fell down and hurt his hand. She was so sweet about it, and bound him up. Then that awful Tiptoft hag began to interfere.'

'I saw. I was watching. But I don't think the young man dismal. I think he's rather romantic with his long eye-lashes, and arm in a sling. He's like an illustration in a Victorian book for boys, or the hero of one of Valentine's novels, though he'd probably do something perfectly awful, if he was out of one of them. He didn't think Tiptoft a hag at all.'

'Perhaps he's not too bad really. Just a lot of competition round about from people who are more dishy. Anyway Barberina bound him up. You never saw anything so professional.'

'Dr Tiptoft didn't think so.'

'She's probably keen on him too. With a jaw like that she must depend on bossing nervous young men round to find a beau.'

'But of course she's keen on him, Fay. Didn't you really take that in? You see much more if you're sitting down like me. I do agree that Barberina is sweet though. She's probably used to patching up Henchman all the time. Did you notice Henchman's face when she was bandaging the young man?'

Louise Beals gave one of her low stifled giggles.

'Obviously the young man's like me, and has developed a passion for her,' said Fay Middlecote. 'That's why they can't shake him off. All the same, I should have thought Henchman capable of shaking anybody off, if he felt like that. He doesn't care what he says. Instead of wanting to get rid of him, he seems positively to encourage Master Jilson.'

'He may tolerate him because Barberina likes him so much.'

'You mean likes him enough to bind him up?'

'Oh, much more than that.'

Fay Middlecote either ignored, or did not notice, Louise Beals's emphatic tone. Perhaps she thought Louise Beals meant Jilson liked Barberina Rookwood more than just a vague attraction.

'Henchman may encourage Robin Jilson just to irritate Gary Lamont. What do you think of Gary?'

'Rather sweet.'

'We've known Gary for ages. He's all right. Some people find him devastating. I wouldn't really call him sweet. We saw a lot of him when Piers was doing the Lebyatkin account. Now Doll's dead, I suppose he's running after Barberina again.'

Louise Beals giggled once more.

'Gary Lamont's chosen a bad moment.'

'Why?'

'Because, as I told you, Barberina's interested in someone else.'

'I suppose she's always interested in Henchman, if she stays with him, however he behaves. Having a passion for him myself, I can see that in a way.'

'She hasn't been interested in Henchman since we've been on this ship. Haven't you noticed, Fay?'

'But, Louise, she's fussing round Henchman all the time. Whoever, then, if you think that? Do you mean she is going to go off with Lamont?'

'Fay, you must have seen it's not the young man getting hints on photography who's got a real fancy for Barberina, though he may be flattered by her liking him so much. It's Barberina who fancies him. She's suddenly tired of living with Henchman. She's just realized that, and fallen for the first attractive young man in sight.'

Louise Beals spoke with such solemnity that Fay Middlecote laughed aloud. She thought the proposition so funny that she lay back on the grass, continuing to laugh with such shrillness that Basically Bach and Marginally Mahler, who were inspecting the Belatucadrus tablet together, glanced reprovingly in her direction.

'Darling Louise, how like you. I love that. How do you manage to think up all the things you say? They are every one of them marvellous. You'd have made a fabulous copywriter.'

Louise Beals looked genuinely puzzled.

'It's not a joke, Fay. That's just what's happening. I'm sure

I'm right. I've been watching them since they first met – after Henchman's collapse at the bar. It was love at second sight on Barberina's part, if you count Henchman as first.'

Fay Middlecote continued to find hilarious the notion that Barberina Rookwood was even a little taken with Jilson, much less in love with him. Louise Beals, smiling her wistful smile, refused to give an inch. Fay Middlecote tried another line.

'What about Lamont then?'

'He hasn't a chance.'

'I'm not sure Henchman thinks that. Or Lamont himself. Henchman's quite jumpy when Lamont's about.'

'That's natural enough after Lamont's earlier thing with Barberina and then turning up like this. I expect he gets on Henchman's nerves anyway. They're so different.

'All the same, Lamont means business. He's got that look in his eye. You can't really believe Henchman's worried about the young man just because Barberina bandaged him. I'm sure it's Gary who gets him down about Barberina, if anyone does.'

'Of course Henchman knows she loves the young man. He knows everything like that. That's why we're all so attracted to him.'

'I don't believe Henchman thinks that for a moment.'

'You wait, Fay.'

'You can't mean Robin Jilson will get her under the noses of both Henchman and Lamont. That would be out of this world. More extraordinary than when she went to live with Henchman.'

Louise Beals looked very serious.

'No. She won't do that. The young man is dazzled by Barberina, but too much afraid of her to take her on. Anyway he's fallen into the clutches of another lady.'

'Which one this time?'

'But you saw the row between Barberina and Lorna Tiptoft about binding up Robin Jilson's hand.'

'What about it?'

'Lorna Tiptoft's got a fancy for the young man too. What's more, he's quite taken with her. She's nearer what he can deal with than Barberina.'

'No, really, Louise. She's got a face like a boot. You can't think he prefers an old sweat queen like Tiptoft to darling Barberina.'

'Tiptoft's not too bad if you take her features one by one.'

'Why should anybody take them one by one? It would be difficult to do anyway, as she thrusts the whole lot of them at you at once. I don't know which of them I dislike most.'

'It's just that she doesn't make anything of herself. I don't think she wants to. She only wants to impose what she is. Jilson may like that. He seems to like being bossed about too.'

'I've never been able to stand looking at La Belle Tiptoft long enough to notice all the good points you say she's got, Louise. She's too forbidding.'

'She is a bit forbidding, I agree.'

Again Louise Beals gave one of her secretive laughs. Fay Middlecote went into attack.

'You must have a fancy for Robin Jilson yourself to think every woman on the boat is mad about him.'

'Well, he is nicelooking in his tired way. But it's Henchman for me, like you, Fay.'

'Yes, I do think Henchman, even if I couldn't stand him for long. I mean even apart from . . .'

'I absolutely understand why Barberina fell when she was only fifteen or sixteen, though it was sophisticated of her not to mind his looks. And he has got a lot of charm. I can't make up my mind whether he's really nice or not. Sometimes I think one way, sometimes the other. I expect, like so many men, he's only nice when he's in a good temper. He doesn't often seem to be that.'

'Louise, oughtn't we to be moving on? We don't want to be left behind. Night will fall, and we shall be raped by the ghosts of Roman soldiers.'

Louise Beals gave way to a sequence of her muffled giggles, a mannerism that had perhaps played a part in capturing Beals when they first met, as it had nothing about it between appeal and irritation. The spectral threat adumbrated by Fay Middlecote did not seem greatly to disturb her. The two of them rose, all the same, from where they had been lying, and followed in the direction of the rearguard of the tour. This still remained in sight, though by now some little way ahead.

27

The *Alecto*'s dining saloon, lacking space to accommodate all her passengers at one sitting, operated a First and Second Service. The number of places at its tables varied, some of the larger ones seating as many as a dozen; the smaller, as few as four. Lamont inclined to take the Second Service, rather than the First, to avoid risk of dining beside Henchman and Barberina Rookwood, who tended to use the earlier sitting. Lamont's tactics were directed towards seeing as much of Barberina Rookwood as possible when she was alone (which was rarely achieved), keep away from her when in Henchman's company. To be with them both at the same table at dinner Lamont regarded as a situation in the highest degree unstrategic. His taste in any case was for unhurried drinking before dinner, which also accorded with choice of the Second Service.

After earlier experience of the encumbering intensity of Mr Jack's impact, Lamont was wary about which seat he took in the bar, the bar nevertheless, remaining his preferred pre-dinner resort for drinking. This created a problem, as to hope the bar would ever be untenanted by Mr Jack was what Lamont would have termed unrealistic. Laying the foundation of a holiday during which he would never be irked by the threat of incipient sobriety, Mr Jack could risk only the briefest withdrawal at mealtimes. Even expeditions ashore offered no absolute guarantee of absence, as he would sometimes cut these. For him not to be on his high stool before dinner would have been unthinkable.

Lamont was reluctant to allow Mr Jack, or anybody else, to obstruct his own daily routine, especially to dominate that by the threat of sheer boredom. It was a matter of power, something Lamont was well used to contesting. He saw that if he were not to give up, sit drinking in the saloon with scarcely less risk of undesired company, he would have to take steps to insure safety from attack in the bar. In general this required no more than a little reconnoitring to arrange a place for himself, which, ideally, would put the complete bar's length between Lamont and Mr Jack; at its most hazardous, never less than three seats.

So far, that precaution had proved effective. There was the additional safeguard that Mr Jack's states of loquaciousness were spaced out at relatively extended intervals, persisting only a short time between much longer bursts of comatose silence. The last were likely to descend as a rule at the approach of mealtimes, the prospect of going among potential non-drinkers at random probably inducing gloom. For obvious reasons Mr Jack always attended the Second Service, an endemic inconvenience for Lamont. Nobody seemed to have heard any specially extravagant stories from Mr Jack in the dining-saloon. These were confined to the bar. He may have regarded all meals as waste of time, hurried through them as quickly as possible.

The tour of The Wall had been energetic. Several of those who had enjoyed the excursion also spoke of feeling rather tired. In consequence the main saloon was fuller than usual, drinks going down easily. Surveying the bar, Lamont considered he was as safe as could reasonably be expected on a stool at the furthest end from Mr Jack, who had an empty seat next to him. Lamont, too, when he sat down, was beside an empty stool. An unforeseen reshuffle of places caused the juxtaposition Lamont had above all hoped to avoid.

Basically Bach and Marginally Mahler entered the bar. After a short altercation as to which should occupy the seat next to Mr Jack, Marginally Mahler, who seemed, domestically speaking, to be the more authoritative of the two (though that may not have applied to musicology), took Basically Bach by the shoulders and firmly set him down, like a child, on the stool. He then ordered drinks, as a measure to endorse the finality of the action. For the time being Basically Bach more or less accepted the arrangement of his sitting there, while Marginally Mahler stood austerely behind.

Then an unexpected thing happened. Mr Jack, who had just finished his drink of that moment, grasped the unhappy partition of a couple always together. No doubt in the course of his travels he had come across similar bifoliate relationships. Stumbling off the stool on which he had been sitting, he spoke in a manner only to be called courtly.

'I can see you two gentlemen would like to sit together ... easily arranged ... No, no you must ... spare place near a friend of mine ...'

Thanking him lavishly, Marginally Mahler accepted the offer of the vacated stool beside Basically Bach, while Mr Jack, smiling understandingly, made his way rather uncertainly to the empty place next to which Lamont was sitting. He had evidently marked it down earlier, unexpected example of his occasional awareness. Lamont was taken completely by surprise.

'Caught sight of you a moment ago, Mr Lamont . . . able to continue that very pleasant talk . . . always nice to come across a man of the world . . . not shocked by the recollections of a rolling stone . . .'

Lamont saw that he had gambled too heavily on his own agility. He would have to project what in business he called a savage re-think. Mr Jack was now well away.

'. . . stories I'd like to tell you . . . two sisters at Southsea, most respectable pair. Never thought about it for a moment, then, before I knew where I was, the question was which to have first, without causing a lot of jealousy . . . before I get on to them, a tale I know would amuse you about the PR job I was doing in Manchester promoting some commodity brokers . . . went out with this fellow and his wife, he was my contact there, we had a good deal to drink, when we came back to their flat all got into bed together for some reason, can't think why, you know how things are after you've had a drink or two. All had our clothes on, of course. Sounds strange now, but there it was, we were younger then. Well, the husband passed out, like a stone. As a friend of mine used to say, we were all three as drunk as skunks, and to cut a long story short . . .'

The gong for the First Service had sounded a few minutes before. Lamont came to a decision. He must change his accustomed routine. He would dine at the earlier sitting. Anything would be better than enduring Mr Jack until the Second Service was sounded. He quickly finished his drink.

'I'll have to hear about what happened in Manchester next time.'

He nodded goodbye to Mr Jack, and moved down from his stool. Mr Jack looked heartbroken.

'Not going to have another?'

'No. I'm hungry after that day in the open.'

Mr Jack's disappointment was more profound than might have been guessed. He was not far from the tears that strong feelings brought on with him. He had evidently developed a hero-worship for Lamont, anyway as recipient of his anecdotes. He hesitated.

'Usually take dinner late. Prefer that for some reason. Not sure I won't come with you all the same. Quite true what you said about a day in the open. I've always noticed that. Makes you peckish. Of course when you're older like me the taste-buds go, you're not so keen on your grub as you used to be. All the same, I'd like to go on with our little talk, if we can manage to sit together, and you haven't any other plans . . .'

Mr Jack abandoned the bar. He swayed for a moment, then before Lamont could prevent him, he took his arm. That seemed to be in order to balance himself, rather than as an absolutely necessary support, the grip being too light even to be thought a presumption, a too effusive cordiality. Lamont had been outmanoeuvred. There was no escape. In the dining-saloon a single spare seat, if sighted quickly, might offer release. Meanwhile, indolently yet with dignity, they crossed the main saloon together, and descended to the deck below.

28

The Beals/Middlecote party usually attended the First Service for dinner. They might occupy one of the few tables laid for only four persons, more usually increasing their two couples by additional diners, according to the varying size of tables available. Their quartet, even at larger tables seating as many as twelve, was apt to form a conversational unit of its own. The fact that they were separated that evening was later held by Beals to have had a decisive effect on future developments on board.

Before dinner had been announced, one of the archaeologists, lecturing on sites visited during the cruise, consulted Middlecote about a matter connected with the showing on television of certain recently excavated finds with which the lecturer was personally connected. He had no means of knowing that such a question was rash, especially as Middlecote, tired after the trip to The Wall, had drunk at least one extra drink. Always liable to pour out a flow of words about his calling, if given opportunity, Middlecote was thereby presented with the rare treat of enlarging, so to speak by special request, on one of his favourite subjects, consumer preference in relation to cultural programmes.

The young man had worded his enquiry in such a manner as positively to excuse Middlecote for giving the motif broad treatment. It was a chance not to be missed, a direct query from an unprejudiced source about a matter that preoccupied so many of Middlecote's waking hours; at times even his dreams, as he himself frankly admitted. Having dealt with the childishly simple problem of the excavations, Middlecote moved on to culture other than archaeological.

He dilated, in fact, on the whole subject of the extent to which the public could be educated in advertising, and in what manner. Naturally the commercial side of the picture had by then been linked on, Middlecote supplying illustrations easy enough for the layman to understand. In fact he branched off into the whole theory and practice of potentially imaginative scope, where multinational brand products (including 'moody' goods like scent and shoes) were concerned, finally straying into byways, comparatively esoteric for the non-adman, such as running costs of reusable slides.

In short, the young lecturer received himself something not much less than a lecture on advertising techniques during the previous two or three years, their weaknesses and strengths, triumphs and disasters, perfections and imperfections. He was able to withdraw only owing to the mere chance that a fellow-lecturer, appealing for his colleague's help in settling an argument that had arisen with one of the more erudite passengers concerning Pictish Ogham, broke into Middlecote's monologue.

Had Beals been present, Middlecote would never have been allowed to indulge himself in such a manner. Middlecote himself would not have risked playing into Beals's hands by giving way to so copious a dissertation about the craft of advertising. As it happened, the Bealses had not yet appeared in the saloon. Louise Beals, declaring she was totally exhausted after her day at The Wall, had rested longer than usual in their cabin, Beals remaining with her.

In the normal course of things Fay Middlecote, too, would have checked her husband's prolixity, had she not been engaged in answering questions about London restaurants put to her by a long-legged freckled young assistant-professor from Colorado, picked up on The Wall. She remembered too late that the gong for the First Service had sounded several minutes before, so that the Middlecotes were committed to eating later. The Bealses hung about for a minute or two outside the dining-saloon, then, fearing they would not find a table if they waited longer, went in. Most of the places were already occupied as they moved across the room, followed only a few seconds later by Lamont and Mr Jack.

29

Beals, unlike Lamont, wanted to see as much of Henchman as possible during the course of the cruise. Henchman fascinated him, even though he saw no way of making use of his semblance in a book. Beals may already have been planning the many stories about Henchman he was later to narrate so widely to his friends. The meeting on The Wall had established good relations. Now, to Beals's satisfaction, he saw that the only three or four seats still free were all at Henchman's table. The Bealses could take them, indeed had to take them, without the smallest imputation of forcing their company. They scarcely had time to sit down before Lamont and Mr Jack, rounded up by the Chief Steward, were shepherded towards the last two unoccupied seats at the same table.

If Lamont had been given to uneasy imaginings, which he can hardly have been, he would never have contemplated anything so inimical to his desired arrangements as not only finding himself a few seats away from Henchman and Barberina Rookwood, but, in addition to that, having Mr Jack on his left. The *places à table* normally prevailing in the *Alecto*'s dining-saloon were set in familial or associative blocks, rather than the more accustomed social usage of alternating the sexes. The last had to take its chance. Thus, husbands sitting next to wives, parents to offspring, friends beside friends, produced the normal pattern of *Alecto* meals.

In this case, Lamont had Louise Beals (whom he did not know) on his right, beyond her Beals. Then followed the Jilsons, mother and son, Barberina Rookwood and Henchman; the American couple called Kopf, who had been at the Captain's table. Professor Kopf completed the circle by having Mr Jack as his right-hand neighbour.

The fact that Mrs Kopf's first-name was Elaine was later, owing to its Arthurian overtones, deemed by Beals to have influenced her husband's choice in making what was evidently a recent marriage. Middlecote would not accept that gloss, pointing out with truth that Elaine was by no means an uncommon American name, and Mrs Kopf's goodlooks alone were quite sufficient reason for her husband to have selected her – almost certainly reselected her – as marital partner. Elaine Kopf certainly seemed unlikely to be the Professor's first wife. How many predecessors there had been was another matter. She was not at all unaware of her powers of attraction, which she at once began to exercise on Henchman, who was sitting next to her.

Professor Kopf gave the impression of being proud, if a little anxious, about his wife. There was always a slight sense of tension when they addressed each other, exchanges to be broadly classified as a rule as cultural, Mrs Kopf being also more or less academically employed; if not now, then at some stage of her life. Perhaps she had been Professor Kopf's pupil. Henchman, though he did not look in too good an humour, showed no immediate sign of dis-countenancing Mrs Kopf's apparent ambition to make a conquest of him. At the same time he encouraged her no further than to direct on her his enigmatic stare.

Dinner opened auspiciously enough with Mrs Jilson's sudden perception that she was sitting next to her favourite author. Until that moment she had not taken in Beals's professional identity, the fact that he was the literary magician who had so often transported her into an easily intelligible, while historically remote, world of the Past. This inconceivable piece of good fortune overwhelmed her. She affirmed that she had read every book Beals had ever written, some of them two or three times.

In the early days of switching from whisky selling to writing, before he acquired the invulnerable status of an unreviewed bestseller, Beals had endured a certain amount of rough humour from friends like Middlecote on the subject of the highly seasoned nature of his historical fiction, the flamboyance of which was undeniable. Possessing few illusions on the subject himself – anyway at the start of his career as a writer – Beals, so far as that may be said of anyone who has ever published a book, had always remained wholly unpretentious about his own standing in the literary world. He would even go so far as to admit that better historical novels than his own were being written. At the same time no author could feel other than gratified by Mrs Jilson's boundless adulation.

The penalty of this homage (a consequence Beals himself later felt keenly) was that Mrs Jilson occupied Beals's attention, while other things more interesting to him were taking place. She insisted upon hammering out every facet of the narrative in every novel. This required mental agility in explaining inconsistencies and anachronisms (of which Beals himself was usually aware), owing to Mrs Jilson's flattering knowledge of his work. Her most beloved was *The Wizard on the Heath* (early in the Beals canon, in his own opinion the best researched), *Nell o' the Chartists* (with a few Disraelian borrowings, a bid, some thought not altogether convincing, to establish the author's social conscience), *Lancelot's Love Feast* (most recent, most erotic, almost certainly answerable for Beals's familiarity with the Fisher King myth and other Arthurian trimmings). Beals later defended his inattention to all that was going on at the table by pleading only human weakness.

'Estimate Mrs Jilson's intellectual calibre where you will, she was able to put her finger on at least one schoolboy howler of which I was unaware, while at the same time offering something not much short of worship. She told me she had not enjoyed any books so much as mine since reading *Little Women* as a girl.'

'Kind hearts are more than columnists,' said Middlecote. 'Literary columnists, that is. You must have felt like Shakespeare.'

'More like Belatucadrus, when classed with Jupiter on the Romano-Briton's shrine. I felt as if I were the tutelary god of the *Alecto*, one of those bearded marine deities with a conch in one hand, and a mermaid in the other. But, by the end of dinner, I was more like a shipwrecked mariner treading water among a lot of sea monsters.'

Mrs Jilson's enthusiasm occupied his attention so exclusively during the opening stages of dinner that Beals was afterwards unable to report with certainty on some of the later outgrowths of what had been a comparatively tranquil inception; the origin of the asperities which took shape between Henchman and Lamont, scarcely less between Henchman and Jilson. Both seemed to have become more than a little threatening by the time Beals took them in.

It appeared that at first Henchman had been content to acquiesce in the overtures proffered by Mrs Kopf (who had shown instantaneous appreciation of Henchman's traditional magnetism for women), without bothering much about what was brewing among the rest of the company round the table. The presence of Lamont was no doubt always an irritation, while Barberina Rookwood's now wholly unconcealed inclination for Jilson may also have displeased him by the conspicuous manner in which it was being displayed, notwithstanding his previous acceptance of that. Such as least was the subsequent diagnosis of Beals.

'Being so solipsistically engrossed myself, through no fault of my own, I missed the opening moves, which are so important in any story. By the time I came to take notice, Henchman was sniping away with indescriminate savagery at both Lamont and Jilson.'

Earlier on, so it appeared, Lamont, hoping to escape from Mr Jack's ramblings, had turned towards Louise Beals. He had been hastily introduced there and then by her husband, released momentarily from the grasp of Mrs Jilson. There was no predicting how Louise Beals would deal with Lamont, known mostly to her from the gossip of the Middlecotes. The choices seemed to be to tackle him either as a newspaper tycoon, or great lover, the latter being his ostensible 'image' on the *Alecto*. Her opening gambit indicated that she was playing the former.

'Oh, Mr Lamont, I'm sure you must know what something is that I'm always reading about in the paper, and seems to be very important – The IMF? Why do countries have to appeal to the IMF? I've always wanted to know.'

Lamont laughed. This was delivery of a sort.

'It's the International Monetary Fund.'

He began to give a told-to-the-children definition of that institution. In normal circumstances nothing would have been more tedious to him than outlining elementary financial matters to Louise Beals – especially as he more than half suspected that she was teasing him – but so welcome was any opportunity to separate himself from his other neighbour, if only briefly, that he threw himself into the explanation, as if answering a *viva voce* examination in economics. In any case Louise Beals was by no means without powers of pleasing. It even occurred to Lamont that a series of articles might be worth considering on such matters for readers at her level. Louise Beals herself, enchanted for a short time to be taken with such seriousness, soon tired of the IMF, and changed the subject.

'Didn't you love The Wall?'

Lamont, too, judged The Wall preferable to international finance on such terms. Knowledge gained from lectures while on board could well be rehearsed, but he might easily find himself out of his depth. Here, again, potential newspaper articles were to be borne in mind.

'I was surprised to hear at the lecture yesterday that the Roman Emperor, Caracalla, gave orders for The Wall to be repaired. I always thought Caracalla was one of the bad Emperors. I hadn't expected him to do something so constructive as repairing The Wall.'

Louise Beals agreed.

'Oh, yes, I'm sure Caracalla did dreadful things. They really went too far, some of those Emperors. I don't think I should have liked any of them.'

This comment, heard by Henchman, distracted him from Mrs Kopf's animated conversation. Mrs Kopf was left on her own, because her husband had been engaged by Mr

Jack, who, abandoned by Lamont at the beginning of dinner, had entered one of his periods of somnolence. Now he came to, and was making himself known to Professor Kopf, who still not yet apprehended what was involved in having Mr Jack in the next seat. Henchman silenced the table.

'I won't hear a word against Caracalla.'

'Why not, Saul?' asked Lamont.

He seemed in the mood to provoke Henchman. That may have been just another means of keeping Mr Jack quiet. Henchman was not at all unwilling to accept the challenge, were such intended, even if his immediate objective was Jilson, rather than Lamont.

'Caracalla was a man of severe consistency,' said Henchman. 'That is something to be admired.'

'Not if he was a bad Emperor,' said Lamont. 'If he was consistent, that meant he was consistently bad. There are quite a lot of people like that, many of whom I've had to do business with. All I remarked was that I was surprised at him repairing The Wall. Or am I muddling Caracalla with Caligula? Weren't they both bad anyway, so it doesn't much matter?'

'On the contrary, it matters a great deal,' said Henchman. 'Caracalla was in love with his mother, Caligula in love with his horse. You must distinguish, Gary, between a man's mother, and a man's horse. Surely you never confused your mother with a mare?'

Lamont ignored the last question, remaining with Henchman's earlier contention.

'But why was it consistent of Caracalla to be in love with his mother?'

'He was consistent, not because he was in love with her, but because he married her. Married her, and lived with her publicly. He thereby expressed the Oedipus Complex – if I may invoke such quaint oldworld terminology – in its most practical form.'

172

'Still, that doesn't make him a good Emperor, Saul. I think it was a most reprehensible thing to do.'

Henchman would not agree. Before he could speak Mrs Kopf broke in.

'Did he do that, Mr Henchman? I daresay he really wanted to reject the intergroup relationship, and there was something compensatory about such extreme exogamy and disregard of the incest barrier.'

'It was certainly sexual mobility in reverse. Caracalla is the foremost example of his kind. He should be the hero of all Mum's Boys.'

Henchman smiled maliciously in the direction of Jilson. Barberina Rookwood was not prepared to disregard that. In such sudden displays of animosity she no doubt knew Henchman's measure to an inch.

'Mum's Boys have often showed their mettle. History and the Arts are full of Mum's Boys.'

Henchman, waving a hand to show he concurred absolutely, turned his smile on her without altering its style.

'I don't deny that for a monent. I am much in favour of Mum's Boys. Surely I have shown my approval more than once. If it comes to that, I could not entirely fend off the soft impeachment – justifiable use of that battered phrase – myself. All I assert is that Caracalla must be hailed as in the forefront of the species. You can hardly call it a fraternity, as the essence of a Mum's Boy is to deny the existence of brothers, should he possess any. Caracalla might be looked on as founder of Mum's Boys' Lib, in so pedantically defining his own sexual situation. I am delighted to hear that, in addition, he repaired The Wall. If I may be permitted to be frivolous about a serious subject, Caracalla was also one of the few men – let alone Emperors – of whom it might be confidently recorded that he enjoyed a Jocasta against himself.'

Beals claimed later that he was the only listener to get that. He managed to catch Henchman's eye, which may have given him a good mark. Professor Kopf would no doubt equally have appreciated Henchman's final pleasantry had he not been concentrating his whole being on conversational release from Mr Jack. For a fleeting moment there seemed some hope of that, because Mr Jack himself, capturing some of the gist of Henchman's talk, had for a second or two ceased to persecute Professor Kopf with his mumblings.

'That's most . . . most . . . remember thinking . . . some boy's mother . . .'

Hechman had by no means completed his peroration.

'Now an example of a boy totally exempt from the Oedipus complex – as far from being a Mum's Boy as any lad could reasonably distance himself – was Master Cruncher in *A Tale of Two Cities*. You will remember that he was the son of Jerry Cruncher, the messenger, who sat outside Tellson's Bank by Temple Bar –'

'Founded on Child's,' said Beals. 'My own bank, as it happens.'

It was an unsuccessful bid to free himself from Mrs Jilson. Henchman gave no help. He simply nodded, and continued.

'Jerry Cruncher was plurally employed, as we say now. He was both bank-messenger and body-snatcher. On the pretext of going fishing, he would at night disenter from churchyards recently buried corpses and sell them to medical men. Nowadays, if that were still a ready market, it would be to ladies too, like Dr Tiptoft. Mrs Cruncher objected to this, and, when she said her prayers, her husband suspected that she prayed he might abandon a business activity, unalluring, like so much else connected with scientific research. To prevent her from engaging in her devotions, he would throw his boots at her. Master Cruncher, whenever he noticed his mother falling to her knees, would incite his father to further boot throwing.'

'Horrid little boy,' said Louise Beals.

'Horrid he may have been, yet an interesting type for the psychological textbook.'

Beals could not resist pressing one point further.

'I'd forgotten Jerry Cruncher used to say he was going fishing.'

'If questioned, he would probably explain it was a night-line,' said Henchman. 'Though no doubt there are other ways of catching fish nocturnally.'

30

Professor Kopf, abandoned by his wife to Mr Jack, had been displaying all this time the traditional American goodhumoured unsurprised tolerance of a neighbour or *confrère* overcome by drink. He was nevertheless unable to conceal entirely a growing sense of uneasiness at his own alienation from the rest of those dining at the table. The weight of having to cope singlehanded with Mr Jack throughout the whole of the meal, while everyone else appeared to be engrossed in lively conversation, was becoming an increasingly threatening prospect.

Mr Jack himself, perfectly capable of handling a knife and fork, was having difficulty in articulation. He was at best disconnected, while evidently feeling that he ought not to appear churlish by sinking too often into silences that were permissible when on his own in the bar. As Lamont was devoting all his attention to Louise Beals, Mr Jack had no alternative to addressing a long discourse on boyhood, and his relationship with his mother, to Professor Kopf, who was suddenly given his chance by Mrs Jilson seeking to reestablish her hold over Beals, after Beals's efforts to get free from her. She returned to *Lancelot's Love Feast*.

'But, Mr Beals, I can never remember what Gawain did. I find those Knights of the Round Table so difficult to sort out.'

Concentration on Beals's novels had caused Mrs Jilson to miss Henchman's animadversions on Mum's Boys. Even if she had grasped aspersions imputed by them to her son, Mrs Jilson would certainly have been prepared to justify her own maternal attitude, either in the past or the present. She was absolutely sure of herself in that or any other sphere. The need did not arise.

Mrs Jilson had been put out, not by Henchman's words, butly Beals breaking off abruptly in the middle of an exposition, as circumspect as he could make it, of one of the more carnal passages in the Arthurian novel. It was where Beals had rather liberally adapted the story about Gawain and the girl who was being boiled in a tub of water. Beals attempted to resume where he had broken off.

'In the course of Malory's narrative, Gawain gives way to temptations of a sensual nature, which he would have been able to withstand earlier in his career. I'm afraid, for instance, that when Gawain was granted an opportunity to see the Grail, he was more interested in the girl who was carrying it.'

Professor Kopf, like an impatient body-snatcher himself, grabbed at a life-line that might not only bring release from Mr Jack, but allow him to take part in general conversation.

As a teacher of English he was becoming increasingly fretted by finding himself opposite someone who seemed from Mrs Jilson's behaviour to be a wellknown British writer, of whom he had never heard, yet was how being spoken of in a manner that would have been fulsome for Shakespeare.

Professor Kopf's total ignorance of Beals and his works was no mere instance of academic detachment from popular reading matter, a donnish foible Professor Kopf regarded himself as rising above. A British academic, existing not too far outside the everyday world, would probably have known of Beals as a popular author, without having read any of his books. For an American, of any literary level, to have heard nothing of Beals was, in fact, natural enough. One of those quirks of international taste in reading matter, by which Beals's sales – to be reckoned in millions from Finland to Japan – caused them to be extremely modest in the United States. For a Beals novel even to lack an American publisher was not uncommon. Beals, to tell the truth, was sometimes a shade irked by transatlantic neglect, but, as with his dismissal by domestic reviewers, he found atonement in accumulated revenues from other segments of the globe. Professor Kopf now leant across the table.

'Excuse me, the maiden who bore the Grail was Elaine. She is usually shown as daughter of Pelles, himself at times equated with the Fisher King, elsewhere as the Fisher King's brother. Elaine is also my wife's name, therefore has special meaning for me.'

'She was the Fisher King's daughter before he was maimed?'

Beals asked the question. He saw dangers looming. He had no idea that there had ever been any question of the Fisher King possessing offspring. In easy cognition of the question, Professor Kopf nodded rapidly.

'Do I understand you to be, like myself, concerned with the Arthurian Cycle?'

177

When he had spoken the name, Elaine, Professor Kopf had smiled in the direction of his wife, as if to indicate a wish to dissociate his intervention from the least stigma of pedantry. At the same time he was plainly excited to find himself at a table with someone also more or less familiar with Arthurian lore. It was evident to Beals that he was likely to be forced to bring up much heavier artillery than any in action against Mrs Jilson. Even so, he was glad to find momentary respite from her ardour, in certain respects as ticklish to satisfy as anything Professor Kopf was likely to put forward.

Beals explained unostentatiously that he had written a great many historical novels, a recent one having the setting of King Arthur's court. That was no more than in accordance with facts. Professor Kopf, speaking with the humility of a man who probably knew a great deal about the subject in hand, continued to add substance and depth to his disengagement from Mr Jack.

'My interruption must have seemed rude, but I am professionally interested. Particularly in the 12th century romances of <u>Chrétien de Troyes</u>.'

'Ah, yes.'

Beals could just recall the name.

'You may have seen the current number of <u>The Bulletin of the Board of Celtic Studies</u>?'

'As it happens, I have not.'

'I brought a copy with me. You must let me lend it to you.'

Beals saw that temporary relief from Mrs Jilson might turn out to have been bought at a high price. He prepared himself for making some sort of a disclaimer, an honest admission of scholarly ignorance, one which would not reduce him too hopelessly in the eyes of Mrs Jilson. Professor Kopf, so far as he was concerned, was determined to prolong any topic which might prevent, at least delay, relapse into Mr Jack's jerky locutions.

'On this cruise we are in the midst of Arthur in more

ways than one. May I ask, Mr Beals, are you one of those who locate King Arthur in the North, as some authorities do, or around Glastonbury?'

'I have reservations about both, but a perfectly open mind.'

'I look forward to Orkney, realm of King Lot, brother-in-law of Arthur, yet his enemy. By some accounts, Lot was also the father of Gawain, of whom you were speaking just now, the Perfect Knight.'

'In different versions the relationships are often contradictory.'

Mr Jack was showing ominous signs of wanting to break in to this conversation. He had begun to breathe heavily. Professor Kopf, noticing that, continued more desperately than ever.

'In the earlier phase of Gawain's own myth there is a suggestion that he might have been a healer, shaman, what is sometimes called a medicine man. That theory has been applied by extension to Perceval, too, in the way in which the Knights are sometimes confused with each other. Perceval was supplanted by Gawain, you recall, in the Grail Legend, or, perhaps more authentically, fertility rite.'

Beals had by then become aware of Professor Kopf's predicament, the reason for this feverish need to keep the cross-table conversation going. Now that they had reached Perceval and fertility rites, things were trembling on the brink of linking both with the Fisher King, the question of whose physical disabilities might at any moment arise. If that happened, Henchman's reaction was impossible to foretell. He might at once accept his own resemblance. That could turn out even more embarrassing than objection on his part, though it was hard to see how he could raise any. Henchman had, in fact, now begun to pay attention to what was being talked about. He broke in.

'Do you think we have a healer on board, Professor Kopf? A Gawain or a Perceval? The ship's doctor, maybe?'

Professor Kopf agreed that would be a suitably Arthurian touch, on what seemed to be a notably Arthurian cruise. Henchman pursued the subject.

'Shamans can ritually raise the dead, I think. That might turn out a useful accomplishment in the light of the passenger-list. They are also of an hermaphroditic nature, unless I am mistaken. We could, for example, have a medicine woman on board.'

Professor Kopf readily concurred.

'In early forms of shamanism a woman would be as likely as a man, Mr Henchman. We must also remember that Aphrodite both loves and emasculates Adonis.'

'We must remember, indeed.'

'That situation is related to my own speciality,' said Professor Kopf. 'The Loathly Damsel.'

Afterwards, Beals claimed, just as the words overheard at the Captain's table had revealed Henchman to be the Fisher King, Professor Kopf, in this exchange with Henchman, was again the medium to disclose – with the utmost clarity, Beals asserted – that Dr Lorna Tiptoft was the Loathly Damsel.

According to himself, consciousness of that came to Beals in a flash. Fay Middlecote used to hold that he had simply mulled things over in his mind later, and attempted to fit Lorna Tiptoft in just to improve the story. Professor Kopf's last phrase seemed to have struck a chord in Louise Beals too. At least she gave one of those secret smiles to herself, without speaking. Mr Jack, on the other hand, suddenly looked startled. A moment before he had seemed likely to enter the debate. Now something deterred him from that. Professor Kopf, delighted to find himself with so comparatively informed an audience, was in full flight.

'I am not concerned solely with the Loathly Damsel herself, but with the myth, in its different forms, of the archetypal female figure of unprepossessing exterior, who reverses the story of Beauty and the Beast. Instead of the

Beast being transformed into a handsome Prince, the Lady's loveliness is restored by the apparent self-sacrifice of the Knight in accepting her as his bride.'

Henchman nodded. He seemed interested.

'You will recall that the Loathly Damsel rides into Arthur's court at Caerleon, mounted on a tawny mule, and carrying a scourge. Perceval, now admitted to the Round Table, after return from the castle of the Fisher King, is upbraided by her.'

'I was speaking of the Fisher King only the other day,' said Beals. 'He is a puzzling figure.'

He wished the Middlecotes had been present to witness this personal triumph. He also glanced in the direction of Henchman to see if any reaction had been produced. That could not be guessed. Henchman, smiling with his usual grimness, was at that stage recaptured by Mrs Kopf. No further liability arose immediately as to the Fisher King, Professor Kopf wanting to continue discussing the Loathly Damsel.

'She was hunchbacked, so the chronicle runs, eyes like a rat, nose like a cat, lips of an ass, beard of a goat, black hair tied in two plaits.'

Louise Beals could contain herself no longer.

'Are you sure about the plaits?' she asked.

'That's what the chronicle says.'

'Then I was at school with her. Don't tell me she's on board. Now what was the girl's name? I shall remember in a moment.'

Henchman once more separated himself from the attentions of Elaine Kopf.

'The theme of men who fall in love in some grotesque or utterly unexpected manner is always absorbing,' he said. 'With women the rules are rather different, though no less interesting. From my own observation, I don't feel confident that Loathly Damsels, once married or possessed, are instantly metamorphosed into beauties – of the opposite process not functioning, a monument lies before you – but the notion that men fall in love only with women who look like film stars, an aberration ceaselessly disseminated by press and media – people like you, Gary – is altogether absurd, bane of the age. I fear your country has not been blameless in propagating that doctrine, Professor Kopf.'

Professor Kopf smiled a little sadly in agreement.

'That might be thought the conclusion of the legend, though some ambiguity is added by the heroine's eventually bestowed fair countenance, in order that they can live happily ever after.'

Henchman laughed.

'Photography brings curious cases of almost every sort to the photographer's notice. I must search my mind for Loathly Damsels who have sat for me, and what has been their ultimate fate. Purely in terms of taking their photographs, I could mention lots of them. That is just the photographer's point of view. What is in question is the fate of a man who takes on a Loathly Damsel as his partner in life, for she revealed to Perceval that what women most desire is their own will.'

31

Some sort of agitation had been perceptibly increasing from the direction of Mr Jack. He seemed once again anxious to join in the discussion, at the same time apologetic as to the form his intervention was likely to take.

'Mr Henchman . . . don't for a moment expect . . . why should you? . . . just wondered . . . especially after some of the things you've been saying . . .'

Henchman stared, as if Mr Jack's intoxicated condition had only just dawned on him, and he found interest in it, rather than amusement or disapproval.

'I would what?' he asked.

'Remember . . .'

'Charles I's last word on the scaffold.'

'Not surprising if you don't . . . must have been thirty years.'

'We are getting nowhere. Do come to the point. Not only for Charles I, but for us too, the minutes are ticking away. Death may not be long delayed. We must not either of us waste time. Loathly Damsels are on the agenda. Have you anything to contribute? Speak, or for ever remain silent, though I fear that is too much to hope.'

Mr Jack took all that surprisingly well.

'That's it . . . just what I meant . . . about visiting you once . . . that <u>dump in Soho</u>.'

Making a marked effort, he managed to emerge from the state of incoherence which for ever threatened him, and spoke quite distinctly.

'I'd fallen in love with a whore.'

'*L'amour est enfant de bohème.*'

Mr Jack was greatly struck by Henchman's words.

'Now that's very well put . . . must try and remember . . . *amour* . . . <u>girl called Theda</u> . . . worked the top end of Dean Street in the afternoons.'

'That situation is not unknown. Major Esterhazy, presiding genius of the Dreyfus case – which produced some really excellent photographs by the way – lived with a registered prostitute for some time, if I remember rightly. So, if not exactly in good company with him, nobody could call it humdrum.'

'Wasn't much of a beat on a wet afternoon . . . I'll come to that.'

Unusual as this conversation was, two or three people at the table disregarded it. Beals stressed that. He himself was anxious not to miss a syllable, but Mrs Jilson continued to torment him, and he did not wish to give offence to his most passionate fan. More significant was the manner in which Barberina Rookwood and Jilson were too deeply engrossed together to notice any singularity in the topic being discussed. Mr Jack, as alcoholics will, had suddenly sobered up.

'Trouble about falling in love with a tart is, if you're seen about with her too much, you're liable to be pinched by the coppers for being a ponce. Never knew that before I met Theda. Hadn't thought about ponces much. I suppose if you live on women, you're bound to be seen about with them some of the time. Theda was always dinning that fact into me. About the only sign of affection she ever showed. The only time she treated me fairly well was one afternoon when she was out in the street with rain coming down in sheets, and I turned up, and gave her a chance to get under cover. She wasn't too bad that afternoon, but, believe me, even then I never saw her with all her clothes off. I suppose, if she wasn't ever very loving, she didn't want me put inside.'

'That was nice of her,' said Henchman. 'I've known girls when I was younger show less good will to a lover.'

'Don't expect it would have redounded to her credit with her colleagues. Indicated a careless disposition. I mustn't say too much against her. Theda wasn't a bad girl. Just liked money rather a lot. I didn't have much of it at that time, nor since, if it comes to that . . . but what I was going to tell you, Mr Henchman, was about the photograph. I wanted a photograph of Theda and myself.'

Henchman's manner suddenly changed. Mr Jack's story had struck a chord. The penny had dropped.

'My God. I remember now. Of course I remember.'

Mr Jack became more apologetic then ever.

'Call it sentimental, if you like. A photograph of the two of us was what I wanted. That was when all the ponce trouble came up in a big way. Theda wouldn't hear of it. Anyway, she said, her time was money. She didn't want to spend working hours being photographed, unless there was some profit in it.'

Lamont spoke in a low voice to Louise Beals.

'Reasonable enough. Just what I felt myself, when Saul wanted to photograph me.'

'Oh, I'm sure you were flattered,' she said. 'I know I would be.'

'Well, the more Theda put difficulties in my way, the more I went on pestering her about the photograph business. I told her I'd give her what she normally got for our romp together. It worked itself absolutely into my system that I have this photograph of us together, so one day she told me there was a man just round the corner from her place, who lived in a bombed-out building, which housed several girls she knew on the lower floors. He was in the garrets, and took photographs of all sorts.'

'In giving that definition,' said Henchman, 'she was right.'

Mr Jack paused. He seemed afraid of going too far.

'If I may say so, Mr Henchman, you were surprised at what I wanted.'

Henchmen laughed a great deal.

'Surprised? Of course I was surprised. When people brought tarts to see me in those days it was usually to be photographed practising some little speciality that pre-occupied them. You know the sort of thing I mean. A chap in a bowler hat and a starched collar would arrive with a suitcase packed with easily portable instruments of flagellation and torture. Arriving pillion with the Loathly Damsel and her scourge would have been less unexpected than you, had the mule been able to manage the stairs. When you turned up with your girl I thought you'd want to record some special humiliation, or hitherto unachieved position. Anything but a straight photograph.'

'I was just in love.'

'With by no means a slip of a girl, if I remember rightly.'

'Forty, if a day.'

'You seem to have combined giving gold away and rubies, without keeping you fancy free. Always an unsatisfactory fusion. You wanted to sit side by side in what passed as my studio. If I had possessed a rustic seat, against a backcloth showing honeysuckle and a crescent moon, that would have suited you to perfection.'

Mr Jack smiled at the memory. He did not dissent, beyond making a gesture to suggest extenuating circumstances.

'Alas, I hadn't the props. I expected clients to bring their own. They usually did.'

Lamont had listened with more attention to Mr Jack's account of this interlude in his life than at its earlier less detailed narration at the bar.

'How long were you engaged in your carefree Soho life, Saul?' he asked. 'Your heedless youth?'

'About as long as you were cub reporter, Gary. Nowadays, of course, one would be regarded as performing a therapeutic duty towards mankind, almost a social obligation for a photographer. Things were different in that unenlightened period. It was even possible to experience trouble with the police.'

Louise Beals leant across Lamont in order to address Mr Jack. As usual in putting any question, she spoke with great earnestness.

'And did the lady whose photograph you wanted taken turn into a beauty, when the picture was developed. I do hope so. I think you deserved that.'

Mr Jack was equally serious in his reply, although the question had otherwise caused some amusement at the table, even to Henchman. When Mr Jack spoke to a woman, which Beals had not hitherto seen him do, it was possible to detect, under the fairly rancid detritus of his past life, a touch of what had brought success in offering himself to so many of them, a wheedling, caressing, entreating tone, one less inconsequent than when conversing with a man. Before answering, he thought for a moment, then made for once a simple direct statement.

'No. No. Never a beauty. I wouldn't have called Theda a beauty either before or after. Just a . . . well. It all petered out, I'm afraid. Matter of money, sad to say.'

Louise Beals persisted.

'And have you still got the photograph?'

Mr Jack shook his head.

'In my pocket-book for a long time. I used to take it out

187

and look at it occasionally. Remind myself that I was doing better than that now. Then the pocket-book got swiped. I don't like to say such a thing, but I'm pretty sure it was swiped by another lady.'

'I fear the negative will have gone too,' said Henchman. 'It was almost certainly amongst a lot of stuff I got rid of for obvious reasons, when I moved to more comfortable quarters.'

He leant back in his chair. It looked as if he were suffering one of his spasms of pain. These were hard to chart from features at once expressive yet impenetrable, concealing as much as they revealed about Henchman's mind or body. He had undoubtedly been enjoying the turn taken by conversation. It had perhaps been less popular with Barberina Rookwood, had she heard anything of what was being said. Beals could never decide whether she suddenly became aware of that, found it distasteful, or simply chosen this as the propitious stage for whatever was in her mind. In any case, Beals said, it was the moment of truth. The die was cast. Beals used to employ a whole series of metaphors to express the finality of the step. However much others might doubt its predictive certainty, there was no way of disproving his assertion.

'I've rather a headache. Robin and I are going to get a breath of fresh air on deck.'

Henchman turned towards her.

'Very wise.'

'Will it be all right if I meet you later in the big saloon?'

'Perfectly all right.'

'The sea has become very calm all at once.'

'The stillness before a typhoon. The sense of oppression one reads about?'

She laughed.

'Perhaps we are having freak conditions in these northern waters.'

'Perhaps we are.'

She went slowly from the dining-saloon, followed by Jilson, who had first muttered something to his mother. In the sense that stewards, anxious to lay the Second Service, were animating diners to depart, dinner was terminating all over the room. To that extent there was nothing un-expected in Barberina Rookwood retiring at that moment, especially if she had some purpose in view. Henchman had just prevented removal of his glass. He now poured into it a respectable residue from the bottle they had been sharing. His only observable reaction to this double withdrawal was stating presentiments of a hurricane, a normal enough comment from him. Now he spoke across Mrs Kopf to her husband.

'I should like to talk more with you, Professor, about Loathly Damsels, the intricate problems of technique they pose for a photographer. I suspect that we have at least one prototype of the species on board.'

32

Beals considered Barberina Rookwood's ascent to the deck that night to be the most decisive step she had made in her life, since taking up residence with Henchman. On deck, such was Beals's view, she must have made some sort of declaration to Jilson, just as formerly to Henchman, when for him she had given up dancing. To what extent Jilson had travelled along some of the same road to meet her Beals found impossible to estimate. He considered Jilson more mesmerized than in love, while admitting the distinction possible to make between those two states to be a highly delicate one.

'Whether or not you think Jilson worth the trouble is unprofitable to discuss. Titania and Bottom, if you like. What you might expect is that, in comparison with Henchman, he would be easy money. Having captured Henchman, Jilson would be child's play. The problem, severing the bond with Henchman. In such matters, however, there is no such thing as easy money – where, indeed, is there? – and one's own predictions are never assured.'

Perhaps Beals was right in supposing that Jilson had been

what he called easy money in the early stages. There seems at least some evidence of that. In any case whatever passed between Barberina Rookwood and Jilson that night on deck could only be conjectural. Many paths might have been explored by them. Fay Middlecote afterwards put forward her own diagnosis.

'You never know how virgins are going to behave. They are an odd type. In this case there may well have been two of them.'

'Don't you mean unicorns?' asked her husband.

All to be called categorical afterwards was that the Henchman/Rookwood association had been shattered; and even that required an additional touch of drama to be certified. Other relationships were plainly altered too. They remained to some extent doubtful. It was the main one that loomed most apparently, most tragically, Beals thought.

'The remarkable thing about it all was Henchman's calm acceptance of what was happening. That was instantaneous, so far as Jilson was concerned. Lamont was another matter. Lamont, too, in his not very sensitive way, saw an upheaval was taking place. Reasonably enough, he could not gauge the extent of it, nor its implications. Lamont, in spite of worldly success, remained at heart a simple fellow, just as Henchman later told him. Not simple, of course, in the meaning of being got the better of in a business deal. Far from that. Simple in possessing uncomplicated ambitions – power, money, publicity – all those sort of prizes that Lamont pursued relentlessly. He didn't know about pleasures like self-sacrifice, even pleasures like having a pride in yourself.'

'You speak as if you were quite uninterested in such squalid things as money and publicity, Valentine,' said Middlecote. 'I'd never particularly noticed that as far as you were concerned, though I would give you a fairly clean bill of health over power.'

Beals denied speaking as if he were outside the contest. 'It's because I'm keen on them all in moderation that I know about people who share those tastes in moderation. I'm not sure that Lamont is moderate. He certainly supposed he could combine worldly ambitions with an ideal marriage. In imagining such a thing his simplicity becomes positively winning. Not many of his type share that illusion. As it happened, Lamont was lucky enough to find Doll, and nearly brought it off. That kept his self-deception intact, while the marriage lasted. When Doll's death knocked him out – as it undoubtedly did – Lamont wanted to have Barberina Rookwood to himself more than ever. Marriage to her seemed not only the best but the only way out. He wasn't interested in how she felt. The problem was to prise her away from Henchman. Lamont, being as I say a simple man, couldn't see what she was getting out of existence with Henchman. Of course plenty of other people failed to see that too. Other people's concern, however, was only hypothetical. Lamont's was practical. Then Lamont grasped that, in leaving Henchman, and going to walk with Jilson on deck, Barberina Rookwood had rebelled. As he could never understand why she was where she was in the first place, he couldn't really understand the form rebellion had taken, but he saw he ought in some manner to make use of that.'

Beals liked to emphasize the lack of sound health common to all competitors in this triune contest, an important, if not overriding, factor in his opinion.

'Lamont was sharp enough to work out that, if poor health were to be advantageous, he could play heart condition as imparting uncertainty as to his own length of days. That was how Henchman put it, when he talked to me. Henchman hadn't been nicknamed The Monkey for nothing. He saw at once that doubtful tenure of life might be used as one means of breasting the tape in a race from which he knew he himself had dropped out. By the stage he told me the things he did Henchman had no longer any hope of keeping Barberina Rookwood. He was just inter-ested in the contest. Jilson, even though still young, had an equally good chance of dying quite soon. That, anyway, in Henchman's view, could make him in a special way attract-ive. Jilson undoubtedly had something special about him even if it took subtlety to see that. No one could accuse Barberina Rookwood of lacking subtlety. Above all Jilson was a failure, a failure who might be turned into a success. What no one bargained for was that Jilson might have his own preferences.'

Beals, possibly recognizing that he had chosen a different path himself, was at that point apt to pause and laugh.

'Jilson wanted to be an artist, if you're prepared to allow that term for a photographer, and was certainly one to be applied to Henchman. Of course there are people who find artist a meaningless definition, but it's an undeniably use-ful one. Barberina Rookwood had by then learnt a good deal about photography herself, through contact with Henchman. She was also an artist, knew what it meant to give that up. She was prepared to take Jilson on, get him to the top. Lamont hadn't the least conception of all this, either in the abstract, or the concrete. That might or might not have been an advantage in what he wanted to do. It certainly goes a long way towards explaining why Lamont behaved as he did.'

If (by no means invariable) Beals had managed to hold the attention of an audience, one of the listeners would persist sometimes in expressing surprise at so beautiful and talented a girl falling for so outwardly poor a specimen as Jilson, notwithstanding all the arguments Beals had put forward in Jilson's favour. To Lamont, they would agree; to Jilson, they would not. Beals, perhaps deliberately, used to hold a trump card up his sleeve.

'I will allow that everyone concerned had a strong will. That's what makes the story so absorbing. Henchman,

Barberina Rookwood, Lamont, nobody doubts the strength of their respective wills. The man they under-estimated was Jilson. He had the tenacious will of the indulged child, one continuing to be indulged into man-hood, because he was ailing. When in good form – which was probably only seen by Barberina Rookwood – Jilson may have had all the elation, the egotism, possibly even the self-disgust, of the type he belonged to. Unlike many indulged children, he also knew what he wanted, which was a wife to look after him as devotedly as his mother had done. When Henchman invoked Caracalla, as usual Henchman knew what he was talking about. Jilson knew too, and may have laughed up his sleeve. Jilson was suffi-ciently well able to look after his own interests to see that it would be a mistake to remain too long under his mother's wing. He wanted to be under another woman's wing, a woman younger than his mother, and much more effective. Until he sailed the northern seas on the *Alecto* he had probably never come across a woman to suit. Then the incredible happened. Henchman offered to coach him as a photographer, Barberina Rookwood – this saintly beauty – took a fancy for him. Not a man in a million would have behaved as he did.'

Beals would stop for a moment after making this last dramatic statement.

'At least one says that because one admires her appearance so much – admires a lot of other things about her too for that matter – but I daresay I do not give sufficient weight to male sense of self-preservation.'

'That's vigorous enough,' said Fay Middlecote. 'God knows.'

'Not always,' said Middlecote. 'I suppose old Jack was an example. What if Barberina Rookwood had decided to look after him in his dotage?'

'I prefer to think of him as Don Juan in old age,' said Beals. 'Don Juan would certainly have been quick to ward off any threat to his independence. Anyway Jilson seems to have felt that Barberina Rookwood might devour him, perhaps by dancing, rather than photography. Then, at the opening stages of all this, Jilson did not know how Henchman was going to react. Being passionately anxious to make himself a good photographer – as great a photographer as Henchman – he could not afford to risk losing Henchman's tuition. How Henchman would behave if he went off with his girl, naturally Jilson could not foretell. It was unlikely to endear him.'

'Unless by then Henchman had supped his fill of her,' said Middlecote.

'How like you,' said Fay Middlecote. 'I often wonder how I have stood it for so many years.'

'I shall come to that point,' said Beals. 'Of what there is no doubt is that Henchman was mad about her. It is possible to be mad about someone, yet, as Piers so elegantly puts it, also to have supped your fill. Think of what Henchman had gone through at one time and another in his life. Then think how he behaved. As Professor Kopf so sagely remarked that night at dinner, Aphrodite loved Adonis, yet emasculated him.'

'But Henchman had been emasculated already,' said Fay Middlecote.

33

For Lamont, the close of dinner had bestowed above all the ineffable benefit of escape from Mr Jack. In any case Lamont had no wish to remain a second longer than necessary in the company of Henchman, now dispossessed of Barberina Rookwood. He was aware that tumult was in the air, while at the same time uncertain as to causes and effects. There was at least a possibility that Barberina Rookwood, separated from Henchman, was now more or less on the open market. Jilson's claims, Lamont scarcely even considered, even if for the moment Jilson's presence might represent the most immediate obstruction. Lamont quietly left the table. He would, as expressed to himself, play it by ear.

In spite of increasingly fidgety waiters, Henchman and Professor Kopf continued to pursue the Loathly Damsel in her myriad shapes, Henchman keen if possible to pinpoint individual instances that had come his way. Elaine Kopf, dissatisfied at her husband supplanting her with Henchman, became restive, insisting on immediate need for coffee. The Kopfs retired with hopes expressed by the Professor that

Arthurian exegesis should be resumed at the first opportunity.

Mrs Jilson, who seemed not at all concerned at her son's apparent subjection to Barberina Rookwood, or leaving his mother to look after herself, showed extreme reluctance to part from Beals, from whose earlier sociability she had been cut off by Professor Kopf's intrusive erudition. She did not conceal that she found unfair this ruthless elevation of the intellectual level of conversation, refusing to abandon Beals until he had promised to clear up later some of the undercurrents in *Lancelot's Love Feast*. When she finally made her exit, Beals, a little exhausted, felt that he had put up a creditable display on two intellectual levels simultaneously.

Louise Beals, who did not drink coffee at night, had evolved a routine of her own, which included taking two or three turns round the deck after dinner, then returning to the cabin, and reading a book. Beals himself did not sit up late as a rule. He would usually hang about a bit with the Middlecotes listening to the band, have a look at the next day's programme, then follow his wife. After Louise Beals had gone to the cabin that night, Beals saw that circumstances had given him an unlooked for chance to sit with Henchman after dinner, and, were Henchman willing, talk about many things in which Beals was interested.

If this was to be, it would also entail the company of Mr Jack, for whom Henchman appeared to have developed an inexplicable liking, after the revelations about taking his photograph in the company of Theda. Henchman offered some encouragement to Beals in accompanying him, at the same time brushing off offer of a hand on the way up to the main saloon. He was certainly steadier on his crutches than Mr Jack on his legs. The three of them found a corner in the saloon. It was some little distance from the dance-floor, round which a few couples were apathetically rotating.

Henchman, using the punitive system of analysis that he had adopted towards Jilson, began to cross-question Mr Jack on the subject of amatory passages in his past life. In principle, Mr Jack could have had no objection to that, the problem for those sitting near him in the bar being to prevent the cataloguing by him of former love affairs. Nevertheless, so far as any consistent attitude of mind was apparent in him, he seemed, as much as Jilson, overawed by the severity of Henchman's interrogation. Beals supposed that concentration on Mr Jack's adventures, while satisfying an anarchical strain in Henchman, also, consciously or not, helped to mask any visible reaction to the sudden and categorical abandonment fallen on him. He seemed determined to penetrate Mr Jack's protective screen of alcohol in order to get down to some sort of inner being beyond that.

'So Theda told you that she loved the life, but hated the clients? That is a striking statement. Try to recollect any more of her comments of that kind, which throw light on prostitution. Did she express any opinion on its dangers to the health?'

Mr Jack took that enquiry to refer to himself.

'Never had any trouble of that kind with her. Always been pretty lucky in that respect. Sole dose I ever caught was from my best friend's wife. Only shows!'

Henchman displayed no interest in that mishap. He continued with the subject he had in mind.

'Commercial love has its special attractions for certain people. They enjoy the cash nexus for its own sake. The only case I can recall at all like your own in the photographic line was a homosexual customer, who wanted a photograph of himself and his boyfriend. He was an expatriate Irishman – one of the Tame Geese, he said – and, when he found me a man of indulgent moral attitudes, he would talk of past experiences. He liked to pick up guardsmen in the Park, and told me, after love had found a way, and it came to a haggle about the price, that the guardsman would sometimes say, when the fee seemed too small, "But what about my honour?" To that my queer customer would reply, "Well, what about *my* honour?" This rejoinder always seemed to me apposite to many mutual relationships between human beings, emotional or unemotional, physical or moral, defrayed or gratis.'

Beals showed more appreciation of this story than Mr Jack, who scarcely seemed to take it in. Henchman added a footnote.

'The same man complained that the male prostitutes of Copenhagen were "common and presumptuous, with small penises and bad teeth". A damning indictment. But we are now getting into a different, to my mind, less interesting sphere of sexual action. When you were on your travels, Jack, did you have any success with the veiled beauties of the harem? I think you said you were a courier in Iran. They had probably abandoned the veil, to which they have now returned, when you were there. I remember taking a photograph in some North African town of a couple necking on a seat, the lady wearing a yashmak and black robe, her beau in a mauve lounge suit, the tint of which I envied.'

Mr Jack smiled dully. He was showing signs of becoming sleepy again. Henchman, who had worked himself into what was for him a state of nervous excitement, turned to Beals.

'Have you ever set one of your novels in the East? *The Arabian Nights* provide a wealth of stories to be worked up into modern versions.'

'It's a long time since I read *The Arabian Nights*. I don't think I remember any of the stories except Aladdin and Sinbad the Sailor.'

'You fall into the common error of supposing Aladdin to appear in *The Thousand and One Nights*. That is by the way. Let me call to mind to you the tale of the Young King of the Black Isles.'

Mr Jack came to for a moment.

'Loved *The Arabian Nights* as a boy . . .'

Henchman silenced him. He wanted to talk himself.

'<u>The Young King of the Black Isles</u> had recently married a beautiful wife, equally young, whom he adored. Their union was at first happy. Then, as women will, she became bored with him. Every night, before they retired to the matrimonial couch, she would arrange for her husband to have a potent drug mixed with his night-cap. The draft overcame him at once, and he passed out forthwith into a stupor. Absolved from her wifely duties, she would hurry off to spend the night with a lover.'

'How badly behaved of her,' said Beals.

He felt some comment was required.

'Quite by chance the Young King of the Black Isles overheard a conversation between two ladies-in-waiting that revealed all was not well with his married life. To cut a long story short – something Scheherazade herself would never have dreamt of doing, except as a temporary measure when dawn was breaking – he caught his wife *in flagrante*.'

Mr Jack, naturally identifying himself with lover rather than husband, showed complete comprehension of this episode.

'Awkward situation . . . bloody awkward . . . thank God, I never quite . . .'

'The lover, as it fell out, was a Nubian slave, who was also a leper and a paralytic. What we now call a deprived person. In the telling of the tale one can detect both lack of compassion and racial prejudice.'

Beals, now remembering a little of the story, began to feel embarrassed. Henchman was thoroughly enjoying his own narration.

'Physically unappealing lovers of beautiful women are a commonplace in Scheherazade's recital. I must draw Professor Kopf's attention to that, in considering the reverse side of his Loathly Damsel syndrome. My own observation by no means divests that surmise of all credence. Let us get expert advice.'

He turned in the direction of Mr Jack.

'Wouldn't you agree, my dear Jack, that the nicest girls often display a taste for some of the most unsavoury scraps of jetsam floating about on the surface of life's sewage farm?'

The question was too elaborately framed for Mr Jack. He had to have Henchman's enquiry phrased in simpler terms. When he had understood, his agreement was absolute. The thought even raised in him another reflection.

'All the same, I suppose I shouldn't grumble. If all the nice girls wanted a Pop Star, I wouldn't have had a lot of the luck that's come my way. Makes me think of one sweet girl . . . only place was the emergency exit of her local cinema . . .'

'We'll keep that for another time,' said Henchman. 'I was just saying that the Young King of the Black Isles found his wife in compromising circumstances with her leprous and semi-paralyzed lover. He was in no two minds how to deal with that eventuality. He drew his sword, and wounded the Nubian all but mortally.'

Beals found his sense of embarrassment building up at an alarming rate.

'Why did he stop short of killing him?' he asked. 'I can't remember. One would have expected that.'

'Because the wife was an accomplished sorceress. Her magical gifts had remained unrevealed at the time of the Young King's marriage. Now she displayed them in all their strength. They did not, however, succeed in preserving her already sickly lover from a state of suspension between life and death. He remained alive, but in a hopelessly groggy condition, far worse than before. Naturally the sorceress was enraged with her husband. In revenge for what he had done, she transformed his kingdom into a lake, his subjects into fish of varying colours, according to their religion. The Young King's own body she turned, from the navel downwards, into stone.'

Beals had to remind himself that, in making a study of Henchman, he must take the rough with the smooth. There was no drawing back now, however uncomfortable he was being made to feel. At least here was plenty of food for thought. Where that might lead when digested was another matter.

'Not content with so savage a retaliation, the sorceress clad the Young King in his royal robes, and set him on a throne in the hall of a palace, within walking distance of the mausoleum (perhaps comparable with Theodoric's), in which she had installed her still breathing, but murderously wounded, lover. Every day, armed with a whip, she would visit the Young King, strip the royal robe from his shoulder, and scourge him with a hundred lashes. We have no record to suggest that even the Loathly Damsel did that. It was a scene that might well have been reenacted in my Soho studio, during my photographic novitiate, for clients less romantically inclined than Jack. At least romantic, perhaps, in another form.'

Beals, hoping to relieve his own growing tensions, asked what had happened to the Young King, whether he was still there suffering these tribulations. He could think of no other enquiry to make.

'By an unexpected piece of good fortune, another King, out on a country walk by himself in that neighbourhood, came upon this sinister palace. Naturally interested in palaces, he entered the hall. There he found the Young King of the Black Isles, on his throne, clad in robes of state. On being questioned, the Young King revealed his own unhappy circumstances. The visiting King took in the situation at once. He concealed himself nearby. When the demon wife arrived on her routine round, he forced her, by a neat trick, to undo the sorcery, then sliced her in half with a scimitar. It is to be presumed, like cutting off a life-machine, this also accounted for the lover.'

'I see,' said Beals.

Again, that seemed the easiest comment to make. When describing what Henchman had narrated, Beals always emphasized that, in fact, he had not seen at all. He was completely at a loss to establish Henchman's reasons for recounting what seemed intended as a kind of parable: whether Henchman wished to identify himself with the Young King of the Black Isles; with the Young King's wife's lover; with the fellow King, who released the Young King from his predicament. The fable might even have been aimed at imparting a moral lesson to Mr Jack, though hard to see quite what lesson. The more Beals reflected on the matter, the less he could decide.

'On the whole, I suppose the first most likely. That at least fits in more or less with the disability of the Fisher King, which should always be kept in mind, the regality, physical incapacity, suffering. On the other hand, the leprous and paralyzed lover has claims in his own right to represent Henchman too. Again, the lover might be Lamont with its suggestion of stealing a beautiful woman belonging to someone else. But then perhaps Henchman had shown himself blind to Barberina Rookwood's art, been punished for that. Possibly Jilson comes in, too, as seen through the contemptuous eyes of Henchman, or even of Lamont. If the first is true – Henchman as the Young King – there is the unexamined possibility of pain suffered, in addition to being marble from the waist down, notwithstanding the royal robes and princely crown of success. Did he smart daily from the consciousness of Barberina Rookwood's sacrifice? Was what seemed to the world so immense an oblation, for Henchman the lashes of a whip? Another story Henchman let fall may confirm the signification of that torment.'

No doubt Henchman had intended to be embarrassing. Beals admitted that, so far as he himself was concerned, Henchman had succeeded. Mr Jack, on the other hand, plainly accepted all the details of the story of the Young King of the Black Isles as adversities that could only too easily fall on any man, king or commoner. He had listened with much more attention than he usually managed to summon up, when anyone else was talking.

'Lucky that other fellow turned up. What a thing to happen. Always risky to take a chance with other chaps' wives. But what a woman. To do that to her husband, when she'd been two-timing him in any case. Don't remember that story when I was a boy.'

'*The Thousand and One Nights* should essentially be read in Burton's translation,' said Henchman. 'Sir Richard, of course, not Robert of *The Anatomy*. Burton reproduces all the cruelty and obscenity of the original. Most of the former, and all of the latter, get bowdlerized in the illustrated editions or those for children. Burton's footnotes are excellent too. For instance, a modern touch is added to the story of the Young King of the Black Isles by his witch wife drugging her husband with cannabis. It is called bhang, but, in an exhaustive note, Burton explains that cannabis is meant, and goes into the effects and uses of the narcotic. Cannabis somehow brings the story nearer home. After hearing Elaine Kopf talking about her campus life, I told her I should in future call her Mrs Wiggs of the Cannabis Patch.'

Mr Jack shook his head.

'One of the girls I knew . . .'

Henchman, still wanting to hold forth, cut him short again. He addressed himself to Beals.

'Stories, as I'm sure you will agree as an author, are agreeable only if, like Scheherazade's, they develop. Otherwise, especially in the form of anecdotes, they can be a burden. I have some considerable experience of hospital treatment, therefore of doctors who vary greatly in demeanour. For example, one of those who treated me long ago was a very shy man. He was also, as it happened, an internationally known athlete, with all the acute, even painful, nervous system that so often accompanies over development of physical skill for public performance. I should have supposed that temperament agonizing for someone wholly concerned with attempting to cure human infirmities, but there it was. This doctor found me in every respect a difficult patient with whom to establish contact. I readily sympathize. I find difficulty in establishing contact with myself. My appearance, disablements, personality, can be disconcerting even for a medico.'

'Always tried to keep out of the hands of doctors,' said Mr Jack. 'Come away from them iller than when you went in.'

'As a specialist, this man arrived to inspect me only at intervals some distance from each other. There was therefore no continuity of intercourse to build up a relationship by conversational exchanges. I was in some pain at the time, my temper not always of the best. This doctor would try and relieve awkwardness created through my condition by immediately telling funny stories on his arrival at my bed.'

'Like a good story,' said Mr Jack. 'Hopeless memory for them myself.'

'Thank God for that,' said Henchman. 'My medical man was in much the same condition. At least he always told the same two stories. Whether he possessed a larger supply, I do not know. Perhaps I always happened to hear the two Wednesday stories, or hit some other routine principle. The practical effect was that, over and above what were still fairly serious wounds, I was reduced to near nervous prostration, not much short of the doctor's own, by waiting for the stories' rehearsal, worrying that they might not be the same two stories this time. That somehow would have brought bad luck. A new anecdote could well have had a fatal effect on me. Fortunately they never varied.'

Beals, since he thought the question expected of him,

rather than because he desired the information, from which he feared further embarrassments, asked if Henchman could remember the stories.

'Remember them? Calais was lightly pencilled on Bloody Mary's heart compared with the manner in which they are etched on my consciousness. The first had old-world charm. The doctor would begin: "Did I ever tell you about the paragraph written in our parish magazine by the vicar, in which he thanked his parishioners for contributing to a fund for improving the church organ?" I would shake my head. He would then repeat the vicar's words: "Owing to your generosity, our organist can now change his combinations without taking his feet off the pedals." I used to ponder long on the organist's under-clothes. Perhaps, an old man, he had never altered the habits of boyhood. The unworthy thought also crossed my mind that the organist might be a fetishist in female undies.'

Mr Jack saw it from another angle.

'Knew a lot of girls who wore combs.'

'You have perhaps hit it. A lady organist. I had not thought of that. It lends a faintly erotic flavour. But the vicar used the masculine pronoun.'

'And the other story?' asked Beals.

He felt he had got off lightly.

'That has far deeper implications. At the time I was less aware of them. After telling the story about the organ – indecent possibilities as to the word itself happily avoided – the doctor would continue: "Talking of church matters, I expect you know what the child said when asked at Sunday School the difference between the Saints and the Martyrs?" Again I would profess ignorance. "The child said the Saints were very good people, and the Martyrs were those who had to live with them."'

Henchman made one of his frightful grimaces.

'Both stories have in them something of my own pious childhood, the latter especially strikes a chord.'

Mr Jack laughed throatily. The stories had appealed to him.

'I must remember the Saints and the Martyrs. Tell my brother.'

34

Then took place the incident, which was in one sense the high spot of the cruise. That is, if it did take place, Beals used to add. Afterwards its reality seemed doubtful, even to Beals himself. He had not been drinking level with the other two, and was contemplating immediate retirement to bed. In retrospect, he could not imagine why he had stayed up so late, which normally he disliked doing. Hope may have lingered that Henchman would utter further revealing comments, following up suggestion of martyrdom in living with the good. Henchman, Beals remarked, must have had a certain amount of experience with the other sort, so was in a position to speak. No doubt he would have grumbled about them too.

Henchman himself, who had been drinking at least as heavily as Mr Jack without appearing at all surfeited, after making his own determined contribution to the conversation, seemed once more to possess an insatiable appetite for also imbibing huge draughts of Mr Jack's sex life. At first Beals hoped this unending saga might, with modifications, yield material for fiction. The expectation proved vain, the stories being continually trivial, scrappy, lacking in all the local colour Beals required.

When the thing happened, Beals, half asleep by then, granted the best account was later given by Basically Bach and Marginally Mahler. Accustomed to exchange their blue blazers and skittish T-shirts for soberly dark suits of matching cut, though different shade, when they dined, they were sitting not far from the place where Henchman, Mr Jack, Beals, had come to rest. The music-loving couple must have been kept up by the peculiar bitterness of that night's argument. Beals had caught the words 'post-Wozzeck orchestration', followed by a cutting retort, then a sentence about 'the expressionist intention of later dodecaphonic Weber'. The mere fact of each breaking off simultaneously from the heat of such a controversy showed how startling the incident had been.

The sudden wonderment that had shaken out of themselves Basically Bach and Marginally Mahler – not to mention the rest of those who remained in the main saloon – was of musical interest only within the context of the band playing selections from *Swan Lake*. The apathetic couples had ceased to circle the dance-floor, individuals were increasingly slipping away to their cabins, when, metaphorically speaking, the bomb burst. Everyone capable of giving an opinion, no doubt many who were not, agreed that Tschaikovsky had often, even usually, been better rendered than anything the band at that moment was achieving. In any case its muted notes were almost drowned by the chatter of those determined not to retire to bed.

Beals had actually risen from his chair, turned towards his companions to say goodnight, when Barberina Rookwood came through the glass doors of the saloon.

She was alone. She stopped for a second, an odd look on her face, while she took in what was being played, then she made quickly for the dance-floor. When she reached the polished square of deck she began to dance. All talk ceased instantaneously.

It was a day or two before Beals's fulldress version of the occasion was wholly organized. That night, the Middlecotes after dinner had gone up to the small saloon on the deck above the main one, where Middlecote had continued to hold forth on advertising techniques. Several fellow passengers were hypnotized by his volubility on the subject of monitoring the product through the computer system to avoid fragmentation of suppliers. Beals, accordingly, had later much to recount. He let himself go.

'When I was writing *A Musket at Meerut*, I remembered a poem about The Mutiny I'd had to learn as a boy. It was by Whittier, like Poe not much in fashion now, but interesting for an American, not to mention a Quaker, taking a pro-British line, when nowadays treatment of anything Indian over here in fiction is always devoted to raking up every anti-British angle the author can lay hands on. The poem was called *The Pipes of Lucknow*. I don't suggest it's a very good poem – though I quoted a verse in my book – but some of the lines absolutely hit off how I felt watching Barberina Rookwood do that dance.

> Like the march of soundless music
>   Through the vision of the seer,
> More of feeling than of hearing
>   Of the heart than of the ear.

That tells you what the performance was like, just as if taking place on some transcendental plane. The musicians were immediately aware that they were participating in an act of magic, an act without precedent in their professional careers. I'm far from being a musicologist, but the abrupt change in the way they were playing was galvanic. It wasn't just me thought that. Those two Americans went off their heads. The band put all they had into what was obviously for them a passionately intense occasion – which it was, of course, for several other people too, not all of them present, though the band couldn't know that.'

Listening to Beals with her hands clasped together, Fay Middlecote was no more able to tease as usual, than the Queen of Sheba to pull Solomon's leg about pride in his possessions. She never ceased to express regret at her own absence from the scene.

'It must have been marvellous. God, I wish I'd been watching. What a super girl she is. I do love her.'

Even Middlecote had to accept the score for Beals. He did what he could to reduce that.

'It certainly sounds a neat *coup de théâtre*. Do you think she had been planning it for months, just waiting for an appropriate piece of ballet music to be played by some band?'

The occasion seems to have gripped the imagination of every onlooker, not so much for its implications (no one could guess them) as for the *pas seul* itself. Beals was very insistent on the time element, or rather the complete subtraction of time as an element, the fact that all was over in a matter of minutes, almost of seconds, yet the dance seemed to exist in eternity. Both sensations were present as in a dream. When, as a matter of cold fact, Barberina Rookwood had ceased to dance, both Basically Bach and Marginally Mahler at once stood up.

'Bravo! Bravo!'

'Encore! Encore!'

'*Bis! Bis!*'

Marginally Mahler had the last word, but there was to be no second chance. Considering how many passengers had gone off to bed the applause was very loud indeed. The stewards and barman, who, by the instinct that something stupendous was on, had extracted himself from behind the bar, joined in ardently. The band stood up.

Their leader, who wore dark spectacles and looked a man not to be trifled with, bowed again and again.

Barberina Rookwood stood there laughing. She remained like that just for a brief minute. She kissed her hand to the band, then to the room, where people were still clapping. She looked round about, evidently seeking Henchman. When at last she saw him, and those with him, in their corner of the saloon, she made her way between the tables, moving with that peculiar weightlessness, as if borne on the air itself. Beals was still standing, gently clapping. Mr Jack tried to rise from his seat, succeeding only for less than a second, collapsing into a chair before she reached them. When she came up, Henchman inclined his head.

'Very fine.'

'Thank you.'

'Worthy of Pavlova, Karsavina, Lopokova, Fonteyn, anyone else you like to mention. I swear you danced better than all of them.'

'Don't be absurd.'

She laughed, but was rather upset. In fact almost in tears. Beals said he noticed the little scar. It seemed to quiver. Henchman too, shaking a little, was very moved.

'The *pas seul* before the curtain?'

'If you like.'

'Naturally I feel a little sad.'

'Me . . .'

She did not, perhaps could not, finish what she was going to say. Beals, while admitting that he had drunk perhaps two drinks more than usual that night, nevertheless maintained, even when completely sober, that he could remember no moment in his life at which he had felt himself more moved by a matter that did not in the least personally concern him. He found himself unable to explain that, either at the moment or later.

'Henchman always greatly interested me. There was that

to it. Then – just as the Masai of Kenya hold that all cows in the world belong to them – so all girls one finds attractive seem in a sense to belong by right to oneself. That was all. Apart from such things, neither Henchman nor Barberina Rookwood meant anything to me. It was something about their mutual recognition that the dance showed ritually their relationship had come to an end. The absolute lack of any need for explanation, when something mattered so much. The horror that they were going to part hit me, too, as if below the belt.'

Then, while she looked rather agonizedly at Henchman, it was clear that she had come to ask what must have been one of the routine questions of their daily life together. It had to be asked that evening as much as any other.

'Are you ready to go to your cabin yet?'

She was finding the crisis less easy to carry off than he. Henchman smiled. For once, said Beals, the smile did not chill the blood. In the background, people were still sporadically clapping, in the hope that she would dance again. She took no notice of them, perhaps did not hear. She only looked at Henchman.

'Are you ready?' she asked again.

Her voice trembled a little. Apart from private emotions, dancing again in public – if only on the dance-floor of the *Alecto* – had deeply stirred her. Henchman shook his head.

'Not yet. The night is young. Young, at least, compared with our friend here. In any case, I will look after myself. At worst, one of my drinking companions will assist me, though I hardly think I shall need that. I am more likely to be called upon for help for my afore-said friend. As you know, I have not the least objection to looking after myself. I did it for many years. Having been for so long now treated with a care and consideration that I neither require nor deserve, it will be just as well to make a start on a new, less benign, more bracing regime.'

That again was a bad moment. Beals thought one or other might break down, perhaps both. It passed.

'Are you sure?'

'Quite sure . . .'

'Dancing again made me feel a little wrought up.'

'Naturally enough.'

'I somehow knew I had to do it.'

'Inspiration must never be ignored. I hope it will visit me again too, one day.'

'With other things.'

'With other things, as you say.'

'You understand?'

'Perfectly.'

'One of the nicest things about you is that you always do understand, even if understanding sometimes has odd side effects. Now you must be philosophical.'

She said that, Beals thought, to show that she could compete with him in steadiness of nerve, perhaps even in brutality. It was a rather brutal phrase. None the less, the worst was over, so it seemed to Beals. The scene had been decidedly painful.

'This is an appropriate moment for me to thank you for all you have done – also for closing things in this elegant, even glorious manner.'

Henchman pretended a regally dismissive gesture. Smiling, she made as if to curtsy, but did not do so.

'Goodnight, then.'

'Goodnight.'

Infinitely graceful, she withdrew from the room, turning just before she reached the doors, laughing, again making the suggestion of a curtsy, as if in a theatre. People began once more to applaud, beg for more, as she disappeared beyond the glass doors.

35

After this conjuncture, Beals, as he said, required a moment or two to recover breath, take bearings, generally consider a new set of circumstances. He was not sure, for one thing, how seriously Henchman had referred to the possible need of help from friends to get him to bed. If so, Mr Jack was hardly to be relied upon, though he now showed signs of throwing off the lethargy which had descended upon him when attempting to rise in acclamation of the dance. Recovery was sufficient to cause him to resume some anecdote interrupted when the room had become so electrified.

'Well, there was the bed. The question was . . .'

The subject of the question was never brought to birth. Henchman raised one of his crutches, and, not particularly gently, tapped Mr Jack on the crown of his head. The action, if a trifle schoolmasterish, was not unfriendly.

'Enough, Jack, enough. Even Scheherazade, when as Burton picturesquely puts it, she saw the dawn of day, ceased her permitted say. As the hour is getting comparatively late, you too must obey the law of supply and demand. We will, if we so choose, hear more of your amours at a later date. Meanwhile, to use a tiresome current phase, enough is enough.'

Henchman now made preparations to retire for the night. He must also have been turning over in his mind plans for the immediate future. Things were going to be very different. In spite of his own self-control, he could not have been unaware of the turmoil that had overtaken his private life. Beals was about to speak, ask whether assistance from him was in fact required, when a new factor arose to be considered. Henchman was the first to notice that Jilson had just come through the glass doors.

'Why, there is that unhappy young man.'

Jilson, who was rather dishevelled, gazed round the room. He was evidently in a state of some anxiety. Whether he was looking for his mother, or Barberina Rookwood, was not apparent. It was likely to be one or the other. Perhaps, after an emotional scene with Barberina Rookwood, they had parted, and he now wanted to add something to what he had said. He might wish to tell his mother about whatever had taken place. Conceivably Barberina Rookwood had left Jilson with the intention of seeing Henchman to his cabin as usual, and Jilson had now decided that he, too, should be included in what was likely to be some sort of showdown. Barberina Rookwood could even have been searching for Jilson at that moment to tell him that Henchman, accepting all, needed no explanations. Mr Jack stirred, and rubbed his eyes.

'Wish that girl would dance again . . . loved that.'

Henchman waved a crutch to indicate that Jilson should come over to where they sat. When he caught sight of this signal Jilson seemed astonished that Henchman should still be in the main saloon, probably supposing that he would have been removed below by Barberina Rookwood. Jilson approached. He looked more than ever worried. Henchman did not ask him to sit down, but spoke in a comparatively kindly manner.

'So you have emerged from your ordeal.'

Jilson – understandably, said Beals – received this comment in apparent wonderment. He could think of nothing to answer. Henchman now adopted a meditative tone.

'Who can tell what our relationship might have been had I found myself able to possess her? Perhaps less warm, yet ending just the same in this manner. More likely it would never have begun. I don't expect you've ever read any of the poems of Alfred de Musset?'

Jilson continued to look astonished. He shook his head in reply to the question. Henchman turned the enquiry on to Beals.

'Possibly when younger. I don't remember any of them.'

'You surprise me. I probably dipped into some anthology. For a special reason, which will be obvious to you, one of Musset's poems remained in my mind. Strange as it may seem, he wrote some verses called *Chanson de Barberine*. Not long after Barberina came to me I happened on this poem. Naturally I was riveted.'

He looked hard at Jilson, now sufficiently under control to reply.

'Naturally.'

'You understand French?'

'Only a little.'

'A little will suffice. This is very easy French. I will translate anything you miss.'

'Thank you.'

'I am superstitious in the sense that I believe the curious synchronisms and juxtapositions, physical and moral, in which we all from time to time find ourselves involved, always have meaning.'

Again Henchman paused. He seemed to be asking Jilson a question. If he were doing that, it was answered by Beals.

'I entirely agree. I know just what you mean. I am always

coming across such things in historical research for my novels.'

Jilson, used by now to Henchman's obliquities of speech, even if at the same time scarcely taking in a word of its meaning, also expressed assent. That caused Henchman to smile.

'I now see, however, that *Chanson de Barberine* applies not so much to myself – as I used to speculate – but to you. The interesting thing is that it matches so well, yet not exactly in the manner that the poet himself intended.'

Not unreasonably, Jilson was far from able to cope with all that.

'Let me repeat a verse. You will grasp the romantic tenor at once. It was the high summer of Romanticism. Do not deride that out of hand. Romanticism can often be what is required, supply an answer, be, in short, on the ball.'

This time Henchman smiled at Beals, rather than towards Jilson. Beals urged him to quote the poem.

> 'Beau chevalier qui partez pour la guerre,
>   Qu'allez-vous faire
>   Si loin d'ici?
> Voyez-vous pas que la nuit est profonde,
>   Et que le monde
>   N'est que souci?'

Jilson nodded. He tried to smile, as if he understood, though unlikely that much had penetrated his consciousness. Beals himself had to look out the poem later before grasping all of Henchman's point in reading it. Henchman had spoken the lines of French in a fairly English accent, whether to make them more intelligible to Jilson, or simply because that was the sort of French he talked, Beals was unsure. He suspected the last.

'The poet goes on to explain that the world not only brings cares and anxieties, but the *beau chevalier* supposes

217

that an abandoned love vanishes from memory. Even if that were true, it is, alas, no less true of a taste for fame, which also dissolves into nothingness. Such at least is my own interpretation of Musset's meaning. I think very possibly he may be right. But what does one mean by Love, what does one mean by Fame?'

Jilson made a great effort.

'I don't think I quite get all you've been saying. There was something –'

'You better not attempt that now. It would be difficult, almost certainly painful.'

'But –'

'I think I know what is on your mind. As I supposed, you are just like the *beau chevalier*. All will be made plain in due course. At the same time I want to make one thing immediately clear. My offer to help you as a photographer remains operative. Ways and means will obviously have to be reconsidered, indeed heavily revised. Naturally, after what has happened, I shall not want to have you within my own orbit. In any case I now have no idea what that orbit will be. Its course will certainly be drastically changed. I will, however, make sure that someone else of reasonable capacity takes you on. A means will be implemented to become a photographer, good or bad remains with yourself.'

'Thank you very much indeed, but –'

This time Jilson was not interrupted by Henchman. An altogether unlooked for exterior force came into play. Lorna Tiptoft was standing by them. Either she had come up quietly, or, more likely, Henchman's harangue had too much occupied the attention of everyone present for her to have been noticed. Her white cassock suggested hospital garb, medical status, sanitary precautions.

'You ought to be in bed, young man.'

'I suppose I should.'

Jilson was completely at ease with her.

'Didn't we agree about early hours and freedom from excitability? That's what the motor nerves need. And your muscles generally. I think we concurred about that, didn't we?'

'Yes, we did.'

She had a strange calming effect on him. Her aggressiveness, inimical to some, perhaps most people, was soothing to Jilson. His mother had none of Lorna Tiptoft's categorically domineering personality, but there could have been resemblances under the skin. Mrs Jilson's own immense determination may have explained why she and Dr Tiptoft had a sense of fellow-feeling in their shared cabin, in spite of difference in age. Beals put forward some sort of a theory of pattern of domination that included Henchman, which, aimed at Jilson, in the last resort, expressed Jilson's own will.

'If Mr Lamont hasn't turned in yet, I'll have a look at you in your cabin. I don't think he has, because I've just seen him in the bar.'

'All right, Lorna.'

As doctor and patient, they already seemed on close terms. Jilson spoke obediently, affectionately. He turned towards Henchman.

'Thank you so much for all you were saying — I mean about getting me fixed up. I do really —'

'No more. Off to bed. You are an invalid. Dr Tiptoft is right. Do not argue with your medical adviser. It is never wise. Look where that sort of behaviour has brought me.'

Jilson, resigned, now scarcely at all reluctant, hesitated a moment, as if he still had something on his mind. Then he must have decided to speak another time of whatever that might be. He followed Lorna Tiptoft from the saloon. Henchman watched them go.

'That's a very masterful young woman. Jilson is going to have trouble with her. He has admitted a Trojan horse, more specifically a Trojan mare. She is like one of those physicians in Molierè's comedies, carrying a huge clyster, which she is only too anxious to bring into play.'

Mr Jack, who had been sitting listlessly, since expressing the hope that Barberina Rookwood would dance again, revived for a moment. He must have forgotten, or decided to ignore, Henchman's command to stop talking.

'. . . dear little thing . . . didn't quite know what . . . this other fellow . . . thought himself a card . . . bit of a brute . . .'

This time Henchman was final.

'Jack, if you can get to bed, go to bed. You are a powerful tonic against romanticism in its insidious forms, but there is not much else to be said for you. You embody every proclivity of the lifelong womanizer, to which you have added a few personal touches of your own. Tireless in pursuit, prolix in narration, sentimental in approach, heartless in abandonment, you are insensitive to the feelings of everyone but yourself. Above all, you have that strain of sanctimoniousness, essential to all womanizers in the top class, one which enjoys a delicious sense of guilty horror at the thought of past adventures, and is, at all periods, immensely resentful of other men enjoying the same pleasures as your own. You must never leave me. Become my male Scheherazade, eternally relating a chronicle of aimless amatory encounters, unspeakably wearisome to everyone but yourself, while I photograph, stage by stage, your rapid descent on the escalator of senile degradation. You shall be Falstaff to my Prince Hal.'

Henchman rose.

'Come.'

Henchman and Beals made their way out of the main saloon. Beals saw Henchman down the companion-way. He was allowed to accompany him no further. When they left, Mr Jack had leant back in his chair, and begun to snore gently. The wind had dropped, and the sea was calm.

36

Beyond the lightly quivering curtain of the port-hole the sky was lightening. Beals had been awake for some time. He was not sure that he had ever properly gone to sleep. There had been stages of comparative coma. Now familiar indications confirmed that even short spans of such stupor would not be achieved again that night. There were all the signals that he was going to suffer for having drunk more than usual.

He lay thinking in a disordered manner about the happenings of the previous evening. On return to the cabin, he had found his wife asleep, so that events had not been partially rationalized in the mind by recounting them to her. Louise Beals was still asleep. Insomnia was unknown to her. She gave long soft breaths, and would continue to do so, unless disturbed, for several hours.

The *Alecto* was due to dock at Leith later in the morning. Beals reckoned they must just about be entering the Firth of Forth. He was now fully conscious, head throbbing, mind desperately clear. Rather than waste this artificial lucidity by ruminating on the complex problems of fellow passengers, he decided to attempt a decision about the subject of his next book. During the course of the cruise he had already rejected one or two plots fabricated from circumstances on board, or places visited. All had turned out insufficiently commonplace for his readers. Now, remembering the trip would soon be entering the land of several popular historical figures – if it came to that, the land of the writer to whom in a sense he owed his daily bread – Beals began to turn over in his mind the possibilities of what Middlecote might have called reusable slides.

However unpretentiously Beals looked upon the level of his own writing, once determined on a subject, he would take a great deal of trouble about the material in hand, in obtaining the effects he wanted. Even if rare opinions given in the press taxed him with flamboyance, he was conscientious in the forms that flamboyance took. It suddenly struck him that dawn would soon be breaking over the northern seas, a spectacle to be used with advantage in almost any period novel not set in southern climes. What about Mary Queen of Scots sailing back from France, a sunrise ere long to become sunset? Possibilities began to present themselves.

The so-called sun-deck was likely to be the most advantageous spot for observation. There should be no delay. The fresh air of summer might even dispel some of the ills inherited from the previous night. He put on a dressing-gown, found a notebook and pencil. He was not feeling very well. In her sleep Louise Beals turned over, away from the light of the port-hole. Opening the door very quietly, Beals entered the passage.

This long passage, with cabins on either side, lead ultimately to means of ascent to the decks above. The topmost of these decks was the one towards which Beals aimed. He had not gone very far when he saw someone walking ahead in the same direction. It was a man in pyjamas. Beals recognized the back as belonging to Jilson.

Grasping the fact that Jilson must have risen to relieve himself, having no such facilities in his cabin, Beals recalled a conversation that had taken place between the Middlecotes, after Middlecote had remarked on a man of Lamont's standing submitting to a shared and bathless cabin.

'God,' said Fay Middlecote. 'Gary must have done worse than that in his younger days. Lucky if he had a bath once a week.'

'It's not what he did in his younger days. We all did funny things in our younger days. It's what a rising tycoon does now. It shoes his resolution in chasing that girl.'

Beals had scarcely taken in the fact that the grey-pyjamad figure in front was a back view of Jilson returning to his cabin, when a cabin-door opened in the passage ahead, just at the point Jilson was passing. A man emerged into the passage. It was Lamont. He was fully clothed, but looked in a state of extreme disarray. Seeing Jilson immediately before him, in fact almost colliding, Lamont seemed both astonished and enormously displeased. Evidently he had not taken in Jilson's manifestly natural reason for being on the move at this hour, Lamont possibly even supposing that he was himself being spied upon.

In the days that followed, when the story was being dished up all round in many different forms, Jilson let it be known that, hoping not to disturb Lamont's sleep, he had slipped from the cabin quickly, silently, not bothering with a dressing-gown, not even glancing in the direction of Lamont's bed. He had never been quite at ease with Lamont – probably even less so after the interlude on deck with Barberina Rookwood, who had no doubt explained Lamont's presence on board – the night before going to sleep, happy that Lamont was not there to threaten some sort of confrontation.

Now, in the passage, Jilson seemed even more confused by the sight of Lamont than Lamont by Jilson. Jilson may not have been fully awake. At first he could have supposed that he had arrived back at their shared cabin sooner than expected – had noted the numbers on the doors incorrectly – their cabin the one Lamont was now leaving for the same reason as himself. That was the impression conveyed to Beals, because Jilson stood politely aside for Lamont to pass, as if Jilson himself were about to enter the cabin Lamont had just vacated. The fact that Lamont was wearing his day clothes, rather than pyjamas, may have added an unsettling factor in the mind of Jilson.

Whether or not Jilson's intention was to go into the cabin, Beals was uncertain. Some sort of misapprehension undoubtedly took place. Whatever that was appeared to enrage Lamont, in any case having all the air of suffering extreme inner disturbance, far from the slick operator, always on top of the world, which he normally set out to personify. Lamont retreated half a step, as if to make sure that he had closed the door effectively, in particular against Jilson. Then he almost pushed Jilson aside. Before Beals could grasp exactly what was happening between the two of them, the door opened of the cabin immediately opposite that from which Lamont had just come out. Henchman, in pyjamas of crimson silk, leaning on his crutches, stood at the threshold.

'I knew one of you was in there. I could hear a man's voice for hours, and recognized Barberina's tone when she is upset. I had not guessed it was both. Did you have an enjoyable threesome?'

Afterwards, Beals made no bones about having hidden himself with the direct object of observing what would happen. He offered no apology for that. A small recess (leading to the cabin where the ship's laundering was done) lay at one point between the two lines of cabins. Beals quietly withdrew there, and waited. Drama was only beginning. The cabin from which Lamont had come – as Henchman's words had made plain – belonged to Barberina

Rookwood. She now opened the door, and looked out. Beals did not later minimize to Middlecote this vision in a black nightdress.

She showed no surprise at finding Henchman standing in the open doorway of his cabin. Jilson's presence in the passage was evidently far less explicable to her. Beals thought she gave Jilson a look at once wondering and tender. None the less, she was perfectly calm, mistress, as ever, of the situation. The only exception to that habitual composure had been exhibited the night before when, during the process of bidding goodnight to Henchman, there had been moments when it had seemed to Beals she might break down. She smiled at Lamont. It was rather a sad smile, disapproving, not unkind.

'I think, Gary, you should explain what has been happening, so that things look rather less like one of those oldfashioned farces, with everyone running in and out of everyone else's bedroom.'

Lamont laughed rather harshly. The closer Beals examined him from the recess the more disordered Lamont seemed. He was perhaps still a bit drunk from the night before. All the same he was showing signs of being able to carry off what was, on the face of it, an undignified predicament, whatever subsequent explanation of the circumstances might come to light.

'Yes, Barberina, I think I should. I was put off my stride for a moment. I didn't expect to meet your young friend in the passage like this. I still don't know what he is doing with himself.'

Jilson showed some spirit at that.

'I just got up in the night. There's no law against it.'

Lamont stared at him. Such a contingency had for some reason not struck him.

'Taken short? I see.'

Henchman moved a shade further into the passage.

'Don't trouble to explain, Gary. Let me offer my own

solution to *The Mystery of the Alecto's Passenger* – the answer being that there was no mystery. Not as I see it.'

Lamont laughed again, this time not so much harshly as hysterically. He was no doubt suffering not only from the previous night's drinking, but untold frustrations, not all of which he himself fully understood. Those were coupled with lack of sleep, anxiety about the job in prospect, worry about his heart condition. Any or all of the these could be playing a part. The encounter in Barberina Rookwood's cabin had unquestionably been an upsetting one for him. What form that had taken remained for the moment veiled.

'As I see it, Gary, you sat in the bar as long as you could, then wandered about the deck in a drunken state until the small hours, brooding on the lack of success you've been experiencing in getting Barberina to yourself during this cruise.'

Henchman had changed his stance to a more comfortable angle. One of his facial contortions suddenly took place after saying that, an intermittent spasm of pain having at that moment stabbed. He was looking as gruesome as a man well could, said Beals, but in high spirits.

'Having earlier had the forethought to mark down the number of Barberina's cabin, you became obsessed by the idea of going to it. Being a poor sleeper, I heard your arrival there. Your own tortured state recommended a bold method of attack. You would enter, at best go to bed with her – as you attempted to do, with pertinacity, but without success, a few years ago – at worst discuss, in private and without fear of interruption, your new and favourable status as widower. Perhaps persuade her to marry you, and return to dancing. Am not I right?'

'Not so far wrong, Saul.'

Lamont showed no particular resentment at Henchman's analysis of how he had been engaged during the last few hours.

226

'Even had there been no other ominous signs, the charming display on the dance-floor last night would have left me in no uncertainty that I was going to lose her. What I am, however, uncertain about – though I would hazard a guess upon which I would stake a lot of money – is the extent to which you were successful in putting either of those not necessarily conflicting propositions to the test.'

Henchman had not managed to utter the sentence about losing Barberina Rookwood with quite his accustomed panache. His voice went so hoarse that it was scarcely audible. The hoarseness was of a different timbre from Henchman's night-after throatiness. Henchman looked so ghastly, Beals said, that death could then and there have been about to intervene. For the second time, in observing these scenes played out, Beals found himself deeply moved.

'Oh . . .'

Barberina Rookwood's face seemed to become twisted with tears. Whether or not she had begun to weep, she shook her head, and withdrew, closing behind her the cabin door. Henchman, looking more dreadful than ever – as if about to have a fit – watched as she disappeared from sight. Jilson, trembling violently, seemed in a state of terror. Only Lamont remained no more than coldly furious. His voice showed all he felt.

'So far as I'm concerned, Saul, you can set your mind at rest. But you're right in thinking you're going to lose Barberina.'

That was addressed to Henchman, who continued to rest on his crutches a little ahead of the doorway. He did not speak. Lamont turned to Jilson.

'In the past, I used to think it a pretty galling experience to be turned down in favour of an impotent man. I'm not sure it isn't even more humiliating to be turned down on account of you.'

This comment had the effect of causing Henchman to make a recovery from the imminent doom that seemed a moment before to be hanging over him. Either he felt physically better at once, or made an immense effort of will to overcome whatever anguish consumed him.

'Thank you, Gary. That was most gracefully put. We know you to be a master of invective in newsprint. I had not given you credit for being able to express yourself so fluently in extempore speech. With quite a lot of journalists, politicians, publicists, to choose from – all the mob of four-letter men with three-letter first-names – I would award the palm to yourself for vulgarity of mind. No wonder you are spoken of with respect. But believe me, Gary, plenty of people beside yourself hate me simply because I am a cripple. The condition in itself provokes a kind of perverted envy, which in a way I understand.'

Lamont continued to smile. He was far too angry to be in the least put out by anything Henchman, or anyone else, said or implied. He was beyond denunciation for mere effect. He spoke from the heart. Henchman, Barberina Rookwood, Jilson, all exasperated him equally. There was nothing to choose between them in Lamont's eyes. He continued to rage.

'But you would not disagree, Saul?'

'On the contrary, agreement was what I had hoped to make clear. I was not lamenting your mental ignobility, lack of taste, failures in appreciation. I was trying to express admiration for the manner in which you confirmed about yourself so much that had already struck me. Like you, at first, I found what undoubtedly seems to be, not only improbable, but impossible to believe. But, as my friend – our friend – Jack so often makes only too evident, in love nothing is impossible.'

Again Henchman spoke the operative word a bit hoarsely, as if still a shade too painful for him to articulate easily. That was only for a split second.

'At the same time, Gary, you practical men miss things. In certain fields you are not quite so smart as you think yourselves. Life is sometimes very obvious, sometimes not obvious at all. You've got to have the right instinct for when one is happening, when the other. Have you never noticed that even poets and writers function largely by not knowing what the world is like at all from one point of view, perhaps very well from another? For instance, every-one agrees how unexpected it was of Barberina to come and live with me in the first place. She recently re-commended me to be philosophic about that drawing to a close. To achieve a philosophic state regarding my loss I shall not, I admit, find easy. I concede that at once.'

'Has no one told you what a bore you are when you go on like this?' said Lamont. 'If not, let me do so now.'

Henchman smiled, but scarcely paused.

'I have given only part of the picture, as we used to say in the army. I suspect something confronts Barberina as well, which may demand philosophy. I am not sure, I con-fess, just what is going to happen. If my suspicions are correct she, too, may have to rely on philosophy to mend a damaged heart. Will she prove equal to that? We shall see. I expect she will. Women can be unexpectedly tough. Meanwhile, I am naturally happy to receive confirmation on a point which – as you so delicately put it – is outside my own terms of reference. None the less, I have never been able to feel indifferent as to it. Incidentally, I gather from Barberina that you are also having trouble with your heart of a quite unmetaphorical kind.'

This flow of words showed Henchman back in his old form. Depth of feeling had not, as seemed possible a minute or two before, overwhelmed him. Listening to this dialogue, the notion struck Beals that mere lack of a bath-room would be a small matter compared with what now faced Lamont and Jilson in their shared cabin accommoda-tion. Before he could develop the idea to himself, even before Lamont had time to answer Henchman with vigour, as he clearly intended to do, Jilson himself, silent since explanation of why he had been roaming the passage at night, suddenly took over the scene. He had been in a state of growing distress. Now he leant against the wall, and groaned.

'I say . . . I'm sorry . . . one of those bloody . . .'

Beals decided that was the juncture to make his own presence known by lending a hand. If he moved quickly he could prevent Jilson from falling to the ground, which no one else showed any sign of doing. That, at least, was Beals's story, thereby recording the only occasion on the cruise when opportunity was given him to behave as a man of action. Even then the action was beneficial, rather than in any manner decisive to the course of events.

Later, Beals always tended to exaggerate the farcical nature of his assistance, perhaps to cover up or excuse indulging curiosity in a manner that over fastidious people might have looked on as a shade furtive. He emphasized that any such imputation did not in the least worry him. A touch of forgivable slyness had been amply vindicated by helping to alleviate so awkward a contingency. In fact, Beals insisted, it was hard to know what would have happened had he not appeared so opportunely. Henchman, comfortably aware that he himself could not possibly be called upon for help, had taken in the situation at once.

'I think your stable companion needs a hand, Gary.'

Considering the circumstances, sentiments recently uttered by both parties, Henchman did not speak the words with undue spite. Without Beals, the problem of an all but inert Jilson was solvable only by allowing him descent to the ground, then to lie there until more assistance arrived. Over and above any lack of relish on Lamont's part to help him back to the cabin, Jilson's state of collapse made that almost impossible to attempt singlehanded. Beals launched himself from the laundry recess, and immediately became useful in mitigating Jilson's prostration.

'Has he had another fall?'

Beals asked that without otherwise commenting on the reason for this tableau staged during the small hours of the morning in the passage: Henchman in his doorway; Lamont fuming; Jilson huddled against the wall. Henchman did not take long to enquire the cause of Beals himself being about at this time. Perhaps he suspected Beals, too, might be tracking down Barberina Rookwood.

'We all seem very early risers on this boat. May I ask what gets you up at cockcrow after our potations last night? Perhaps the answer is obvious enough.'

Beals spoke what was entirely true.

'I was on my way to watch the sunrise. It's going to be pretty spectacular, I hope. One wants to get one's money's worth out of the cruise. I know nothing of photography, but might not the dawn coming up like thunder be worth your own consideration?'

Henchman gave the matter thought.

'I'm glad you asked that question. I also admire your powers of recuperation after sitting up with that hardened old bugger, who probably wakes up quite unaware that he drank anything but water the night before. I do not do that sort of thing often, therefore feel the effects. Thanks to your being fit to do so, you have saved the situation.'

Beals had already begun to prop up Jilson, who showed no sign of recovery, rather the reverse. Lamont continued to take no action. Henchman withdrew from the threshold without shutting the door. For the moment he disappeared from sight.

'Ought we to knock up the ship's doctor?' said Beals. 'Or shall we just get him to bed?'

Jilson himself took that in. He did not sound very well, but was quite firm about what he wanted done.

'No, don't get the doctor. I'm only too used to these things. They pass off. If you can help me to the cabin, I'll be all right there till the morning. Then the doctor can check up.'

'Sure?'

'Absolutely.'

'We'll tell the doctor in the morning.'

'No, don't do that, now I come to think of it. If some-body could let Lorna Tiptoft know, she'll look after me all right. No fuss. I've talked to her about my trouble.'

Beals looked towards Lamont to see if he were prepared to help. There was no real alternative. Lamont nodded. His agreement was far from gracious. They took hold of Jilson on either side, hauled him upright, started into motion. Jilson was full of apologies at not being able to walk alone.

'Sorry about this . . . happens . . . sometimes . . . I'm . . .'

'Where's the cabin?' asked Beals.

'This way,' said Lamont.

'Have you got hold of him all right on your side?'

'Just about.'

Lamont was surly. He was not going to give an inch. The three of them had just set off down the passage, when Henchman's voice sounded.

'Wait a second.'

Beals and Lamont, turning to see why Henchman had given this sharp order, were forced to bring Jilson at least halfway round with them. Otherwise he would have fallen to the ground. There was a click, a slight flash. Henchman had taken a photograph.

'If available, I always prefer the human touch. Nature has never quite the same appeal for me. This will go into my private album, which few – I think only Barberina – have ever seen. After taking what I hope will be rather a good photograph of the three of you as you now are, my conscience as an artist will be clear. I shall feel exempted from the necessity of photographing the northern dawn. Instead, I shall try and get some sleep. I never seem to achieve that until it is light outside, even on nights less full of incident than this one has been.'

Henchman closed the cabin door.

37

Speaking as an internationally popular writer, one prepared to carry language to any length dictated by sales promotion, Beals used to say that the expression on Henchman's face, above the crimson pyjamas as he shut the door, was beyond any powers known to him, or to any novelist with whose works he was familiar. Beals was quite well read, so his word could be accepted that Henchman had looked fairly terrifying.

In the same connection, Beals would add that, when telling a story, order of events was everything. There lay the key to the clarity demanded by his readers. He insisted that they required clarity, just as much as heart-throbs. The problem, therefore, was which subject to tackle first, so that the rest fell logically into place. Beals must have known to some extent what he was talking about to acquire fanatical readers like Mrs Jilson, who would speak of the excitement they experienced from the very opening page, fevered attention which carried them through events in the highest degree improbable.

Even Beals himself allowed that certain historical periods

were what he called (probably borrowing the term from Middlecote) shelf-dated. They were to be employed with that limitation in mind, so far as chronological mutations of psychology were concerned. Different historical eras demanded different imaginary acts. He said these things had bearing on retracing, with anything like assurance, the happenings of what was essentially an interim period on the *Alecto*. In short, he admitted difficulty in deciding what events deserved that priority he considered so important for lucid narrative. Like his novels, they belonged, so to speak, on different historical levels.

In the personal relationships undergoing upheaval, effects were easier to recognize than causes. Certitude as to individual motive was often blurred. The main focus of commotion naturally emanated from Henchman and Barberina Rookwood. That was accompanied by scarcely lesser whirlpools of feeling, which, while also involving Barberina Rookwood, converged on Jilson and Lorna Tiptoft. Sometimes one axis seemed the more pivotal; sometimes the other. The period Beals found most hard to chart – which he compared with these inherent difficulties in constructing an historical novel – was that spent in and around Edinburgh, after the *Alecto* had docked, when passengers were devoting themselves to sight-seeing in the city, or visiting places of interest round about.

Had there been grave need to isolate a patient, no doubt a cabin would somehow have been assigned. The *Alecto* did not normally dispose of a sick-bay, as such, Jilson remaining in in his usual accommodation, rather than removing to special quarters. Knowing his indisposition likely to last only a day or so, he himself seemed to have decided that; although what had passed between him and Lamont might have made any chance of separation welcome. If that was ever on offer, the opening was not taken.

Perhaps what Beals had called the tenaciously strong will of the indulged child had come into play. Jilson, in whatever contempt Lamont held him, was prepared to show moral superiority by completely disregarding the offensive speeches Lamont had spoken; in short, prove that he could stand up to Lamont. If that attitude had been in Jilson's mind, the strategy was no bad way of confronting Lamont, who was likely to find unaltered confinement with Jilson at least equally obnoxious.

Fay Middlecote, after hearing about the scene in the passage, was particularly outraged that Jilson and Lamont should continue to be closeted together. Louise Beals, on the other hand, simply gave way to quiet laughter. As it happened, exterior circumstances – spoken of by Beals as creating one of his problems in narrative priority – intervened.

So far as Jilson's relegation to the sick-list was in question, the major force to take immediate effect was Lorna Tiptoft. When, as a matter of routine, the ship's doctor was called in, she explained her special interest in muscular conditions, particularly cases where failure of normal conduction of the motor nerve impulse was symptomatic. To look after Jilson during the short period throughout which he was likely to stay in bed would be positively instructive to her.

The ship's doctor would certainly have done his duty by Jilson had that been required. He saw no reason to stand in the way of a qualified practitioner, who wished to widen her experience in a specific case. In addition, the ship's doctor normally accompanied excursions on shore. When these took place, Dr Tiptoft proposed to remain with the patient. To attempt to thwart her would, in any case, have been unwise. She had set her heart on looking after Jilson, and had long experience of getting her own way with a man so intractable as her father.

The ship's doctor did not attempt to obstruct Lorna Tiptoft's intention. As a matter of fact, Elaine Kopf, stung by a wasp, fearing an allergy, was, after initial consultation, taking up a good deal of the ship's doctor's spare time. Mrs

Kopf found herself sometimes on her own at moments when her husband had managed to corner Henchman for further talks about the Loathly Damsel. So far as possible Beals used to discourage Professor Kopf's parleyings with Henchman – then at his most expansive in moods of self-revelation. He tried to guard against these confessional moments suffering interruption. Henchman, left to himself more than formerly, seemed ready to spend his time about equally, talking of his own past to Beals, or giving a hearing to the scholarly theories of Professor Kopf, whom he only mildly teased.

The submission of Jilson's health into the hands of Lorna Tiptoft (Mrs Jilson being allowed to play only a very small part in the nursing of her son) appeared to suit him well enough. Jilson had already shown signs of finding Lorna Tiptoft unusually sympathetic as an acquaintance. That she had now become what Henchman called Jilson's medical adviser turned out a mutually satisfactory extension of their friendship. Lorna Tiptoft's intermittent presence in the cabin was also to be foreseen, so far as he might make use of it during the day, as an inconvenience to Lamont.

According to Beals, an important aspect of the Jilson/ Tiptoft relationship was the protection Lorna Tiptoft's professional status offered in relation to Barberina Rookwood, from whose net Jilson now seemed anxious to detach himself. His wish to escape might have been because her highly charged emotions terrified him, or – in spite of what Henchman himself had affirmed to the contrary – Jilson saw her as an impediment to his own career as a photographer. No matter what help of a new sort Henchman might put forward, to be involved with this dancer was more than Jilson felt able to take on. His capture by Lorna Tiptoft confirmed the latent threat to Barberina Rookwood's hopes to which Henchman had cryptically referred.

Another element influencing the lack of decision Beals

experienced in deciding his so-called narrative priorities was weight to be accorded to Sir Dixon Tiptoft. Beals had even gone so far as to contemplate using Sir Dixon as lead-in for initiating the latter sequences of his story. Sir Dixon, far from a pivot himself, was quite by chance the bearer of pivotal news.

Throughout his career, the relationship between the civil service and the press had much engaged Sir Dixon Tiptoft's attention. According to Middlecote, former colleagues used even to hint that he had shown himself at times over anxious to insinuate his own name into public dealings, in their eyes preferably anonymous. That may or may not have been true. Sir Dixon's persistence in pursuing Lamont on the *Alecto* in no way disowned the assertion. He even went so far as to persuade Lamont – who showed no sign of wishing to discuss such weighty matters while on a holiday – to make a semi-appointment to discuss 'over a cup of tea' the appropriate relationship between Whitehall and Fleet Street, such outer areas as television naturally being understood.

That goal had never been achieved. The meeting, anyway in Lamont's eyes, had been only vaguely agreed, and, at the hour fixed, Lamont had been seen by Sir Dixon sitting with the Radio Officer in his small cell. Lamont was conversing and laughing with the Radio Officer, showing no sign of abandoning that for Sir Dixon's company. On the contrary, when conversation with the Radio Officer was at an end, Lamont moved straight on to the bar, which, whatever its dangers from Mr Jack, might be regarded as a recognized sanctuary from Sir Dixon.

Lamont may have been arranging a personal matter involving radio communication. It was by no means impossible that he was not collecting information with a view to running a series of articles on some such subject as radio's neglected facilities in everyday life. Whatever it was, Middlecote chanced to hear of the cutting of Sir Dixon

Tiptoft's appointment, an incident made into a comic story by him, only on account of Sir Dixon's extreme annoyance at such a thing being possible.

There was probably more in the circumstances than Middlecote appreciated at the time. In fact Middlecote's view of himself (said Beals), as a man who never missed a trick in seeing well ahead of everyone else in what was happening, took a serious knock. His mind could only have been on other things.

Lamont's frequentation of the ship's radio-reception centre must have been linked with the arrival of a message finally to dash Sir Dixon Tiptoft's hope of a long session picking Lamont's brains; possibly, in addition, he hoped to take a photograph of him, as Sir Dixon's cameras (he had several) were now playing an increasing part in his scheme of things. In short, the news broke – suddenly spread all over the ship – that Lamont had been appointed to the not-to-be-sneezed-at job for which his name had been hanging in the balance.

Sir Dixon Tiptoft's irritation at Lamont's cavalier treatment of what amounted to an offer of friendship on the part of a former high functionary to – whatever might be said of Lamont's capabilities – a buccaneering journalist was mitigated by being the first to announce the news. That is to say Lamont's decision to leave the ship. This scoop may have been consequent on Sir Dixon scouting round the radio-office. More probably he heard of Lamont's imminent departure from his daughter.

Lorna Tiptoft would have learnt from Jilson that Lamont was relinquishing his allotted portion of the cabin. Various administrative arrangements must have been made. Lamont, within his own limits a goodnatured man, may well have told Jilson in so many words what had happened. He could even have expressed some sort of apology for regrettable phrases used under severe emotional stress during the encounter in the passage. Available channels of information indicated, if by no means established, such conjectures as possible. They also reported Lamont's extreme satisfaction at finding himself in the job. All else seemed forgotten. These were the tidings Lorna Tiptoft seemed to have passed on to her father.

Lamont himself appears to have been surprised that the decision in London had been taken so quickly. After the original confirmation that he was to fill the post several more radio conversations seem to have been exchanged, which demanded his presence on the spot with the least possible delay. That instruction suited Lamont well. He must have seen it as proof that his luck, anyway up to a point, was holding. He might have been unsuccessful in love this time, in other spheres (which, on reconsideration, may have meant more to him) he was not only laying his hands on a plum, but, after undergoing in public vicissitudes, amatory and social, he was at least afforded means of making a prompt, relatively dignified, exit from the *Alecto*'s stage.

38

Outwardly, the break between Barberina Rookwood and Henchman would have been invisible to anyone uninitiated into the mysteries of this story. The two of them went about together in much the same manner as before, even if less inseparably. Barberina Rookwood would be seen talking with Fay Middlecote, with whom she had become friendly. In the evening she would retire early. Henchman played about with his camera more than formerly, or held the conversation *à deux*, which Beals valued so much. Henchman was also seen from time to time with Mr Jack, over whom he seemed to have established a stranglehold, cutting down his drinking, transforming him into something not much short of Henchman's private body-servant.

Nevertheless, all was changed. What had passed, if anything in the form of words, between Barberina Rookwood and Jilson remained unknown. While confined to his cabin, Jilson had been, by definition, under the charge of Lorna Tiptoft. It would not have been easy for Barberina Rookwood to see him, even for purposes of a showdown, had she planned something of the kind. Their close relationship, come so quickly into being, seemed to have been dissolved similarly in a flash; perhaps not without mutual pain, especially on her side.

How much the Tiptoft parents knew, or cared, about their daughter's concentration on Jilson was not apparent. They showed neither approval nor disapproval of a situation to which they could hardly have been blind. In their eyes Lorna Tiptoft's comings and goings to Jilson's sickbed may have represented no more than professional zeal, a side which no doubt played a substantial part in all her behaviour. In any case she made her own decisions. Even to mention the matter might be unwise, after what her father had said of Jilson.

Sir Dixon Tiptoft, unless personally concerned, was in any case disinclined to notice the behaviour of others, even his own family, if not inconvenient to himself. This indifference to people as individuals eased his own relations with the rest of the world, in which, as he said, he looked for results, rather than methods of achieving them. Middlecote remarked that, unlike some lesser apostles of rudeness – who, as with Aladdin's lamp, expect good manners in exchange for bad – obtuseness of sensibility in any case protected Sir Dixon from taking amiss the acerbities of others. For example, Henchman's discouragement, even downright incivility, had not at all damped Sir Dixon's determination to put further questions on the subject of photography. This was made clear when the *Alecto*'s passengers were visiting a mansion, predominently eighteenth-century in architecture, in the neighbourhood of Edinburgh.

As it happened, on the morning of that excursion, Fay Middlecote had been talking about the ballet to Barberina Rookwood, whom she came across on deck. Barberina Rookwood said she had a headache and was going to stay on board, rather than see the house. They were chatting of this and that before the Middlecotes went ashore.

Suddenly Barberina Rookwood remarked, quite casually, that she was thinking of going back to dancing. When she returned to London she proposed to make a few enquiries in the appropriate quarter with that end in view.

This news about herself was presented in the most heedless manner imaginable. She even affected surprise when Fay Middlecote expressed astonished delight at hearing of that possibility. Henchman was not mentioned. Nothing was said of what he might do, when Barberina Rookwood was once again leading the life of a ballerina, nor whether their separation was now taken to be an eventuality recognized by everyone, too wellknown to deserve reference.

All was treated with the greatest calm on Barberina Rookwood's side. Fay Middlecote, on the other hand, could hardly control herself at this announcement. She wanted to give it out on the loudspeaker. The two of them continued to talk together for a short time, then, when the excursion was about to start, Fay Middlecote hurried off to find Louise Beals, and tell her this hot piece of news. They were still talking about it when they reached the great house, which was to be visited.

Later that morning, Beals, wandering by himself in the grounds, saw Henchman sitting on a seat under one of the two colonnades which curved outward from each wing of the house's façade. Henchman was alone. He beckoned Beals with a crutch. Beals strolled across the grass, and sat down on the seat on the side away from that where the crutches rested. Henchman looked more exhausted than usual, but in good spirits.

'Collecting background for a novel about Bonnie Prince Charlie?'

Beals was always impressed, even if resentful, of the manner in which Henchman seemed able to penetrate the reflections of a romantic novelist. The Young Pretender had indeed been in his mind as a possibility, even if a last resort. Henchman also mortified him by the manner in which their talks together seemed always to terminate with Henchman having learnt more about Beals than Beals of Henchman. This time, however, having given that particular matter some thought, Beals was fully equipped for refuting the taunt.

'The family who lived here wouldn't have been on Bonnie Prince Charlie's side. I suppose a story could be written from the Whig angle for a change.'

'Show BPC rebuffed by the beautiful daughter of a haughty Whig lord, when he tried to seduce her, revealing anything but the bonny side of his character. I've never liked BPC. Worth trying.'

They were interrupted by Sir Dixon Tiptoft, who, carrying two cameras and a tripod, had been inspecting the exterior of the house. Seeing Henchman, he ceased from this, instead making for the seat. He sat down next to Henchman's crutches. Henchman went into attack at once.

'Good-morning, Tiptoft. How goes the optical density?'

No doubt recognizing the facetious nature of the question, Sir Dixon made no answer. He shaded his eyes with a hand, and gazed at the house, as if trying to make up his mind how best to reproduce its architectural niceties. When he pronounced judgment that was to make a general observation.

'I'm never sure whether I like Adam.'

Henchman at once expressed hearty agreement.

'No – a bastard.'

Sir Dixon looked surprised at concurrence with his opinion going quite so far. Beals, too, found the personal nature of the apprehension unexpected. Henchman enlarged on his views about Adam.

'The sort of man not to be trusted with a woman. For that matter, the sort of man a woman couldn't trust. Rather like our fellow passenger old Jack. He was here a minute or two ago, now gone off to find what he referred to as the shit-house. But to return to Adam for a moment, God was right to expel him. Bastard, in the circumstances, is perhaps an imprecise term. I withdraw it. I will say, however, that Adam was not the sort of man one would care to have created oneself, legitimately or illegitimately. Personally, I never wished to create anyone, even in days when that was feasible. In doing so I am inclined to think God undertook too grave a risk. It cannot be said to have come off well. Expulsion from Eden was the only possible outcome. In any case, Eden always turns out to be a less satisfactory place of residence than might be supposed. Everyone gets expelled sooner or later. Haven't you found that? Perhaps you have been wise enough never to have camped out there. There's a lot to be said for keeping clear of Eden. What seems so strange is that Adam apparently expected to be an exception. Even if the lesson of history was in front of him rather than behind him, he could have used his own intelligence. That in itself would have told him that he could not expect to go on living in Eden indefinitely. With a woman too.'

Sir Dixon showed no sign of listening to any of this. If he listened, he had either not taken in what Henchman had been saying, or dismissed it as not worthy of attention. He had his own ends in view. No matter at what cost, he intended to reopen the subject of photography.

'I meant the brothers. When you are taking a photograph of an eighteenth-century building –'

'The brothers? Cain and Abel? As a child I was always on Cain's side. I should have done the same myself. I read a lot of the Bible as a boy, or had it read to me. I came of a very pious family. That may have disadvantages in other respects, but nothing is more to be recommended than reading the Bible. I mean, of course, the real Bible, not the appalling modern translations nowadays foisted on the English-speaking world. The Bible tells you how human beings behave. It always gives a useful standard of perspective. A realistic one.'

The arrival of Middlecote brought Henchman's speech to an end. Sir Dixon tried again.

'Perspective is just what I want to ask you about. The focus –'

'Have you heard that Gary Lamont has jumped ship?' said Middlecote. 'He's got the job.'

Sir Dixon saw that his plans had been thwarted. Having himself been the first to make public Lamont's departure, he was not prepared to listen while Middlecote expatiated on the consequences of Lamont's new appointment. On this subject Middlecote was going to spread himself.

'My gut feeling was that Gary would get it. I'm sorry he's left us like this. I wanted to dish up with him the turnabout in the ITV network in relation to intensive consumer research.'

39

Under huge Norse skies the *Alecto* slowly sailed through the waters of Orkney's clustered archipelago towards the little north-facing port. Here they were in a new dimension. Certain things going to end. The story was drawing to a close; if any story could truly be said to have a close, let alone the story of the Fisher King, Beals said.

By the time the first bus reached The Ring – the Circle of ancient Stones spoken of by Professor Kopf, and by Henchman – rain, borne on a menacing breeze that threatened at any moment to dilate into a gale, was coming down hard. The bus drew up by the side of the road, a place from which the Stone Circle could be seen. Preceded by the young archaeologist who was to lecture there, the first sortie moved along the track leading to the site.

The group had not gone far when a taxi appeared on the road behind. The taxi passed the parked bus, and stopped in front. Mr Jack stepped out. His air was sober, even rather nervous. He had exchanged the Panama hat for a cap not unlike that worn by Lorna Tiptoft, though of more ancient fashion. He still looked as if taking part in some performance, this impression increased when he turned towards the interior of the taxi, and withdrew two crutches. He helped Henchman out of the vehicle, on to the road, then handed him the crutches. Henchman, camera swinging from neck, established himself in a characteristic position. He looked round about, contemplating the green headland, the Circle of Stones, the loch beyond.

When he had taken in the landscape, Henchman paid the driver, at the same time issuing some instruction, which probably had bearing on a return journey. While he was doing this, Mr Jack, who seemed completely to have reverted to past years of courier or PR duties, unloaded various objects from within the taxi; a rod-case containing two fishing rods; a tackle-bag; a creel; a kind of haversack or satchel; the last, in spite of Henchman's reservations about picnics, perhaps containing provisions. Mr Jack slung the tackle-bag and haversack crisscross over his back, shouldered the rod-case with one hand, and held the creel in the other. The taxi drove away.

Henchman and Mr Jack followed the party making for The Ring. They were not too far behind the last stragglers of the group from the bus. Henchman swung along on his crutches, Mr Jack keeping up with quick shaky strides. So far as could be judged from his face, Henchman seemed in tolerable form still. Mr Jack, on the other hand, was at his most subdued. Seeing the two of them likely to augment a potential audience, the lecturer delayed his opening words until they were in earshot.

'Sorry about the weather. I'll keep what I have to say as short as possible. Unusually, in this type of henge monument . . .'

Orcadian rain drove across the coarse grass of the headland, detonating tiny explosive drops, like shot, against the wrinkled surface of the megaliths. From a conjectural sixty or more Stones only thirty or forty had survived four or five thousand years of upright conformation. Lack of symmetry in their roughly circular grouping suggested ring-a-ring-o'-roses played a few millenia before by ghostly beings of superhuman stature, who, before some of the players had time to rise from the ground at the game's finale, were instead frozen by a magician into petrifaction. Discontinuity of pattern in no way lessened a sense of awe dispensed by the place.

'. . . That's all I'll tell you now. Oh, yes, and there are Norse runes on one of the Stones . . .'

Several of the visitors, among them Henchman, had begun to make a tour of The Ring before the lecturer's talk had come to an end. Mr Jack, as if arranging a small private sacrifice of his own, had piled the luggage he carried into quite an impressive heap under one of the Stones, a votive offering perhaps later to be consumed by fire. Then he followed Henchman.

'Ah, as I hoped.'

The surface of the first three or four Stones was entirely covered with the modern graffiti, of which Henchman had spoken earlier, and was now examining. These were mostly confused jumbles of names, carved or scratched with little or no attempt at craftsmanship, especially when efforts to record both christian name and surname had proved un-expectedly onerous. Sometimes two persons' names were linked together, souvenir of an expedition to the Circle with emotional rather than archaeological overtones. After the first few Stones had been passed, scribblings gradually died away, as if persons inspired with transitory hope of drawing the attention of posterity to their names had lost heart in the presence of so many megaliths, such im-memorial antiquity. Henchman examined carefully the face of each Stone.

'I shall photograph some of these. Here, for example, is an effort at once barbarous and painstaking, a dreadful combination when merged in the human spirit.'

He had paused in front of the last Stone to be at all heavily defaced. Mr Jack, moving like an automaton or robot, the machinery of which had been insufficiently oiled, jerked to a halt too. The name that had caught Henchman's eye was incised not only in the largest lettering of any hitherto seen up to that point in the Circle, also executed with far the greatest skill. The carver had even made an attempt to add serifs to the capitals in which name and date were set out.

G ISBISTER
1881

Henchman set about gearing his camera into play. Mr Jack watched gloomily, fidgeting with his shirt-collar, changing his weight from one foot to the other. Trans-formed temporarily into Henchman's factotum, though perhaps only for the day, he was evidently feeling the strain.

'Give me another film.'

While Mr Jack was searching in the haversack, which he still carried, probably having been ordered to do so, Fay Middlecote came up. The lecture had finished. She was clearly anxious, if possible, to glean from Henchman more information than was known to her at present about recent developments on board the *Alecto*. She stood watching him photograph the Isbister inscription, which Henchman was doing from different angles.

'Just look at the size of that name. What a frightful thing to do.'

Henchman did not turn in her direction.

'I am looking at it. In fact I am recording its horror by photographic means.'

Fay Middlecote was not at all intimidated by this show of indifference to her. As usual she stood her ground.

'Do you think the man who carved it was a relation of Isbister, the portrait painter? Perhaps there was creative art in the family.'

That caused Henchman to laugh. He even followed the question up.

'Wasn't the painter called Horace?'

'As I remember.'

Henchman retained a goodish mood.

'Isbister is also an Orcadian place-name. Excavations are in progress there at the moment. Accordingly, the epigraphist is likely to have been a local, rather than tourist. One pictures him returning day after day with hammer and chisel.'

'We've got to remember Byron carved his name on the pillar of the temple at Sunium,' said Fay Middlecote. 'This is much the same typeface. A good one for a certain kind of ad.'

'Byron no doubt appreciated that fact.'

'Of course we've no proof Byron did it himself. It may have been put there by an admirer.'

'So far as I can remember, Byron and Shelley both scratched their names in the Castle at Chillon. The existing evidence is therefore against Byron. He was a thoughtless man in many respects. It never seems to have occurred to him, for instance, that, if Grecian breasts had not suckled slaves, the economic basis of the Hellenic world would have been drastically incommoded.'

Grecian breasts brought the attention of Mr Jack, who must have been cold sober to have taken them in.

'Never thought of that . . . beautiful line . . . Maid of Athens . . . when I was taking a party there . . .'

Fay Middlecote grasped that she was getting no further with this conversation. Henchman's fencing was too adept. She saw no prospect of working round to what she wanted to talk about. At least a touch of directness was required, a snub risked. Henchman's mood was unlikely to improve, rather the reverse. He had even shown amusement at Mr Jack's rise to the surface. She was alone with him (Mr Jack's presence scarcely counting), and the chance was worth taking. At worst she could switch the subject to archaeology, always available in the circumstances, apparently acceptable to Henchman.

'Is it true you're going to leave us? Stay up here and fish?'

'Fish and take photographs.'

'That will be very peaceful.'

'What makes you think so?'

'Surely it's very peaceful in Orkney?'

'Is peace a condition familiar to you?'

'Well, sometimes.'

'You surprise me. I can't say the same.'

'You mean . . .'

Henchman allowed her implied interrogative to remain in mid air. He smiled. Fay Middlecote knew now that, in risking trouble, she had found it. Although far from being at his most sadistic, Henchman clearly saw no reason why he should not torment her a little. To forgo that would have been to depart from a natural habit of behaviour. In any case he may have felt, possibly reasonably, that inquisitiveness has to be paid for by submission to torture, even if of a mild nature, merely moral spasms.

'I was not sure one could do that on this cruise.'

'Do what?'

'Leave the ship, I mean. Harbour dues, that sort of thing, if passengers disembark permanently. Of course Gary Lamont did.'

'Yes, he did.'

Henchman fixed her with his speculationless eyes. Fay Middlecote (as she admitted afterwards) felt herself blushing, something she had not done for years. Henchman made as if he wanted to help her out – certainly far from his intention – pretending that he did not altogether understand her purpose. He assumed the puzzled expression of someone who hoped to answer any question she might wish to put to him, while wholly at sea as to what any such question might be.

'I have made special arrangements about the sort of thing you mention, like leaving a ship which is primarily a cruise ship.'

'I suppose one can.'

'I can.'

Fay Middlecote floundered. She was being more than a little reduced by all this. If things went badly, she had envisaged a brutal snub, quickly over, leaving the possibility of taking refuge in runic inscriptions, even the architecture of the Cathedral of St Magnus. Henchman was not going to allow anything of that kind. He proposed to skin her quite slowly.

'It's been so nice meeting you – and, of course, Barberina, who's so sweet.'

This was conceding defeat. Henchman recognized that. He saw no reason to be magnanimous. He had by no means finished with Fay Middlecote.

'But I haven't answered your question,' he said.

'My question?'

'The question you wanted to put.'

'How do you mean?'

'If Barberina is staying here with me?'

'I naturally –'

'Very naturally. But that was what you intended to ask, I think.'

'Of course I was interested, but –'

'Barberina is going to enjoy the rest of the cruise on her own. She does not at all mind being on her own. She is a girl full of resources in herself, as people call it. In her own way she makes friends easily. She has made two nice friends already – very nice friends – who will see her through. I rather think, by the way, that she has become quite a friend of yours?'

'Yes, of course. We have had a few talks. I would love to become a friend of Barberina's.'

'You may have heard that Barberina is returning to the ballet?'

'She did say something about it.'

'To you?'

'This morning.'

'Did she. I'm interested. We shall all look forward to seeing her dance again. It will take a little arranging, but all will certainly be well once everything is *en train*. You have two more questions, I think.'

'I've always got a lot of questions.'

Fay Middlecote spoke quite humbly.

'Foremost among them in your mind will be, first, Barberina's relations with Lamont, secondly, with Jilson.'

Fay Middlecote nodded. She told Louise Beals afterwards that she was afraid she was going to cry, which would have been a dreadful humiliation to her. She felt tempted to say that she knew how awful all this was being for Henchman, and for Barberina too, who had once given up everything. She herself was ashamed of just feeling trite curiosity about it all. She wanted to tell him that.

'You need attach significance to neither.'

'That's what I thought.'

'I mean in any intimate sense.'

'I was sure.'

'You were quite right.'

What further details Henchman might have supplied remained unsaid, because at that moment Middlecote joined his wife, immediately followed by the Bealses. Fay Middlecote found relief in a burst of formally amicable sentiments, which her voice did not simulate with entire success. It shook a little.

'Saul is leaving us. We shall all have to bid him goodbye here. He is going to stay and fish.'

Until then she had never called Henchman by his christian name. Their talk together had given her a sense of being uncomfortably close to him, almost as if she had gone to bed with him, she said. To address him as Saul seemed for the first time permissible, even required.

'I did hear a rumour,' said Beals. 'If you remember, you hinted quite early on that you might be tempted by the fishing.'

Beals felt unusually triumphant. There could be no doubt now of the Fisher King identification.

'We shall all miss you,' said Fay Middlecote.

While they had been talking another bus had drawn up on the road. Its passengers, led by the Kopfs, were already beginning to penetrate The Ring. Professor Kopf, who knew too much about the site to require the introduction, now being repeated by the lecturer, made his way at once to where Henchman and the others were standing.

'Here we are reminded more than ever of the characteristic proximity of water to these Stone Circles. At least five lie near the Atlantic Ocean. I know the loch to be important to you, Mr Henchman, for you spoke of it at the start of the cruise.'

'I am actually proceeding from these numinous Stones to the loch itself, after I have taken a few photographs. Jackie here has kindly agreed to accompany me for the day. My personal water-bailiff, though water is an element with which none of us associate him.'

Louise Beals spoke in her softest voice.

'Valentine always insisted that you would fish sooner or later.'

'So did Elaine,' said Professor Kopf.

Beals wondered if he referred to Mrs Kopf or she who bore the Grail, mistress to Lancelot. More members of the intrusive bus-load were now appearing. Among them was at once noticeable a distinctive trio. Of this, two were men, one a woman. The men were Basically Bach and Marginally Mahler, who were wearing identical beige trench-coats, ornamented with heavy rectangular epaulettes and small shoulder capes. The woman was Barberina Rookwood. She too was equipped against the weather with no less chic an outfit of yellow oilskins.

Beals said, when he saw her at that moment in The Ring, he knew at once that she would be able to confront with elegance the strange concatenation of circumstances, which had placed a woman of her strength of will in such a predicament. Having apparently every advantage on her side, she had been defeated. That was one of the occasions when he wondered whether he ought not to have made her, rather than Henchman, the core of his story. He meant, of course, the story for those he knew. Unspoken – in a sense even unacted out – stories were no good for his public, and this one he regarded as in any case explicable only in magical terms.

'When the Jilson business hit her, she was like a woman who had taken a love potion. In fact I've sometimes wondered whether things might not have been reconstructed in terms of Tristram and Iseult, rather than the myth I chose.'

He said that when they were all discussing the *Alecto*'s cruise long after the event.

'Tristram and Iseult might have been an improvement,'

said Fay Middlecote. 'I could never see how Barberina Rookwood fitted into your Fisher King stuff. She wasn't the girl who brought in the Cup, because that was Elaine, and Elaine was Mrs Kopf. I wonder whether she's still married to the Professor.'

'I can't be tied down,' said Beals. 'Fanciful analogies mustn't be pressed too far. You know that from the ads Piers produces. Look at his Deucalion Mineral Water. You're behaving as if I'd infringed the Trades Description Act. Try and be less pedantic, Fay darling.'

'Well, the great thing is to have Barberina Rookwood back dancing. She ought never to have given it up. Not even to look after Henchman.'

'Even better if she married Lamont,' said Middlecote. 'Been left a relatively rich widow. Then she could have danced as and when it suited her. How were we to know it was the kid's last fight?'

'But if she looked after Henchman because she liked doing good, it seems a pity that she sacrificed her sacrifice,' said Louise Beals. 'People do so fancy themselves doing good. I can't understand it. I always say it was simply because she loved him. Then she just stopped loving him.'

Beals closed this discussion, which he had often had to suffer before.

'Anyway, you must admit that Perceval was snapped up by the Loathly Damsel.'

That last fact had been confirmed in The Ring, confirmed even a little dramatically. Among those who had arrived in the rear echelons of the last group were Jilson and Lorna Tiptoft. Standing in front of the first graffiti-laden Stone, they were lightly holding hands. Neither the Tiptoft parents, nor Mrs Jilson, were with them. Mrs Jilson, always at the head of any queue, had, in fact, been on the earlier bus. Professor Kopf well expressed what seemed to be happening.

'These circles seem to have been meeting places for ceremonials, where important tribal events were celebrated. What can King Lot have thought of these ancient Stones? Perhaps that they were carried here by Merlin?'

Henchman had been the first to notice the entry of Barberina Rookwood with her two musical companions. Whatever parting had taken place between himself and her must already have been sealed in private. He waved, and kissed his hand. She saw him, also kissing her hand when she waved back. Then she turned once more to the Stone that the three of them were examining. Henchman made a sign to Mr Jack, who was sunk in his own thoughts.

'Come. Let us leave these pilgrims seeking forgetfulness of the Present in a Promised Land of the Past,' he said, 'Like the impotent man at the Pool of Bethesda – so far as I know the first recorded example of queue-jumping – we will make for the water.'

Mr Jack gathered up the impedimenta stacked in its propitiatory pyramid. The two set off together from the narrow promontary on which The Ring had been built such a long time ago.

The rain had abated a little, though not altogether. In spite of foul weather there was exhilaration in the northern air. The leaden surface of the loch was just perceptibly heaving in the wind, still blowing from time to time in fairly strong gusts. On the far side of the waters, low rounded hills, soft and mysterious, concealed in luminous haze the frontiers of Thule: the edge of the known world; man's permitted limits; a green-barriered check-point, beyond which the fearful cataract of torrential seas cascaded down into Chaos.